Code Word for Chaos

by

E.C. Farrell

Code Word for Chaos

Cover Art by *The Wild Rose Press, Inc.*

The Wild Rose Press, Inc.
PO Box 708
Adams Basin, NY 14410-0708
Visit us at www.thewildrosepress.com

Publishing History
First Edition, 2023
Trade Paperback ISBN 978-1-5092-4899-5
Digital ISBN 978-1-5092-4900-8

Published in the United States of America

A distant snap sends cold shock through my limbs. *Slingers*.

We spring off our sleeping mats. Cal throws the lever to slide the false floor over our mats as I turn off the lamps and shove my half-eaten dinner into the pocket of my tool belt. Though the Slingers can't see us in the railroad car, if they get close enough, their whips will pick up the frequency the lab embedded into our DNA. Home will no longer be safe. Better to risk running.

Jumping out of the small hidden door at the back of the railroad car, I brace myself for impact. Old injuries ache as I hit the ground, but I push myself forward. Together, we sprint into the cloud-dark night. Damp air slaps me in the face as we head in opposite directions out of the protective circle of cars and shipping containers. Splitting up hurts, but it also makes it harder on the Slingers.

I barrel through a cloud of sewer steam. Stagnant water splashes around my feet, catching light from the billboard screens towering over the streets ahead. I kick over an empty diesel canister to draw the Slingers away from Cal. Images of them catching her with the tips of their whips and dragging her away into some dark vehicle flash through my head. Fear sours my stomach.

Gasping for breath, I hook left around a corner and skid to an almost immediate stop right in front of a group of soldiers blocking my path. My pulse jumps into my throat as their whips light up blue.

They look up, and a man shouts, "Freeze! You're suspected of being one of the Expired—"

Dedication

To Mom and Dad, who always read the good, the raw, the messy.

Chapter One

Sephrim

We never run out of dirt in our railroad car.

It cakes every corner, crevice, and cranny, chafing our skin, rubbing it raw and red. No matter how much I shake out our sleeping bags or beat our shoes against a wall, I can't get away from it. But anything's better than the pristine lab where my sister Cal and I grew up.

"This stuff sticks like engine grease." I huff, trying to muck out my boot tread with the end of a dulled screwdriver. "The storm didn't help at all."

"Storm, noun, a heavy fall of rain, snow, or hail, or a violent outbreak of thunder and lightning, accompanied by strong winds." Cal mutters the words, then shoves up from her stomach onto her knees. "Think they'll come tonight, Seph?"

She leans forward to peek out the door. Fear wrenching my gut, I jerk one strap of her canvas overalls. Cal rocks back and lands on her rear. The goggles she always wears slide off her head and onto the tip of her freckled nose, leaving tracks of red across the pale skin of her forehead. Our tools jitter in the gray metal compartments screwed into the roof.

We wince at the noise. Hold our collective breath. The clinking stops as our gadgets still. Sweat stinging my lower back despite the bone-numbing cold, I strain to hear past our walls and into the train yard beyond. This far from the city, we can't even hear murmurs from the ever-glowing billboard screens. Only the final sounds of settling metal interrupt the silence.

Sighing, I tug the collar of my hoodie. "I don't think so, but just in case they are out there, let's not make it easy for them to see us before we can run, huh?"

Cal's lack of self-preservation drives me nuts. Like someone much younger than a fourteen-year-old, she acts without thinking way too often—one of the side effects of spending her early years as a lab rat. I've got my own neuroses, but impetuousness isn't one of them.

Cal nudges the eyewear into her dirty blonde curls. Rolling back onto her stomach, she digs a thumbnail into the pink crayon she's pulled from her pocket. Never much bothered by the filth, she maps intricate designs into the wood next to her sleep mat almost every night. This evening, her fingers trace a sleek handgun on the floorboards.

Artwork covers the walls on her side of the railroad car. The battery-powered lamps hanging from the corners of our home spread dim light across the drawings. Pink cats chase blue dogs, flocks of purple birds sweep across the black steel background, and a legion of white frogs drink tea around a mushroom table.

All preferable to the guns she draws for work.

I set my screwdriver onto a shelf, then focus on Cal's current drawing. Watching her process helps distract me. I chuckle a little at the incongruity of a childish coloring utensil planning a deadly weapon. Dr. Gayle—the scientist who helped us escape the lab—calls it a coping mechanism. The motion calms her while the subject matter excites her.

With a piece of chalk, I carve another one of our days—1,822—in a tally mark into the wall. I squint at the white lines. If I've counted right, that makes it…October 5, 2035. Satisfied I can spare an hour or so to rest and eat before heading to work, I brush chalk off my hands and sink onto my sleeping bag. "Toss me that FudPak, would you?"

Cal shoves the crayon into the pocket of her overalls and pulls a small silver packet from a toolbox. "You call this food?" She glares at it before tossing it to me.

Every time. Every dang time we get a new stash, she makes a comment about the contents of the rations. I snicker a little. Her consistency is kind of comforting, even if it doesn't improve the taste of the FudPaks.

"They're edible anyway." I pinch it open and wrinkle my nose at the smell of metallic rice and beans.

"I miss meat."

"We have meat."

She points at the bag in my hand. "I don't know what that is, but it's not meat. I miss Fun Food Friday." She shuts her eyes. "What food do you miss most? I'd kill for a pineapple pizza."

"French fries doused in cheese." I squint at the FudPak ingredient list, then think better of it.

"I'll get you some for your birthday next week. Seventeen is a big deal. Maybe—"

A distant snap sends cold shock through my limbs.

Slingers.

We spring off our sleeping mats. Cal throws the lever to slide the false floor over our mats as I turn off the lamps and shove my half-eaten dinner into the pocket of my tool belt. Though the Slingers can't see us in the railroad car, if they get close enough, their whips will pick up the frequency the lab embedded into our DNA. Home will no longer be safe. Better to risk running.

Jumping out of the small hidden door at the back of the railroad car, I brace myself for impact. Old injuries ache as I hit the ground, but I push myself forward. Together, we sprint into the cloud-dark night. Damp air slaps me in the face as we head in opposite directions out of the protective circle of cars and shipping containers. Splitting up hurts, but it also makes it harder on the Slingers.

I barrel through a cloud of sewer steam. Stagnant water splashes around my feet, catching light from the billboard screens towering over the streets ahead. I kick over an empty diesel canister to draw the Slingers away from Cal. Images of them catching her with the tips of their whips and dragging her away into some dark vehicle flash through my head. Fear sours my stomach.

Gasping for breath, I hook left around a corner and skid to an almost immediate stop right in front of a group of soldiers blocking my path. My pulse jumps into my throat as their whips light up blue.

They look up, and a man shouts, "Freeze! You're suspected of being one of the Expired—"

Electricity from their whips singe the air as I spin around and sprint toward the city, breath shredding my throat. My perfectly designed genes give me an edge. I weave in and out of alleyways. Avoid areas with cameras, stoplights, traffic cops. Sweat soaks my T-shirt and hoodie. My shoes squeak.

On a last, sharp turn down a deep alley, I slide behind a large dumpster and crouch, air trapped in my raw lungs. A light on the corner wall buzzes, blinking in and out. Staring up at it through the strands of my hair—

even darker than normal from humidity and sweat—I count five rounds of this, dropping my gaze to the sewer lid a few feet away when the sound of boots pounding and whips snapping finally reaches me.

I crunch my back against the cold brick wall. Unless they come down the alley, they'll never pick up my frequency at this distance. If they do, if they slow for even a few steps, I've just trapped myself in a corner with no way out.

At least until they leave.

Then the pounds and snaps and shouts fade again. Worry for Cal's safety twists my gut. I siphon air out of my lungs, pull it back in, let it out, and pull it back in. With every inhale I tell myself to wait. With every exhale I tighten my grip on the sticky underside of the dumpster.

On breath number ten I lean out an inch. On twelve I crawl to the sewer, wrench the lid open, and slip into its cold, clammy depths.

Murky water filled with unspeakable things sloshes in the dark. Slurping, slapping, splashing. Cal says they whisper secrets. Every muscle strains to run, but even at this slow pace, my shoes slip on the algae coating the ledge. If I fall into the sewage, I can expect one of two scenarios—with luck, I'll shiver and smell until I can shower and get dry clothes; with bad luck, I'll break a limb. Better to slow down. Getting injured won't do Cal any good. I keep counting breaths to calm my frenzied mind.

Twenty.

Twenty-five.

Thirty.

At breath number sixty, I climb another ladder, this one marked with a neon-green X. I nudge the sewer lid up an inch, glance around, then wriggle out onto the damp concrete and scurry to the fire escape. Daniel always positions the garage dumpster just close enough for Cal and me to reach the rungs when we need roof access at night. It still requires a bit of a jump.

My palms chafe on the wet metal as I climb. When I clear the roof, I'll find Cal safe and back to work on her project. She shifts between one stressful event to another much better than I do. This late-night escape will hardly even register as much more than an inconvenience.

Fingers anchored into the top of the cinder-block wall, I hoist myself up to a view of an empty roof.

Empty.

Panic grips my chest. Did the Slingers—

Cal slams into me, arms wrapping around my ribcage. She drags me the rest of the way up. Neither of us say a word. We just gasp, clinging to each other. Tense in my arms, she stays perfectly still, her pulse pounding against mine. After the hundredth breath—the one that finally comes deep and slow and no longer shallow and shredding—I nod, and we turn to peek down into the street. Our knees grind into the cold cement.

The black-clad soldiers search the alley below.

Each time one of their electric whips slaps a corner, Cal spins a gear on the gun she built from scrap metal and keeps in the pocket of her overalls. Her fingers shake. I clench the edge of the roof until the rough cinder block bites into my palms. Pain always distracts from fear.

The patrol finally passes. I shut my eyes, then turn and slump to the ground.

I rub my scraped palms on my stained jeans and glance at Cal. "How's the project?"

Pushing her goggles up so the curls spiral skyward with one hand, she tilts the gun so I can see with the other. Light from yellowed bulbs in the cinder-block wall pour over the black metal. Apart from them, only the faint glow from distant billboard screens breaks the shadows around Daniel's garage.

"Coming along nicely. Need a few more parts, but it's on its way. Then I'll find some charges and bam!" She closes one eye and aims the weapon at a pigeon.

It ruffles its feathers, pecks at the bare ground, then launches into the air. She follows the bird's path with the gun, making exploding sounds until it disappears into the white billboard lights. Others follow from different directions, a swarm of flying rodents, their wings like the sound of Slingers marching.

"Pigeon doesn't taste so good anyway. Though in a pinch…" I wrinkle my nose and glance over the half wall again.

Two lamps with busted bulbs stand guard on the pothole-ridden street. Repair crews don't make it around often, but if they do, a well-placed rock darkens the bulbs easily enough. I crane a little to get a better look. Still out. Beyond them, night-blackened buildings—some government tenements, others abandoned office buildings—form a protective barrier around the garage, their windows mostly smashed or covered with tinfoil against heat and cold.

A single gap in the circle gives us an almost movie-perfect view of downtown Washington DC. There, sleek, metal-plated buildings reflect the bright glare of billboard screens, a shining city on a mound that only makes the dark places around it that much darker.

An ad plays on the closest screen. Nausea floods me.

A Designer Kid with lab-perfect symmetry smiles at the camera to the sound of a voiceover. *Get your own custom-made child under the age of ten. Select from a variety of personalities, genders, and skills. Design your own or choose from our catalogue.* The pace of the voice speeds up. *Privatized since 2019. All expired children will become productive members of society in state-of-the-art workhouses.*

The image shifts to groups of children dressed in crisp, clean uniforms. They chatter and laugh, type on laptops, and solve math problems. *There they will learn life-affirming skills that will allow them to enter the workforce when they reach the age of eighteen.*

I swallow disgust.

Child labor laws don't cover kids over the age of ten, even if they are Designer Kids. *Especially* if they're Designer Kids. No one cares about the rejects. Not when they don't sell for whatever reason. Well, no one cares besides the Slingers, the task force whose electrically charged whips can wrap kids up good and fast and sling them right back to the lab.

I shove down a new wave of nausea and stand.

"Off to your other job?" Cal squints at me, one eye closed.

I stretch, back cracking, then pull up my hoodie. "So long as I don't run into any more Slingers. Or one of Hellen Jacobs' crew." I shiver.

With work so slow at the garage, we only make enough for a FudPak box or two a week. Leftover change—if there ever is any—goes into the tin can Cal rigged into a makeshift safe. The extra money pays for emergencies, like medicine for a cold or bad cut, but on rare occasions, we spoil ourselves, her with a coloring book or ammo, me with a new torsion wrench or hook pin.

Gun aimed at the sky, she makes another explosion sound. "Getting a new assignment?"

"Should be."

She tightens her grip on the weapon so hard the tendons spring out. "Be careful. Don't piss Felix off." *Pop, pop, pop, bang!*

I pause at the peeling door that leads to the garage, anxious tension tightening my jaw. Facing Felix is almost more dangerous than dealing with Slingers. At least I can predict the soldiers' movements. My boss, the crime lord, kicks the crap out of people for shits and giggles.

"And, Seph?"

"Yeah?"

"Don't die. The streets would be so boring without you."

A smirk jumps onto my face. Typical Cal. Always protecting me from my own mental spirals. "You either. Stay out of sight. Back in the morning." I pull the door open, then jog down the stairs and attempt not to think about the danger I leave her in every time I go to work.

Chapter Two

Cal

After Sephrim leaves, I focus on the pistol. Pursing my lips, I blow metallic-smelling dust from its barrel. Just a few more strokes to perfect.

"Perfect. Adjective. Excellent or complete beyond practical or theoretical improvement. Entirely without any flaws, defects, or shortcomings."

I recite definitions without thinking, words scientists and lab techs repeated throughout my childhood. Defining things gives me some power over them. Somehow, that helps.

Designer Babies. *Perfect* children. No genetic flaws. Exactly what individual parents, politicians, or dignitaries want. Usually. Not many reject their orders, but it happens. I knew from the age of five they would reject me, especially after a conversation I overheard on my fifth birthday. Something about being on the "spectrum" and the lab wanting to "retire" my donor sample.

I asked Dr. Gayle for the definition. She frowned, her eyes full of tears I didn't understand, then wrote the words down in her near illegible doctor's scrawl.

Spectrum, noun, any of a group of developmental disorders marked by impairments in the ability to communicate and interact socially.

Sephrim grimaced when I told him my new word. Brow wrinkled in clear confusion, he eventually waved a hand to dismiss it, then poked fun at the scientists for saying I was impaired. After that, we imagined where we'd run away to when we aged out or, as the lab calls it, expired. Sephrim wants to see the ocean. Me, snow.

I squint at another interloping pigeon. It hops off one of the rusted vent pipes, searching for scraps with its pointy little beak. "You could take an eye out with that thing." I glare at it. "If I died up here, would you make a feast of my face?" A nervous laugh bursts out of my throat.

"Perfect. Excellent or complete beyond practical or theoretical improvement." I run my tool over the barrel again. "They can put you all together in a petri dish but can't fix personality. Even with programming. Unless…" I aim the gun at my temple and make an explosion sound with my mouth. "They turn your brain to jelly. But you don't have to worry about that, Mr. Pigeon. Your brain's too small for personality."

The bird pecks at the ground again. Wind kicks stray twigs and leaves around it. Tires wail against asphalt on the street below. A horn blares. Ruffling its feathers, the winged rat waddles to a small puddle near the edge of the roof.

I tilt my head. "Wonder how much meat you got on you."

"I'd advise against it. Pigeons taste lousy."

With a sharp gasp of fear and surprise, I sweep the detached barrel toward the disembodied voice. I arch a brow at the top of the metal stairs and the half-open door that leads down to the shop below. "Who goes there?"

Two hands slide around the frame. "I come in peace.

Hopefully not pieces."

I laugh, and the tension in my chest uncoils. "Come on up, Danny-Boy, but only if you bear gifts."

"How many times I got to tell you to call me Daniel?" One of the hands drops, then reappears with a paper bag. Grease stains darken the corners of the otherwise unmarked package. "How's a burger topped with bacon and cheese?"

Scrambling to my feet, I get fully upright, then attempt to shove the gun pieces into the pockets of my overalls while sprinting to the door. Daniel steps out and presents the bag, his fingers dark brown against the white paper. Their color and texture—not quite even and rubbed raw in places from mechanic work—have always mesmerized me. Black, white, brown, green, every Designer Kid's skin is smooth, uninterrupted by scar or callus. Daniel's work-worn hands are the most beautiful things I've ever seen.

"Who knew angels delivered pork products?" I clutch the bag and pinch it open.

The smell of bacon and beef well into my face. Steam coats my skin with moisture. My mouth fills with saliva. "Sweet merciful meat." I cross my legs at the ankles, spin, and sink to the ground, back against the ledge of the roof.

He chuckles, then sits across from me. He doesn't even seem to mind the fact that he'll get his slacks dirty. Not that he isn't used to grease and grime, since he owns the garage where we work. Still, unless he's tinkering with a car, he dresses for success, as the lab techs used to say: pressed khakis, button-down shirts, maybe a vest. He looks like one of those old-time Hollywood stars, especially when he wears a pageboy hat.

He grins as I bite into the burger. "Not bad, is it?"

"Is it possible to have a food-gasm?" I ask through a mouthful.

He rolls his eyes. "Where did you even learn a phrase like that?"

I shrug. "TV show."

After weeks of plastic-flavored food, a half-smooshed burger tastes of absolute nirvana. No matter how much we save, we'll never have enough to buy something like this on our own. Too expensive now even for normal people, what with all the new government regulations.

Daniel laughs again. "Save some for Seph."

With a groan, I let my head fall back, mouth stuffed. "You know—"

"Finish what you're eating before you monologue."

I snort, chew quickly, then swallow and stick my tongue out the way I used to after the lab techs administered daily meds. "As I was saying. Seph and I were just talking about how, in the lab, we used to eat the best food. Though, I gotta say, my favorite thing about being on the street is bacon. They never let us have bacon."

"Yeah, but they let you have that fake, vitamin-enhanced cheese junk." He drapes both arms over his knees, restless gaze on the ground. "Sephrim at Cade's?"

I wipe my chin with the back of a hand, the burger losing taste and drying out all at once in my mouth. Forcing the bite down takes a moment, but when I manage to do it, I nod, focusing on the tops of my scuffed-up tennis shoes. Why does avoiding eye contact make facing a hard truth easier? Dr. Gayle would probably say it has something to do with vulnerability.

Eyes as windows and all that.

Daniel sighs. "I know he's got to have the work, but still, bad scene."

Bad scene. "A response to an unfortunate occurrence or anything with negative connotations. Urban Dictionary." I pull down my goggles, tinting my world yellow.

"Worried about him?"

"Always."

He pauses a moment, then speaks slowly, hesitant maybe. "Least he's not mixed up with the Jacobs crew. Even worse scene."

Licking a trail of grease from my forearm, I shrug and keep my eyes angled down again, this time at a caulk-filled crack in the cement. "Both a bunch of cuckoo birds. Give me regular birds any day. But their credits work."

Hyper-militant and probably voted most likely to try and overthrow governments while in school, Hellen Jacobs runs the half of the city that doesn't bend the knee to the Cades. Rumors circulate that at one point the two crime families were actually one and the same unit, but a falling out split them up.

Daniel adjusts his hat. "Still don't think you should be selling to Jacobs. She's got delusions of grandeur. Makes her dangerous. Felix doesn't care what goes on around here as long as it doesn't get in the way of his business. Hellen…well, she thinks she ought to run the country."

"Judging, Danny-Boy?" We've only had this conversation a zillion and one times.

"Worried is all. Felix Cade is a bad dude, but at least he follows discernable rules. Hellen Jacobs doesn't have any kind of code. Except maybe chaos."

Inside my pocket, I trace the butt of my gun. The feel of its solid surface and sharp angles calms my nerves, steadies me, anchors me to reality. "At least Jacobs' initiation isn't a beatdown. You saw Seph after Felix's boys 'welcomed him to the club.' "

Bruised. Broken. Bleeding out. He needed a hospital, a healing tube, but we couldn't risk that, not without an ID chip, not with our perfect features and weird frequency embedded into our skin. The food hardens in my stomach and flips over like a poisonous pancake. I fold the greasy paper and set the burger on the ground.

"Yeah, I remember." Daniel scratches his forehead with a thumb.

"Besides"—I pull out the gun barrel and file the inside with my tool—"if I sell to the Cade clan *and* Jacobs' rebel crazies, I'm really just leveling the playing field, right?"

"And if they find out you're dealing weapons to both of them?" His voice gets all low and gravelly, a sure sign of worry.

I draw a pointer finger along my throat, then let my eyes roll back and gag.

He rubs his eyes. "Cal—"

"They won't find out. Don't worry. It's why I don't tell Seph and why I never sell stuff that looks the same."

I push myself upright and carry the leftover burger to the makeshift tent we keep ready for nights on the roof. Stuffing the bag under a rough plaid blanket, I then grab my coat and slip into it before turning to face Daniel. "Don't wait up, Danny-Boy. And don't worry. I'll be fine."

****

Rain splatters the ground again about the time I reach the drop zone. Well, not really rain, more like cloud spit. Strands of my hair stick to my face and neck, and fog breathes across my goggles. I wipe them with a jacket sleeve. A nervous pulse beats against my temples. Only an idiot wouldn't be scared to meet Hellen Jacobs.

As I trot down a half-collapsed stairwell and under a long-forgotten overpass, the rain increases. Bare brown twigs stick out of cracks in the cement like reaching fingers, bits of rain-soaked paper plaster themselves to the ground, and water stains darken the space under a slimy gutter.

When me and Sephrim first came to the streets, my overly sensitive nose picked up every gnarly smell from every corner. With each new "discovery" I complained. Even defining them didn't help much and sometimes just made the nausea worse. Now I barely notice. Weird how the olfactory senses work.

Newscasters' voices from the billboard screens ricochet off the walls. Even this far away, white-blue light from the massive TVs vanquishes the shadows under the overpass. I have to crawl the cement slope all the way to the top for darkness to cover me. Once settled, I watch the alley below with narrow eyes.

Bats hidden in the gloom above screech as a group of women march into view seconds later. Hellen Jacobs occupies the center. The shadows try but fail to soften her angular features. Sharp like the beak of a bird—a zombie bird who would pick flesh off bones and throw it away out of spite. Egret thin and only a head and a half taller than me, she could easily blend in with a group of middle-class soccer moms, given the right wardrobe.

Funny thought, particularly when she stops halfway across the cracked road, wind lifting the ends of her elbow-length dark hair and the sides of her open trench coat. Somewhere, hidden away, she carries a personalized gun I designed nearly a year ago. Silent, accurate, and crafted to fit perfectly in her hand, it makes her already uncanny aim terrifying. Not soccer-mom friendly.

One corner of Hellen's mouth hitches in a smirk. "Are you there, Little Shadow?"

Shadow. Noun. A hint or faint, indistinct image or idea, intimation. Not the substance of the thing. Heart thudding in my throat, I stand and fish the gun out of my pocket.

"Filling the corners," I say, using our code—without which Hellen would open fire—then trek down the slope toward the group. A few feet from the bottom, I pause, glance between both sides of the overpass, then lay the firearm flat across my hands. They tremble faintly, like an idling tailpipe.

Hellen's smirk broadens into a smile when she sees the weapon. Hands still in her coat pockets, she closes the space between us, then bends forward an inch to examine the gun. Her breath, unusually cool, spreads across my skin. "Beautiful."

I grin. Terrifying or not, she recognizes a well-made piece. Unlike Felix, she understands, appreciates the craftsmanship that makes it unique. It's more than metal and charges, stock and barrel. It's art—oily, sleek, weighty—something to admire as much as to use.

She takes the gun and turns it over to study the design more closely, first the butt, then the barrel, followed by the grip. "Perfect."

Palms pressed into my thighs, I take a minuscule step back. "It just needs a charge, and it'll be ready to go."

"Tell me, Cal." She aims her gaze down the rear sight with her right eye closed. "What do you think of our country?"

A swallow clogs in my throat. I curl my toes to stop the urge to rock back and forth. "Not much. The second you're not worth something, they throw you out."

"Yes. You would be so easily gotten rid of." She lifts the gun and aims it at me.

Cold panic skids through my chest and back, but I cement my face muscles in place. I don't breathe. *Hellen wants a reaction. Don't give it to her.* Besides, without charges, the gun won't do a whole lot of damage.

Damage, noun, injury or harm that reduces value or usefulness.

She laughs. "My, my, Little Shadow. You certainly are brave. You liked to give the lab techs hell when you were in the lab, didn't you?"

In my pocket, I trace the worn screw on my wrench. "Any chance I got."

"Good. Then you'll understand what I'm trying to do. Maybe not right away, but eventually."

I don't even have a chance to turn. Something collides with the back of my skull, knocking out all light and feeling and sound.

Chapter Three

Sephrim

Felix Cade holds court beneath the city, away from Slingers, cops, and cameras. An abandoned warehouse would've been too conventional. Instead, he opts for an abandoned subway tunnel.

With every step down toward the center of the cavern, dread constricts my chest. Reinforced with steel, it makes an ideal weapons depot and training facility. Felix, however, spends a baffling amount of time covering up the ugly goings on with beauty. Elaborate rugs hang from the smudged, gray walls, and paintings, all stolen, fill the space between them.

Music pulses in my ears—an odd blend of classical and rock—as I pass the guards in the entryway. Longing to hide under my hood, I duck my head and weave through the thick crowd. Felix refuses to allow me this security blanket. It would be a shame to cover up such a pretty face, he says. These words burn embarrassment and resentment into my skin. Maybe if the scientists hadn't created me to look so ridiculously perfect, people wouldn't gawk so much.

I can't even freaking add a scar to remove the effect. While my body can definitely break and bleed, burn and swell, it all remains internal for the most part, injuries that heal perfectly, particularly when it comes to my face. Another wonderful addition to my stupid, unnatural DNA.

When I first ran to the street with Cal, I tested it out, breaking my stupidly perfect "Roman" nose with a rock. A few days later it snapped right back into place where it belonged. Out of desperation, I shaved my hair—a silky chestnut—but it grew back so fast I gave up. Not worth the effort.

Strobe lights glance off shot glasses full of rainbow-colored liquid, costume jewelry, and watches. No one carries phones. Two rules reign the guests at Cade's—check all cellphones and weapons at the door, and do not, under any circumstance, approach the family without permission.

No one breaks these rules. At least not twice.

Behind closed doors, men and women bag, sort, and distribute drugs, stolen goods, and weapons. Some of the stuff I steal goes to outside buyers, some into Felix's personal collection. Same with Cal's guns. It all pumps through the club like glittering blood, flowing back out to who knows where. Better not to think about it.

Felix sits at the back of the room, legs draped over the arm of an overstuffed chair, a glass of his drink of choice—scotch—in hand. A crowd gathers around him, their rank evident by their seats. Highest—and most beautiful—lounge on carpets, lowest on the bare, metal floor. Felix and Marcus alone have chairs.

Marcus, Felix's dad and the deep pockets behind the operation, rarely gets his hands dirty. Ever present at his son's side, he has no official authority. But everybody knows better than to piss off the man with the money. When he speaks, everyone listens.

Only the lowest of the low look up when I approach,

glancing at me out of the corners of their eyes. A few stare, some sneer, and I again have to resist the urge to hide under my hood. Their reactions make sense. Even they rank higher than a thief, and most everyone feels either disdain or desire around Designer Kids.

I hover at the very edge of the circle, arms at my sides, empty palms exposed, the standard protocol to show I've come unarmed. Blood pounds in my head well above the sound of the crowd. No matter how many times I come to Cade's, fear saturates every second here under the ground.

A full measure of music passes before Felix acknowledges me with a casual flick of his wrist. I walk into the circle, bypassing each level until I reach the crime lord. I lift my hands to shoulder level.

A bodyguard steps forward. As he waves the wand-like scanner under my arms and between my legs, it hums, a frequency entirely unique to a Designer Kid's skin. The man grins. "Four point three seven hertz." He quirks a brow and lowers his voice. "Four point three eight now. Must have you riled good."

Blood creeps up my neck, but I don't respond. The bodyguard chuckles, then shoves me the last foot forward. I crouch, one knee on the ground, head low.

Felix swings his legs from the arm of the chair and stands.

"Ah, my favorite thief, early as always." He grabs my jaw and pulls me upright. The strobe lights illuminate his genetically altered white eyes as he smirks. "Reliable as ever."

I choke on the cologne-soaked air. Both hands shake as nausea fills my throat and mouth. Images flash through my mind, memories of scientists inspecting me

E.C. Farrell

every morning, searching for defects. I lock my jaw. Beneath Felix's tightening grip, the bone aches. Members all around snicker and mutter about "freakish lab babies." Every breath stops short of my lungs.

"I never will get over how"—Felix tilts his head, voice low—"perfect you Designer Kids are. Ready-made and ordered off the menu, right down to these lovely green eyes of yours. It's unsettling. Beautiful. Nevertheless." With a final shake, he lets go of my chin and straightens, resting a hip against his chair. "Next available job's in a few hours. Not a solo mission this time."

I stiffen.

"Problem?"

Flexing my fingers, I shake my head. "No problem."

"It's a private job," he continues. "Local fat cat with a Fabergé egg that will be a perfect addition to my collection. You'll be going in with my most trusted operative, Darby."

A girl sitting on one of the carpets to the right of Felix's chair stands and steps forward, her dark-lashed eyes narrow. I've seen her around, but we've never talked. Though close to my age, someone who ranks that high wouldn't have spared me much more than a glance without a direct order from Felix—but I'd spared her more than a few during my visits to this dungeon.

She walks a silent circle around me, then stops between Felix and me, arms crossed.

Kind of hot, even with that grimace souring her heart-shaped face. She's built a bit like a video game character. An old-school one anyway. Dark denim hugs her muscular legs just enough to show off the shape, and her leather jacket cinches at the smallest part of her waist. Heat burns through my gut as she scans my body. I fight to shut up the little voice in my head that wonders what she thinks of me.

"Still don't think I need a thief, but if he's as good as you say he is…" Darby shrugs.

"Darby, my dear, you are brilliant with locks and alarms, but that safe is beyond your skill. Besides, I don't want you distracted from your other mission," Felix says. "You need him."

I smirk. That's the kindest thing Felix's ever said about me. He'd be an idiot to think otherwise.

Ten years in a government lab, with state-of-the-art locks and safes galore and curiosity matched only by ingenuity, turned me into an expert lock-picker. A few more years on the streets honed my craft, expanding my opportunities to work with more primitive tools. Now, at sixteen, I can get past pretty much any lock or alarm system.

Arms still crossed, Darby pouts a little and rakes me up and down with her eyes. "Fine. But he'd better not get in my way. If he trips an alarm, I'm leaving his ass behind for the cops or that lab-funded task force. What is it you Designer Kids call them? Slingers. I'll leave you behind for the Slingers."

"Feeling's mutual," I say in a low voice.

Unless I'm asking a question, I don't usually speak in Felix's presence, but I do let slip the occasional bit of snark. Depending on the circumstance and his mood, Felix finds it amusing and won't beat the ever-loving snot out of me.

Barking a laugh, Felix claps. "You two will get along swimmingly. Darby will give you the details. I expect delivery by morning." He waves a hand and turns back to his chair.

As Felix tilts to speak to one of the guards to his right, I glance at Marcus and meet his gaze. The older man ignores his son, and his ever-present grin widens. Too much oxygen fills my head. Shitty timing, but really, when's an anxiety attack actually welcome? I resist the urge to rub my chest and force my thoughts somewhere else.

I recall Dr. Gayle's soft voice, her grip gentle on my shoulders as she coached me through what Dr. Troy called "tantrums."

Your lungs are working. Just slow down. Don't breathe too quickly. That's why you're getting light-headed. Take it in slow. In through the nose, out through the mouth...through the nose, out through the mouth...

She would breathe with me then, pausing only to count every so often whenever I hyperventilated. All the while, her focus never broke from mine, not even amidst Dr. Troy's litany of snark.

Then Cal's voice pops into my head. *Creepy creepster.*

A perfect Cal-ism. I press my lips together to suppress a smile as my breathing stabilizes. White-eyed like his son, Marcus scares the shit out of police and politicians alike. Because of this, he can protect runaway Designer Kids to a point, as long as they pay for it. I steal for Marcus and bring Cal's weapons as tribute, but I'll never bring her to the Cades. Not if I don't have to. Not with their cruel initiation standard.

"Come on, thief."

Darby's voice breaks me from Marcus' stare. She bumps my shoulder as she heads into the crowd, dark-red braid swaying in time with her tread. I rip my gaze away from the old man and follow her to a room in the far-left corner opposite the bar.

The newsreel from earlier in the day replays on one of the TVs mounted in the corner, an announcement about the upcoming meeting of the United Nations right here in DC. As the president speaks, her words trail across the bottom of the screen accompanied by helpful emojis.

"A week from today will mark fifteen years since the United Nations dissolved. Back then, in the wake of increasing tensions over global pandemics, nuclear threats, and botched foreign politics, our relations with the rest of the world threatened to burn to the ground when hotheads prevailed. Only our scientists held us together by the barest thread as they worked to eliminate world hunger—"

I snort a little to myself, missing part of her speech.

"…the common cold and share the Genetic Modification Program. Now, as rebel groups and criminal organizations threaten every nation, leaders from across the globe have agreed to meet for the first time since 2020. In a week, people from every tribe, tongue, and nation will gather here, on American soil, to join together once again in a unified front against those who would keep us divided. If—"

"Get out the drums, Danny," Cal had said when we watched it this morning. "And find the lyrics for Kumbaya. World peace is on its way."

Darby stops at a door, fists on hips, lips puckered. Again, she looks me up and down. "I work alone."

Hands stuffed back in my hoodie pockets, I shrug. "So do I, but I'm not risking my payday by pissing Felix off."

"Neither am I, but just because he vouches for you doesn't mean I don't need proof." Darby glances at the locked door, then back to me. "Pick that, and we'll talk."

I scoff a little.

"Are you above an audition?"

"Back up. You're in my way."

Calm settles over me as I squat in front of the handle and study the lock. Primitive on the surface. Then again, Felix doesn't do primitive. I scan the frame. From my tool belt, I fish out an old-school screwdriver and pry open a small, metal panel near the floor.

As I study the switches, Darby sighs. "You're going to set off the whole system."

"Nope." I flip a switch and grin when the faint hum around the doorframe falls silent. "I'm not an amateur." Right eye shut, I pull out a tension wrench and pick rakes, then wriggle them until the last driver pin clicks. Always a satisfying sound. Straightening, I step aside, pride welling in my chest. "Give it a try."

Lips pursed yet again, Darby twists the knob and pulls the door open. "Easy lock." Crossing her arms, she looks me up and down, then sighs. "Fine. You seem proficient enough. Meet me at the Tuttleson mansion in an hour."

I roll my eyes—so much for impressing her—but agree. This is going to be *so* much fun.

Chapter Four

Matt

Computers have their own way of talking. Not everybody gets their ones and zeros, their hums and clicks, but I do. Honestly, I get them better than I do most people. Technological tongues. The superpower I've honed since I was five. Nine years later and I've pretty much become a techno-genius. It makes me valuable, indispensable, and I have to be indispensable.

If I'm not, I'll get tossed out like a faulty CPU.

Like most every day, I sit scrunched behind a metal table crowded with thin-screened monitors. My loyal minions. Lips pursed to one side, I hunch over my keyboard, creating complex patterns of technological wizardry. My good eye skips back and forth as each new line forms.

When the door snaps open and Hellen steps into the room, I shoot to my feet, standing at attention like a soldier. The chair rolls back and crashes into the wall. I tense, my gaze zipping to the metal hide-a-bed built into the wall, then to the area around the small trash can. I sigh with relief. No sheets stick out. No crumbs litter the floor.

Mess, flaws, mistakes, all as dangerous as being expendable.

Arms crossed, Hellen glares, a look that always

makes my brain freeze up like an overloaded webpage. "Is the bit reprogrammed, Matthew?"

"The code's almost in place." My voice croaks. My hand twitches to rub my damaged eye, but I drop it again, shoving it into a pocket to trace the piece of broken motherboard I keep there. "I just need a few more minutes."

With a sneer, Hellen sidesteps the desk. In her heels, she towers over me, but I don't try to meet her gaze. Instead, I stare at my bare feet. Loose strands fraying from my jeans splay across them and fan out along the slick, gray concrete. A crack splits one of my toenails straight down the middle. I press the bottom of my other foot over it to hide the damage.

An inch away now, Hellen grips the back of my neck, and I restrain a wince.

"How long?"

Shifting my eye to the screen, I squint at the numbers through the strands of my dark-blond hair. In the harsh light, my vision blurs, burns, swims. "Just another minute."

"Work quickly." With a pinch of her fingers, she forces me back toward the computers and pushes until I'm bent over the keyboard, bowed like a worshiper before his god.

There her hand stays as I type, sweat stinging my brow. It coats my shaking fingertips, leaving dots of moisture on each key. Seconds tick by too fast. I hold my breath, toes curled into the floor. Cramps seize the muscles along my spine. As the imaginary buzzer goes off in my head, sounding the end of the minute, the last number falls into place.

I lift both hands. "Done."

Without releasing pressure, she leans forward, as if she could actually understand my minions' words. Her cold breath rushes past my ear. "And it will work?"

Palms now braced against the sharp edge of the table, I choke down a sticky swallow. "It should, but there's no way to test it unless—"

"But the data is uploaded and the bit modified?"

"Yes."

"Eject it."

I click the program and hit eject.

Hellen wrenches the small device from the port and slips it into her pocket.

My entire being screams at her to be careful, but I keep my trap shut tight. One wrong twist and she'll destroy the thing she's dumped so much hope into. But it doesn't matter how logical the warning is if I break her rule—don't talk unless she asks "a damn question."

She digs all five nails into my neck. "If you screw this up…" She lets the sentence hang, then straightens and walks to the door.

Through clenched muscles in my throat, I manage to ask, "Mom?"

She stops. "I've asked you repeatedly to call me Hellen."

My chest tightens. "Sorry. Hellen." I stay hitched over the table with my hands still clenched on the edge.

"What?"

"I…I…"

"What. Is. It? I'm pressed for time."

"I need a new cord for screen four. It's starting to short out." Not what I meant to ask, but I can't get the right words out.

"Walter will be around soon. Ask him." She waves

her hand in front of the pad on the wall next to the door and, without so much as a glance back, leaves the small, dark room behind.

****

Darby

In a back room at Felix's compound, I face off with one of his guards, my ritual before every assignment.

Alura stalks in a circle, a mirror of my own movements. Harsh white light burns my eyes as I track every flinch of muscle, the set of her stance, the position of her hands. Though she's good about not telegraphing her attacks, every fighter has a tell. My concentration, however, doesn't want to center on her.

It keeps slipping back to that Designer Kid.

Felix's fascination is easy to understand. Lab perfect, Designer Boy almost doesn't look real. Like someone airbrushed him into existence. I wanted him to fail my test. To show some flaw or glitch. To prove he isn't, in fact, perfect. Instead, he assessed Felix's system like a pro, thinking of things that never even entered my mind.

Alura bursts forward with a straight punch. I block. Jam an arm into her neck. Ram a knee into her gut. I only land one hit before she drops weight. She drives a shoulder into my ribs. As her arms lock around my waist, she lifts my feet off the mat.

Can this Designer Kid even fight? Defend himself from guards or police or Slingers?

Growling, I hammer the side of my fist into the back of Alura's skull. Once. Twice. Three times. Finally, she wobbles. I hook a leg around one of hers, an arm around her neck, locking up tight until she wheezes. She squirms. Claws at my arms. Then taps out.

I let go and take a few steps back. If Designer Boy's lived on the street, he has to know how to fight. He wouldn't have survived this long without learning some kind of self-defense. Even if it's ugly. Besides, Felix is a jerk, but he's not dumb enough to employ a marshmallow. At least not after the last guy screwed the pooch.

Or whatever.

Alura waves me off, hands on her knees as she catches her breath. I nod and back up to one of the benches. The gray mat wheezes under my feet. With a towel pulled from my bag, I wipe sweat off my hairline. In a flinch of movement, Alura throws a surprise hook. I duck under it, then pop up, and slam the bottom of my boot into her stomach. She stumbles across the room, then lands on her ass, legs in the air.

I sling the towel over a shoulder and head toward the door.

If things do go sideways, I'm not bailing Designer Boy out. I've got my own shit to take care of. I'm not a babysitter. No matter what Felix says.

Chapter Five

Cal

This is not the angle a neck is supposed to turn and definitely not the angle it's meant to be slept on. Chin pressed hard into my chest, I struggle to breathe in the sterile air through my nose. Straps cut off the circulation to my arms and legs, dig into my shoulder blades. Each blink blurs the ground below. Then the rounded, black tips of a pair of shoes appear in my line of vision.

Hellen's shoes.

The moment they do, latex-encased fingers press against the base of my neck. Terror and revulsion prickle my arms.

"Where am I?" I don't expect a response, but the question splutters from my chapped lips anyway. Chapped. Always chapped.

"You're awake. Good," Hellen says next to my left ear. "I would prefer to explain the procedure before it happens."

"Procedure?" My voice squeaks, and I cringe at how young it makes me sound. Fists clenched, I pull at the restraints until they pinch my skin, until tears squeeze from the corners of my eyes.

"Now, now, don't struggle, Little Shadow. You'll only hurt yourself." The latex-covered hand smooths the hair at the back of my head. "I've no desire to sedate you.

It disrupts the process, and you should at least understand what I'm trying to accomplish and why."

Chewing the inside of my cheek, I huff but go still. *Crazy. Adjective. Mentally deranged, demented, insane. Unofficial definition? Doing the same thing over and over again yet expecting different results.* If I keep trying to get out of the restraints, I might pass out or worse. Not an option. Better to learn my enemy's plans.

"Fine." I uncurl my fists. "Talk. Why am I here?"

"You're here to change the world."

Anger clenches my teeth together until my jaw clicks. I try to release it with a breath. "What—"

"You said earlier you enjoyed giving the lab techs hell."

Those cold, latex-covered fingers graze my bare shoulder, and I shudder.

"I assume you watched the press conference this morning, heard the grand plans the nations have of coming together, the plans the scientists have for children like you. Tell me, do you think they intend anything good?"

Sweat stings the skin along my spine. "No. Whatever they have planned, it'll probably make things worse."

Hellen's fingers move farther down my arm to brush my elbow. "A wise assessment. But then, you are a genius, aren't you? That was part of the order that brought you into this world. IQ beyond the normal scope. And yet…"

I close my eyes. And yet the customer rejected me. "What's your point?" My tongue sticks to the backs of my teeth.

"This is why I like you, Cal." She laughs. "And why

I chose you. Of course, your proficiency with a firearm helps."

I set my nails into the sides of the metal table and let a breath out through my teeth. "What does that have to do with me?" Dumb question, but I need to hear the answer.

"Isn't it obvious? You're going to be my smoking gun." Hellen strokes my arm again. "And really, I'd love to give you a choice in the matter, but I can't leave anything to chance."

I squirm as Hellen brushes the hair off my neck. "What are you doing? Stop!"

Wriggling makes no logical sense, but I do it anyway, fear and fury driving my limbs. I don't need Hellen to clarify. Not after I gave her that blank chip at our last meeting a few days ago, a chip that can serve two potential purposes—identification or mind control. Though the rest of the world believes the latter hypothetical, all Designer Kids know the truth.

Chips. Noun. Implantable devices used for neural pathway reconstruction. Programmable. Meant to help addicts overcome dependency. Success rate, none. Because everyone either goes crazy or dies. So much for a "better world."

I thrash, but the straps hold me in place. Just like in the lab. My head swims, and I shout every curse word in my verbal tool kit.

"Stay still, Little Shadow." She presses a cold, metal tube against the base of my head. "I have a very steady hand—I was a med student once upon a time—but one false move could damage you. I know what you're thinking. But I can assure you, my programmer has resolved the trouble they've had in the factories. You will only lose your mind at the appropriate moment."

Sharp pain tears through the back of my head. Horrified, I scream. *Unconscious. Adjective. Knocked out, stunned...*

****

Sephrim

A passing glance at the Tuttleson mansion eases any doubt that the owner can do without a measly Fabergé egg. Then again, most people Felix has me steal from don't want for much. Taking up almost half the block, Aaron Tuttleson's home stretches nearly as high as it does wide. Its silver-painted walls reflect the moving patches of moonlight. On the other side of a twisted, iron gate, uniformed guards march a path along the purple grass.

No joke. Freaking purple. When did green stop doing it for people?

Tugging my hood farther over my face, I press my shoulders against the rough bark of a large beech tree, then glance at the normal-colored turf under my feet. Cut brutally short and uniform in length, not a single blade is faded, dry, or brittle. No water restrictions in this neighborhood. Tipping the toe of my shoe, I kick at the roots, tearing a small patch of imperfection and filling the air with the smell of damp earth.

I grin at the mess.

"Thought you were a professional."

Terror snaps through my muscles as images of Slingers or one of the Jacobs' crew sneaking up on me tear through my mind. I spin around to meet Darby's tawny eyes. Or at least I try to. Shadows blot out most of her face, and she's stuffed her red hair into a black beanie. A dark backpack hangs from her shoulders, its straps snapped tight around her waist. As she stands staring at me, she tugs on her gloves.

I glare. "What?"

She points at the brutalized grass. "No evidence."

Huffing, I roll my eyes. "Hope you brought something good to deal with the guards."

"I can handle it. Hope you came prepared to deal with that fence."

"I can handle it."

"Right then. I'll take out the walking security. You take out the fence. Follow me."

Annoyance shoulders out excitement. I scowl but don't argue. Better to take out the guards first anyway. I checked the system on one of Felix's computers before we left, and while shutting it down won't set off any alarms, taking away the human element increases our odds of success exponentially.

We keep to the shadows as we run to the far end of the mansion. Anticipation sweeps from my gut to my chest when Darby and I crouch at the edge of the fence. This close, her scent fills my nose. Honeysuckle? Whatever it is, it's a nice break from mud and grease, gas and grime.

I roll my eyes at the rabbit trail my mind chases. *Focus. Now is so not the time.*

Darby slides a small device out of her backpack with a pointer and middle finger, then edges it toward the purple lawn. I grab her wrist. Her elbow hitches back into my ribs so hard I lose my balance and land on my ass. I bite my tongue to cut off a yelp but hold on tight.

"What the hell are you doing?" Her question comes out in a sharp hiss.

Air filtering back into my lungs, I scan the street, then point at the space between the fence and the ground. "You're going to set off the alarm. I need to take out the sensors first. Unless that thing works from the sidewalk."

"Let. Go."

"Sorry." I let go of her wrist.

Her upper lip twitches, then she scowls. "Take them out. You're wasting time."

Silent, I crawl to the stone pillar about a foot away, then pull a small wrench and a metal wire from my tool belt. Fingers pressed against the crevice between the pillar and the sidewalk, I shut my eyes.

"What are—"

"Shh."

"But—"

"Thought you were a professional." I smirk as my nails scrape the thin divot of the emergency power panel.

Using the screwdriver, I pry it open to reveal three thin slots. This access point is set in place for government technicians alone, so not many know about it. Even fewer can handle the delicate touch required to cut the power. One bad move will set off every alarm on the block.

Nerves alight with adrenaline, I slide the wire into one of the slots. Almost instantly, I find the small indentation at the very center and apply the bare minimum amount of pressure. Heat vibrates into my fingers. The dull hum snaps off. A thrill shoots through my limbs, powering a grin onto my face. I glance back at Darby, who rolls her eyes and lifts her device again.

"Is it off?"

"Zap away." I shove the tools back into my belt one-handed, sucking my scorched forefinger and thumb.

They taste of metal.

Darby pivots on the balls of her feet and pushes the little black box onto the purple lawn. She then jams a middle finger into the button on top and backpedals. Power puckers the air around its front end. A series of thuds puncture the silence as the device stuns anyone in its path. I straighten, but she pulls me back down. Pulse rapid, I steady myself on the pillar.

Darby doesn't let go until a final thump comes from the yard and even then, holds on a second longer before she meets my gaze. "What's your entrance plan?"

Head cocked to one side, I motion upward. "We climb."

"We what?"

I press my fingers into the spaces between the bricks on one of the pillars that mark each corner of the fence. "We climb. Less eyes out here. The front gate doesn't have an external lock to pick."

"I heard that part. What…why don't we just pick a lock in the back or something?"

Looking over my shoulder, I study Darby's face. Patches of moonlight illuminate tense features. Hand at her side, she taps her fingers against one leg, a rapid beat. She glances up at the pillar, then back at me.

"Something wrong?"

Darby crosses her arms. "No." She says it too fast, talking over the end of my question.

I pinch my lips against an amused grin. "How 'bout this? I'll hop over and pick it from inside."

"What makes—"

"We're wasting time." I tug on a pair of gloves, pull my hood farther over my face, then plant a foot on one of the iron bars. Bracing myself against the pillar, I launch myself upward.

At the top, I swing both legs over to the other side and glance down at Darby. She frowns, then hits the button on the device to turn it off and offers me a nod. I drop to the ground. Rocks and sand crinkle under my shoes. I dig my fingers into the cold grass, eyes darting around the yard. Small mounds lie along the front of the mansion, the still bodies of each guard Darby's device knocked unconscious.

I glance up at the windows. All dark.

At the street. Empty.

Over my shoulder. Nothing but the iron fence.

Lips quirked to one side, I weave between the lumps to the front gate. With a final glance at the mansion, I pick the front lock and ease the gate open an inch. Risky, but I need to get Darby inside apparently.

She slips in, fast and silent like a puff of car exhaust. "Shut it. Quick."

I mutter to myself but do it anyway, then relock it for good measure. "Do all that for someone scared of heights and get chewed out for not moving fast enough."

Meeting her at the front door, I crouch next to the lock. Genetically coded. Worthless. Well, only worthless if I hadn't killed the system. A lesser thief might've knocked out the electricity completely, causing the doors to deadbolt from the inside. But I'm not a lesser thief. I toss Darby a small smirk, and she scowls.

"What?"

"Take a breath and hope like hell this works."

As her eyes bug, I slip my tools into the lock.

Chapter Six

Cal

Revolution…assassination…bit… "Expire…"

I wake up facedown to the same straps, the same cold table, and a shiny, new, splitting headache. It throbs from the injection site straight to the space between my eyebrows. Groaning, I wiggle feeling back into my fingers and toes. The pinpricks of sleep scatter and dissipate. Too bad the restraints won't do the same.

Restraints. My heart rate picks up. I chew the tip of my tongue and dig a definition out of my memory banks. *Restraint. Noun. The state or fact of being restrained, deprivation of liberty, confinement.*

What I wouldn't give to pee. *There. That. Focus on that and not the fact that you can't move and have a mind-controlling chip in your head that makes everybody in the workhouses go nutso…*

"Hey!" Panic drives the word from my mouth. "Hey, revolutionary crazies! I have to pee!" I don't want to face Hellen again, and yet the bladder wants what it wants. My voice bumps off the walls, but otherwise, nobody answers. "Hell-o-o. Anybody?"

Then the door opens with a heavy thunk. I flinch and sweep my eyes toward it. A shadow splits the light in two as somebody pads in on what sounds like bare feet. They stop a moment. Hesitant, maybe?

Bare feet? What the what? I scowl. "Hello?"

"Sorry. One sec."

I wrinkle my brow, completely confused. *A boy? Well, that makes zero sense. Nobody my age should be in the same vicinity as a loony lady.*

The door slides shut, and the feet move again. In a single, glorious rip, the straps lift away from my arms and legs, but before I can push myself up, the boy says, "Hang on. You need to move slow after…" He clears his throat. "Just go slow."

"Solid advice." With a sigh of relief, I grip one corner of the table and roll onto my side, looking up at a boy about my age.

A smile cracks across his face, revealing a slightly crooked front tooth and two uneven dimples. Faded pink scar tissue seals his right eye shut from one end of his brow to the top of his cheek, and in the harsh light of the operating room, his hair looks a little like straw. It sticks out over his forehead like the bill of a hat, then kicks upward at the ends. As he looks at me, he digs both hands into his jean pockets and sways between one bare foot and the other, shoulders scrunched.

The imperfections make him, well, kind of cute. Nothing cute belongs in this nasty place. It would die like a plant without sunlight. Suspicious. Highly suspicious. Might be some kind of trap Hellen has sent in to distract me. As soon as the room stops swaying, I'll have to do something about him.

I rub the spot between my eyebrows with a knuckle. "Whew. Okay, this'll have to work for a minute. You weren't kidding. Make the room quit rocking, would you?"

"Actually, I can. With this." He pulls a small, silver

stick out of his pocket. "Can I…" He gestures to my head.

I blink. "Can you… Oh, uh, sure."

His grin flickers but then holds fast as he walks to the other side of the table and brushes back my hair. I shiver. The tips of his fingers are soft, gentle. Usually, I don't love being touched, but my skin reacts to his gentleness, and I'm actually a little disappointed when the contact lasts only a second.

Something beeps—probably the device—and the room settles.

"There," the boy says. "That should make it—"

I fling my legs over the table, then plant my feet and lunge at him, pressing one arm into his throat as I drive him into the wall. "Okay, listen up. You're going to help me get out of here, got it?"

With a fragile clink, the little stick hits the cement floor, and the kid lifts both hands. His mouth works but produces no sound.

I glare. Is he scared? This guy, one of my captors? No way. Has to be a trick. Hellen has weaponized his cuteness. "If you can come and go and unstrap prisoners and fix this monstrosity in my brain, my guess is you know how to work the security system, right?"

The muscles under my grip tense and shake with nervous energy, and he doesn't even try to fight me off. I purse my lips, brows pinched together. Scared. Definitely scared and about to have an attack of some kind. It might be a good act. On the streets I've met the best of the best liars, kids who can fake tears, fainting spells, even death with the right drugs, but something about this feels real.

Pupil shrinking, skin going clammy, the kid freezes

up. His breath comes out fast and shallow the way Sephrim's does when he goes into panic mode, frozen up like a busted compressor. Then his legs buckle, and I catch all his weight. With an "oof" I help him sit and grip his shoulders.

"Hey, that's no good. If you pass out, then where will we be? Get it together, and then we can talk. Promise I won't use my fists."

The boy flinches and nods.

"If I let go of you, will you run tell Hellen?" I ask.

Blanching, the kid glances up at the cameras in the corners, then shakes his head, a rapid, minute motion. Words finally come from his still working lips. "No." He forces a slow breath that doesn't do much to steady his voice. "Hell no."

I tilt my head. "She scare you?"

His left eye twitches. "Big time."

Nose scrunched, I let him go, sit back on my heels, and hug my middle. "Me too." I drag my lower lip through my teeth. "What's your name?"

Fists clenched on his knees, the boy swallows. "Matt. And you're Cal. My mom, uh, Hellen, talks about you all the time." His mouth flinches into a smile.

My eyes bug. *Mom? Who the heck let her reproduce?*

"She says you're a genius," Matt continues. "Says I'm pretty smart but no genius. She also says you're a Designer Kid. Never seen a Designer Kid up close before. Do you…" He stops, swallows again, and looks at his feet.

I blink. "Are you broken?"

Matt rubs the back of his neck. "I talk too much. Start rambling. Hellen says I get too excited and need to learn to shut my trap. She's probably right."

Shut your trap, a rude or angry way of telling someone to be quiet. I frown. That sounds like Hellen. How in the heck did she manage to pop out a kid like this? "She's not. It's okay. I don't mind." I glance at the metal stick next to his foot. "What is that thing anyway?"

Matt lifts the little device. "It controls the chip. It can't turn it off, though. See, the chips've been failing in the workhouses because they haven't figured out how to regulate it externally. It's really not that hard of a fix. All I did was create a remote and pair them together. Not sure why they haven't figured it out." He grimaces. "Sorry it's in your head."

I rub the incision spot. It stings under my fingers. "Yeah."

"Look, I…" Matt lifts a hand, apparently to rub his injured eye, then freezes and lets it drop. "I can't help you get out."

I scowl but then notice his gaze shift to the corners of the room again. Cameras. Duh.

Matt continues quickly. "But if you're hungry or still need to go to the bathroom…"

I grin. "Bathroom first."

****

A socially unacceptable moan slips from my lips as I bite into the slice of pizza. Warm, cheesy goodness fills my mouth. I shut my eyes and let my head drop back. Mouth still full, I look at Matt and say, "Food-gasm part two."

Sitting cross-legged about an inch away, his back against the gray, metal door, Matt grins. It lifts his features, making the injured side of his face a little less noticeable. He wipes his mouth on a paper napkin. "That good, huh?"

"I don't remember the last time I had pizza. At least not one that didn't start off frozen. And this basil! I could kiss you." I cock my head. "Think I will actually." I lean forward and plant one right on Matt's nose. Impulsive? Possibly, but if all his cuteness *does* turn out to be a trap, it serves me well to try and get him on my side.

Blood reddens Matt's cheeks. "It came from my garden, the basil I mean. Hellen lets me go out once a day to water it. I have this room that gets really good sunlight. It's nice. I don't get to see a lot of sun."

I rest my elbows on my knees. No. He definitely doesn't look like he gets out much. If the rest of Hellen's hideout looks like this room—all cement and metal furniture and appliances and cold white lights—then… I cringe. Poor guy. At least the Designer Kid lab had solar bulbs and plant life in every corner.

"She's a tyrant more than a mom, huh?"

"Yeah. When she left my dad, she dragged me along with her, but only because I'm good with computers. You need a hacker when you're stealing government secrets and selling them to foreign countries and laundering money and all that. Otherwise, I'm not worth keeping around." Matt picks at his pizza crust.

Anger burns in my chest. Just like "shut your trap," the phrase "not worth keeping around" sounds like something Hellen would say. I let the fury out in a breath. Raging out loud will probably scare him again.

"Did she give you that?" I brush the tips of my fingers along the bruise darkening his left eye.

Unnatural warmth pulses out from the swollen spot. Sure, he could have given it to himself, but other evidence marks his arms and jaw. Yellow patches and green patches and deep, dark purple ones. Pity crawls into my chest.

"I wasn't working fast enough." His jaw hardens. "On the chip."

Eyes narrow, I knit my brows together. "Is it the one I gave her a couple of days ago?"

He nods.

"You reprogrammed a chip in two days?"

"I should've done it in one."

I drop the pizza and grab Matt's hands. "Are you crazy? Two days? You reprogrammed it in two days? That's insane. No one can do it that fast. Trust me, I'm a genius."

Heat from Matt's skin floods my palms, pulses into my skin, full of nervous, jittering life. He doesn't look at me, maybe won't look at me, but fixes his gaze on our intertwined hands. After a second of slight trembling, his fingers curl around mine, and he shuts his eye.

He looks young. Younger than he did when he first freed me, but definitely old enough to be expired like I am. The softness ends with his hands. A network of pale, white scars sketch a violent story into his skin.

Lower lip caught between my teeth, I trace them with my thumbs. Even if Hellen put him up to some kind of elaborate ruse, made him damage his body to pull empathy out of captives, well, that still amounts to child abuse, doesn't it? I wince at the idea.

"What—" I clear my throat. "What happened to your eye? Your-your other one, I mean."

His nostrils flare, and the muscles in his hands clench.

Cold tension balls in my stomach. "Sorry. You talk too much; I ask too many questions."

"No." He shakes his head. "It's okay. When Hellen went into labor, she had trouble. I was in distress or something. Since she didn't want to have me in a hospital, the person helping her didn't really know what they were doing…they used forceps to get me out, and it smashed my eye. They offered an implant or prosthetic or whatever, but…" His voice cracks, and he rubs the back of his neck, then tries again. "She didn't trust them after that, after a lot of stuff, and said she'd take care of it herself. She used to be a med student. So she sewed it up herself. Says it's a reminder of the system she's trying to change."

A word jolts out of my mouth that would make even the mechanics at Daniel's garage blush. "Whoa, and I thought she'd messed me up with this bit."

"She hates it, though, and I don't blame her. It makes me look like a freak."

I repeat the dirty word again. "No, it doesn't. It makes you look like a badass. An adorable badass."

He chuckles, face going stoplight red. "I…" His fingers tighten on mine, and lowering his voice, he meets my gaze. "I'm going to get you out of here."

I squint at him, suspicious. No way my plan to turn him worked *that* fast. "Wh-y?" Sweet kid or not, damaged or not, he isn't necessarily trustworthy. Maybe Hellen has evil plans that involve letting me go. Plans I need to try and figure out sooner rather than later.

Throughout the stream of these thoughts, Matt's eye flicks back and forth, lips pressed together so hard the color ebbs away. "Hellen's plans are bad. Really bad, and she makes me do crap I hate, and I don't want anybody else to get trapped like me."

Warmth crawls through my chest and plugs up my

throat. *Trapped. Adjective. Unable to be moved as a result of obstruction.*

My eyes drift back to him. I could try and press him on what Hellen wants to do, but somehow, I doubt he'll tell me. At least not yet. For now, I try a different angle. "But can you get this thing out of my head?"

A grimace twists his face. "No. Not yet anyway. I'm working on figuring it out or at least how to disable it. When I do, I'll shut it down. I swear."

"Come with me. If Hellen finds out…"

Our fingers lock tighter together as Matt's gaze flicks up to mine and then drops again. He doesn't answer right away but studies his toes. Dirt darkens the nails and cakes every faint line along the bottom. A few bloody cuts interrupt the grime.

Goose bumps tickle the back of my neck. I slammed him up against the wall. Does Hellen do that to him too? Shame isn't always logical—I didn't have all the facts—but it poisons my gut all the same.

"The streets aren't that bad." I squeeze his hands. "Especially if you're a technological badass."

Matt shakes his head. "I can't. I won't be able to figure out how to deactivate that chip without my computers. And she won't find out. Don't worry about me. I've got it under control."

Bam.

The door snaps open. I nearly jump out of my overalls as Hellen stomps into the room, her fury-twisted face shadowed by low brows. Matt shoves up from the floor, but before he can get straight, his mom backhands him. With a yelp he crashes into the wall. I slap both hands over my mouth but stay frozen in place. Matt's feet tangle but plant themselves fast, and a second later, he steadies himself to face Hellen, hands behind his back.

"What the hell are you doing in here?" Hellen asks between her teeth. "You have work to do."

Rusted on the spot by fear, I stare between them and then the open door, pulse slamming against my temples. If I move fast enough, maybe I can get away. A harsh thought, leaving Matt behind with this horror of a woman, but I barely know him. I have to take care of myself. Take care of Sephrim.

In my moment of hesitation, Hellen slams her palm into a pad on the wall. It beeps, and the door sucks shut again. Disappointment floods my veins followed by fear as Hellen takes a step toward her son. The muscles in his face twitch, then harden, but otherwise, he doesn't move. Pretty impressive. Maybe years under Hellen's tyranny taught him to be his own brand of brave.

"I had to stabilize the bit." His voice holds steady, doesn't even shake at all.

A sneer warps Hellen's lips. "And this?"

She kicks one of the plates so it clatters toward me. It bounces painfully off my knees, and I bite into my tongue to keep from making a sound. Long ago I learned the quiet suffer marginally less wrath than others.

"We don't know how a functional bit will affect her." Matt's nostrils flare. "It's better if she's fed."

Hellen glares at him for a long time. Too long. My muscles tense. What will she do? Beat Matt up? Yell and scream? Probably the former based on Matt's bruises. I hold my breath as she clenches and unclenches her hands. My oxygen-deprived lungs ache, pounding along with my pulse.

Finally, Hellen sticks a finger in Matt's face. "Fine.

49

Feed her. But don't waste any more time. You have work to do. I'll need access to all the news feeds by the end of the week."

She then wheels on me.

Fear grips me, but I lift my chin at the loony lady the way I used to with Dr. Troy. Pretending to be strong usually protected me from the fate others experienced, including Sephrim, who's too compliant for his own good. Like Dr. Troy, if Hellen sniffs out any sign of weakness, she'll definitely use it, and not for anything good.

I press my sweating palms into the concrete floor and give myself a mental pep talk. *Clam up until they line you up in their sights, then show them they don't scare you. Pretend to be strong...strong, adjective, having powerful means to resist attack, assault, or aggression.*

Hellen sneers. "Enjoy your time for now. In a few days, everything is going to change."

She turns and storms back into the hallway. The door snaps shut. I heave in a breath and drag my gaze back to Matt. Arms still locked behind his back, he stands fixed in place, unmoving. Doesn't even blink.

Swallowing, I shove up from the floor. "Matt?"

A flinch breaks his stillness. He won't look at me. "I have to get back to work."

In desperation, I grab his arm as he takes a step toward the door. "Don't leave."

Tension hardens Matt's bicep and jumps along his jaw. His pulse beats visibly under the soft skin on his neck. He lifts a hand to his face, to his damaged eye, then lets it drop again.

I tighten my grip. "Please, I don't want to be alone."

Horribly selfish, especially after Hellen's reaction, but fear's drained my empathy tank dry.

He mashes his lips together, then nods. "I'll talk her into it. Give me a sec."

With that, he presses a palm into the door, disentangles himself from me, and disappears into the hallway.

Chapter Seven

Sephrim

The lock clicks open. Smirk still firmly in place, I
slide inside, back grazing the wall, Darby close behind.
That honeysuckle scent follows her along with the clean
smell of government-grade soap. We used that in the lab.
Antimicrobial? Nowadays, Cal and I use whatever we
can find to get clean. Mostly the harsh stuff Daniel
washes auto parts with. It dries out the skin but cuts
grease and grime fast. Doesn't smell nearly as
comforting as Darby does, though…

I glance around the foyer. Small white bulbs border
the ceiling, lighting the way, but just barely. Shade by
minuscule shade, my eyes adjust. One look at the garish
furniture and I half wish they hadn't. Tacky geometric
print covers nearly every surface, including the walls,
and angular "statues" pose at either end of a neon-yellow
staircase. I grimace.

"Classy," Darby says.

Stifling a laugh, I jerk my head at the stairs. "Let's
go. According to the blueprint, the safe's on the fifth
floor."

We climb upward. Darby's heat seeps through the
air toward me. She's super distracting but nothing
compared to the gnarly decorations. More plastic,
geometric cutouts decorate the walls and banister. By the

second level, sweat prickles my lower back, and by the fifth, it soaks my hairline. Finally, on the top floor we find equally bizarre furniture.

As I creep to the neon door at the far end of the room, Darby heads down the hall.

Brow furrowed, I pause. "Where are you going?" I ask in a whisper.

One gloved hand on the wall, she looks over her shoulder. "I have a different mission. Just go get that egg." She then turns and dissolves into the shadows.

I face the door again, making quick work of the separate alarm system and lock, then slip inside. Unlike the stairs below, these are made of basic wood. Each one creaks under my weight and sends my heart zipping in panic. Small and narrow, the final, windowless room in no way resembles the others below. An off-white, metal door meshes with the plain walls, lit by a flat light overhead.

Sinking to my knees, I glance down the stairs, then turn back to study the lock. A professional locksmith would use high-tech tools to listen as he spun the dial. I'll have to do it by touch. Good thing I enjoy it. Sometimes, when memories of the lab get to be too much, when Dr. Gayle's breathing exercises don't work, I spend hours spinning dials and shifting numbers. The motion calms my nerves, helps me focus on the present moment.

It also refines my touch.

Fingers pressed into the cold dial, I shut my eyes and twist three times clockwise, then back to zero. At each sticking point, I make a mental note, and a few clicks later, the door pops open. Even in the faint light, the jewel-encrusted egg glitters. It winks as I pull it from its cushion, fitting into the palm of my hand, light, painfully fragile.

How much does this thing cost? How many FudPaks could I buy with it? Burgers, even? And valuable because...because...my stomach burns with hunger, with longing. I shake my head, slip the small orb inside the foam-filled box I brought, lock it tight, and shove it into the biggest pocket of my tool belt.

Back at the bottom of the stairs, I ease the door of the secret room open a crack, pulse heavy in my throat. No sign of Darby. Nerves prickle my neck. Should I wait? Every minute we waste inside increases the risk of a guard waking up and finding us. Leaving her behind, however, isn't an option. If I show up alone, Felix might pummel me.

A shadow moves from the hallway. I nudge the door open fully and step out, realizing my mistake a second too late. The figure, too broad and tall to be Darby, turns and springs at me. A hand closes around my throat. I gasp as my spine slams into the wall. The tips of my shoes scrape and scuff the ground, my fingers gripping the guard's arm. Even as fear wraps around my lungs, I lift both feet and kick into the man's stomach.

The figure crumples and coughs out a breath. As he stumbles back a step, I tuck my chin and rip the man's hold off my throat, simultaneously driving my fist forward. My knuckles connect with nose cartilage. Something warm and sticky splatters my skin. Shoving his hand sideways, I ram a forearm into the guard's neck and aim a knee at his gut. Then he hunches, plowing a massive shoulder into my middle and locking both arms at the base of my spine. We roll, bumping into a triangle-shaped chair.

The guard gains the top, straddling me. A blow to my temple sends the room spinning. Eyes squeezed shut against the nauseating motion, I buck my hips, sending the man off-balance. I reach for the meaty arm, but when I try to twist, the guard slams a fist into my jaw, then grips my throat again and pins my legs.

With a grunt, he clicks on a flashlight. "What are you after, thief? Are you the one who knocked out the rest of our security?"

I reach for the choke hold, but the guard's hands shoot out to clamp down on my wrists. Jaw tight with terror, ears ringing, I struggle under the man's weight, gaze darting around the dark room.

Darby, where the hell are you?

The guard squints. "Think we need to make a little call to the police."

Shit. The police can ID me as a Designer Kid. They'll check automatically. Call for Slingers. Send me to a workhouse. Panic pounds in my skull, and my thoughts spiral.

With a sneer, the guard reaches for a screen hooked to his side. I make another grab at his arm. Before I can make the pluck, the man's fist connects with my cheek. White lights burst in my vision, further disrupting the flow of my thoughts. They fade, and I blink at the guard who now holds the screen to his ear. Then a sudden jerk rocks the man's body. His eyes go wide, and he slumps to one side.

Darby stands over us, a thin, black device pinched between her fingers. "Whatever would you do without me?" She grins.

All the air clogs in my throat, and the feeling seeps straight out from my limbs. *No. No. No. Not now.* I cover my face with both hands and try to breathe through my nose, through the panic. It comes in and out too quick, too shallow, filling my head. The floor spins under me.

Great. One stupid mistake and I'm going to pass out on the damn carpet.

Gentle hands touch my shoulders. "What's wrong?"

"Can't…breathe…" I choke on a gasp. "Go ahead without me… I'll—"

"No way." She pulls my hands away from my face. "Look at me. Okay? Slow it down, or you're going to pass out. I don't want to have to carry you back to Felix. I'd break a sweat. No desire to do that." She grins again, but her lips twitch.

I shut my eyes. *Get it together, get it together…in through your nose and hold it. One…two…three…four…five…* Darby's gloved thumbs skim the bare skin along my wrists. I focus on the rhythm and count back down to one. After a few rounds of this, the floor finally stops swaying, and I open my eyes again.

Darby's brows lift. "You okay?"

"Good enough to get out of here. Can you…" I let the sentence hang as she loops an arm under mine and pulls me up. Together, we head downstairs.

My legs gain strength with every step; my breath slows and deepens, bit by bit. As it does, embarrassment sets in. *Way to melt down in front of a cute girl, man. Super smooth.* "Thanks, by the way. How'd you know what to do?"

"When my brother gets upset, I have to talk him down now and again." She slides her arm from around my waist and hooks both thumbs into the straps of her backpack, her voice quiet. "It's not exactly the same thing, but I figured it might work for an anxiety attack too. When he's alone with my mom, either of my parents really…"

"Don't tell anybody, huh?"

A small smile touches her lips. "So long as you don't let anybody know I'm afraid of heights, we've got a deal."

Chapter Eight

Matt

I'm bad at verbal persuasion.

My fingers can coax anything with a motherboard to bend to my will, but my tongue gets tied up when I try to communicate out loud with other human beings. Information gets lost between my central processor and my mouth. Lost or tangled up. Most times, I just choose not to try. But I couldn't leave Cal in that exam room.

Somehow, a half-lie about monitoring the chip convinced Hellen to let Cal sleep on my hide-a-bed. She now lies curled in a ball under my sheets, lit faintly by the monitors. Every once in a while, I stop typing to snag a look at her. I don't trust that chip.

It's more than that, though. I've seen thousands of Designer Kids on the other side of a computer screen. All a little too perfect, but none who've caught my attention quite like Cal. It's not even that she's pretty—though she absolutely is that. It's her fire, her fight, even her funny way of defining things.

She's mesmerizing, and if it weren't for Hellen, I might try to convince her to stay with me.

Grimacing, I rub the scarred side of my face. Bad habit. Annoying habit. But sometimes it really itches. In my peripheral vision, I watch the shiny glass eye of the camera perched above my door. Three more mark each corner of my room and every hallway of the compound. They make my "extracurricular activities" tricky.

Tricky—not impossible.

Chewing my bottom lip, I swipe a new page into place. To anybody else, it just looks like a mess of jumbled coding. Nonsense. But I see a doorway, a connection to Dr. Amancia Gayle. With another glance at the cameras, I type in my password. The screen blinks. A message fills the space between slashes and dots and dashes.

Requesting blackout at 14:00.

With a grin, I type, *14:00. Got it. Full hour?*

The cursor blinks. And blinks. Whenever something delays Dr. Gayle, I have to battle the worst assumptions. Images of the lab's guards dragging her away, or of the evil Dr. Troy tasing her, chase each other through my head.

Creepy-crawlies wiggle through my stomach.

Then text springs into the box. *Full hour. System still good?*

The crawlies settle down. *Functioning. Should get a new cord soon. That should prevent another glitch... Lose anybody last time?* That stupid shoddy cord nearly ruined everything.

No. Everyone made it out.

My shoulders relax as I let go of a breath. *Good. Sorry again about the glitch.*

Not your fault.

Forty-eight hours?

At 14:00. Yes.

You'll have your blackout.

I lean back in my chair, arms crossed, and look at Cal. She's one of those kids I helped spring from the lab.

E.C. Farrell

Now she's back in captivity. Also because of me. A way worse form of captivity. One word and... My lunch sloshes into my throat. I scrape both hands over my face.

I'm bad as my mom and those doctors put together.

Well, I'm not going to let her stay a captive. While the thought of Mom's wrath freezes me like an overtaxed computer, making it impossible for *me* to leave, I can't let her hurt Cal. Not anymore. Problem is I need to figure out somewhere to send her after I break her out. If I just chuck her into the open, Hellen might find her again. Will find her again. I need a plan.

I need Darby.

I pop my knuckles and swivel to the far-right screen. Mom won't let us see each other or communicate, so I have to be creative. Thankfully, she doesn't know computer speak. I cover my tracks with layers of code she could never understand.

Not that Darby is great with tech either. Sometimes she takes forever to get back to me. Doesn't matter how many times I show her how to open the doc. She stumbles over the access codes every time. I don't mind. Not everybody can be a techno-genius. The first time I tried to walk her through a code, she almost murdered a poor, defenseless computer.

"Why won't it do the thing?" Darby wraps a choke hold around her braid. "I typed exactly what you told me to."

I stifle a laugh. "Did you turn off the caps lock?"

"Yes. Why would...oh." Embarrassment tints her cheeks red, and she hits the key at the far end of her laptop, then tries again. As she types—hunting and pecking like a confused bird—Darby speaks the code out loud. This time she forgets one of the slashes. The page

pops up wrong again. She slams the top closed and lifts it over her head.

I let out a squeak and reach for it. "Don't kill it! It's an innocent piece of tech!"

"But it's driving me crazy," Darby says through clenched teeth. She swings the laptop away from my groping hands. "These things are possessed."

I finally talked her down and saved the innocent device from assassination, but I never did get her code savvy. We now stick to a simple form with a dummy-proof password. One she forgets weekly. She might take a little time to get back to me, but it's still faster than a text to her other, *other* phone. She'll know what to do.

I send the message, then minimize the two screens right as the door snaps open and Walter walks in. Gray-haired and balding, the older man has to squint even with thick glasses. The few strands of hair still on the top of his head cling to his scalp. Tiny dots of sweat shimmer on his skin. He carries a big box and smiles when he shuffles toward the desk, revealing a mess of uneven teeth.

"Hiya, Matt," he says in his overloud voice. "You needed a new cord?"

Pointing at Cal, I wave for Walter to lower his volume. "Hey, Uncle Wally, yeah, the other one's busted." Slow and sweet, Hellen's older brother doesn't catch on to things real fast. She keeps him around out of a sense of duty, generally ignoring him.

Walter glances at Cal and puts a finger over his lips. "Sorry," he says in a noisy whisper. He sets the box on the edge of my desk, then pulls out a loop of black cord secured with green Velcro. "This should be the right one. Is this the right one?"

With a grin, I take it and check the connector. "Perfect. Thanks. This'll fix the problem. How's the train coming?"

He grins wider. "It's good. You wanna see?"

"Definitely."

I lean on my desk as Uncle Wally sets the box on the floor and pulls a small, wooden train out of his pocket. The front half is painted in bright reds and greens. As he holds it up to the light, he flicks one of the wheels so it spins. He laughs.

"That looks so great, Uncle Wally."

"Thanks." He spins the wheel again. "Who's that? Does she want to see my train?"

"That's Cal." I glance at the bed. Her eyes swoop back and forth under her closed lids, her own internal computer processing her waking moments. "And maybe when she wakes up."

Walter presses a finger to his lips again and lets out a loud "shhh." He slides his train back into a pocket. "Is she your friend? I told Hellie you need a friend. Darby and Felix never come. I know it makes you sad."

My eye stings. I wrinkle my nose. Crack my knuckles. Besides my uncle, no one comes to see me because they just *want* to. It doesn't make me sad. It makes me angry. The thought of Cal staying, of being around all the time, tears me in multiple directions. She could be my friend. Someone to talk to and not just about business or even trains.

But then she'd also be a prisoner—one Hellen would make do awful things.

I swallow. "Yeah. She's my friend, Uncle Wally. Maybe you could bring her a sandwich too, later?"

His smile widens even more. It makes his eyes

double in size. "Okay. What kind of sandwiches does she like? I have peanut butter and jelly and ham and cheese… We're out of turkey, though." He lifts his thick fingers as he lists off the possibilities. Besides trains, Uncle Wally also really, really loves sandwiches.

I love cooking with him when my mom lets me. She doesn't allow it much, but when she does, we make a glorious mess of the kitchen. Sometimes I take pictures with my mini-screen before we clean it up. I use them as background images on my computers.

"I think she'll like whatever you bring her, Uncle Wally. Bet she'll be awake then and—"

Overhead the intercom crackles. Hellen's voice breaks into the room. "Have you hacked that damn feed yet?"

I flinch. "Working on it. I'll—"

"Just get it done." *Click*.

My pulse jumps. "I'd better get back to work, Uncle Wally."

"Okay, Matt. I know you do important stuff for Hellie. I'll see ya later." He shuffles forward and wraps his arms around me.

With my eye shut and the smell of my uncle's shirt heavy in my nose, I pretend I'm a normal fourteen-year-old kid living with a normal family. No one orders me to break into government databases or hack news feeds or create mind-controlling chips. No one hits me. No one calls me worthless.

Instead, I've got a family who loves me. Cares about me. Wants me just because I'm theirs. Not because I'm useful.

Then Uncle Wally breaks away. He waves, picks up his box, and shuffles back out into the hallway. The door slides shut, leaving nothing but an echo behind.

Chapter Nine

Sephrim

By the time we make it to Cade's, I've gotten control of my legs again, if not quite my breathing. Still shallow and sharp, it fills my head with dizzying amounts of oxygen. I'll just have to manage. Tightening the straps on my tool belt, I stop at the entrance and stare at the black, barred gate. If I can get my shit together, I might survive the transfer to Felix.

Darby crosses her arms and leans against the wall. "I always need a minute before I head down there too. It smells. Feels like..." Her eyes flick back and forth.

"Being swallowed."

She meets my gaze. Moonlight pokes through the clouds overhead, igniting her eyes, soft features, and slightly off-center nose. It gives her the kind of character a Designer Kid rarely has. Genetics center my own eyes and mouth and Roman-straight nose perfectly. In a very small act of rebellion, I always wear my hair as messy as humanly possible. It stands out in every direction whenever I take off my hood.

"Being swallowed." She nods. "Yeah."

One hand clenched around a gate bar, I glance down the dark passageway beyond. Blood pounds against every inch of my face. Damn. All that pain and nothing to show for it. Kind of lame. I rub my jaw as Darby taps her fingers on the brick wall.

"Where'd you learn to fight like that?" she asks.

"How long did you watch me get my ass kicked?"

"Long enough to know you couldn't have learned that on the street."

I focus on the tunnel. "Free classes for Designer Kids at the YMCA."

Darby splutters. "What now?"

I chuckle. "I'm kidding. When Designer Kids turn five, we get pretty intense defense training and even a little first aid. By the time I expired, I knew how to break limbs with my bare hands just as well as I knew how to splint them." I pick at a rough spot on the gate with a thumb. "It's funny. The lab techs and doctors always told these horror stories about life on the street, but their training made the idea of running away a hell of a lot less terrifying, at least for me."

Eyes wide, Darby mashes her brows together. "Why the hell would they do that? Sounds like a really stupid way to create a nice little army out of a bunch of kids who don't like them much."

I snort. "They have ways of avoiding an uprising, at least while we're still inside the lab. Most of the doctors are pretty nice until you get closer to expiration. Guess that's when they start feeling the pressure to sell, make their donors and shareholders happy."

"But I ask again, why would they want to teach you how to do that at all?"

"Child soldiers are easier to sell than regular kids."

Darby swears, then kicks a wall. "That's messed up."

I lace my fingers behind my neck. "Very. So...how'd you end up working for the Cades?"

She scrunches her nose. "Felix." She scuffs a boot against the concrete. "He's my brother."

Shock and revulsion mutate my stomach into a solid rock and drag an almost comical gasp out of my throat. I look back at Darby, blinking a few times before forcing words out. "He's your what, now?"

I just barely keep my voice down and resist the urge to physically back away. After all, she can't help being related to a bunch of psychopaths any more than I can help being created in a test tube.

"I know. He's a maniacal lunatic. Runs in the family. Dad, mom, brother...well, Felix anyway. My younger brother—he's not like them. Brilliant with computers. Lives with my mom. She..." Darby's whole face spasms.

I scrub my jaw again, trying to relieve some of the tension and pain. "They not together anymore? Your parents?"

Her lower lip protrudes for a single quiver before she gets it under control. "They never were, not traditionally anyway. Started as a fling when my mom was in medical school. Besides, they have slightly different opinions about crime."

"Is your mom against it?" I tug a hoodie string.

"Not anymore, not after she got burned by one of her classmates," Darby says. "She just doesn't see the end goal the same way Dad and my brother do. They're all about order, living by a certain code. So long as nothing interrupts their business, they don't care what the rest of the world does. And my mom...well, she's probably drumming up some kind of government overthrow as we speak. Thinks she can run everything better than everyone else. Save them from themselves, or something like that."

A shiver scatters up my back. "Not sure which is worse." The clouds shift again, covering the moon.

"Me neither." She straightens. "How you feeling? Ready to go in?"

I push the gate open. "After you."

This late in the evening, or rather early in the morning, no crowds fill the massive hall. Without the movement of bodies or the pulse of music, the room feels even more like the belly of a massive beast. Still, Felix and Marcus lounge in their chairs, flanked by their bodyguards. One marches out to meet us when we approach.

The guard towers even over me. She pats me down, ignoring Darby completely, then goes back to her position at Marcus' right side. I sink to my knees and peer at Marcus and Felix through the strands of my hair. Now I see the family resemblance, the same set of the eyes, the same clench of the jaw.

Felix grins and slides from his chair. "Excellent timing."

As always, he reaches down, takes me by the jaw, and pulls me upright. With a growl of irritation trapped in my throat, I focus on the back wall, trying to ignore the hungry look on Felix's face. The combination from the Tuttleson safe rotates through my mind: *six, three, six, four…six, three, six, four…* My breathing holds steady.

"Are you done?"

I glance at Darby. She stands about a foot away, arms crossed, hip cocked to one side. Apart from Marcus, I've never seen anyone give Felix that look. Most divert their gazes at least a little. Those who don't usually regret it.

But Felix laughs, lets go of my jaw, and claps. "My little sister. Such spirit. And all business." He adjusts the sleeves of his gray suit. "When you're right, you're right. Let's see that egg."

Though I want nothing more than to rub my aching jaw, I unzip my tool belt and retrieve the small, silver box—fingers shaking. *Damn anxiety attacks.* Why does Felix feel the need to "greet" me that way? Cal thinks it's half power trip, half legit fascination. "You're just too pretty*,*" she often teases, trying to get my mind off my intense discomfort.

Back teeth locked together, I open the case and turn it toward Felix. It teeters. Choking on a breath, I lurch to steady it, but the box slips past my damp fingers. Felix catches it in midair. Upper lip curled, he looks inside to inspect the merchandise, hands it to the female guard, then steps forward and drives a fist into my stomach.

I double over with a harsh cough. A poisonous ache trades places with all the air in my lungs. Felix hits me again. One blow follows the next in a nauseating chain. Knees buckling under me, I sink toward the floor, gagging. Deprived of oxygen, my already damaged face pounds, and my ears ring. Fear floods my muscles.

This is it. Felix is going to kill me. Even with my training I can't do a damn thing about it. With every guard encircling us armed, I'd end up riddled with bullets. Or worse. Better to take the beating and pray Felix gets bored before he permanently damages an internal organ.

Gripping my collar to keep me upright, he pauses in his assault only to brush his lips against my ear. I cringe as he says, "How dare you risk my product," then starts up again.

Pressure builds behind my eyes. I can't move, stalled in place like a car out of fuel. Maybe I'll pass out before my head explodes. My whole body wails for the beating to end.

"Felix, that's enough," Darby says, voice hard and sharp. "Stop."

Letting me collapse in a heap, Felix turns to his sister. "What did you say?"

She lifts her chin an inch. "You're going to kill him."

"And?"

Through waxy vision, I look between Darby and Felix, still unable to breathe, tentatively relieved. I want to curl in on myself, to crawl away, but my muscles won't respond.

"And," she says, "he's a good thief."

"There are lots of good thieves."

"Not like him. The last guy you strapped me with, remember how he screwed it up? The headlines?"

Brow arched, Felix squats next to me, elbows on his knees. He runs a hand along his scruff, then skims a thumb over my jaw. I squirm internally.

"She has a point. Besides, it would be a waste to destroy such a beautiful boy." He grins and straightens. "Very well. At the recommendation of my very wise little sister, you can stay on the payroll." Felix pulls a wad of cash out of his pocket and sprinkles it over me, then turns on a heel and saunters back to his seat.

Air still won't come, but I've got to get up. To get out. One hand pressed into the concrete, I try to push myself off the ground. My arms burn. My vision swims. Then someone grips me around the waist with a strong, taut arm and pulls me to my knees. Darby fishes for the dollar bills and shoves them into my hoodie pocket.

She hoists me to my feet, then hauls me toward the door. A breath finally breaks through. It stings on the way down my throat but finally lets most of the pressure ebb out of my face. I cough and gulp air greedily.

In the tunnel, she readjusts her grip under my arms. "Gonna live?"

"Yeah." My voice is a croak. "Initiation was worse, though not quite so…focused. Thanks for that."

Darby smirks. "Yeah, well, couldn't let my mistake get you beat to a pulp."

"Your mistake?"

"If I'd done my job right, that guard wouldn't've attacked you. And if the guard hadn't attacked…" She shrugs. "I've seen Felix do that before, the stupid face-gripping thing. I know it sets you off. It would set anybody off. It's degrading, obnoxious. The guard from the Tuttleson mansion attacking just made it worse, made you almost drop that egg."

"I guess." I cough again, wincing when pain lances across my ribs. "I've gotta learn to get that under control. It just makes me so damn uncomfortable."

"It should. Try to avoid him as much as you can and don't ever get stuck alone with him. Don't ask why, just trust me. His hunger for power is…" Her muscles tighten against me, and she grimaces.

Revulsion slithers up my spine.

Darby pushes open the gate. A thick mist puffs into our faces, cold and sticky and smelling of exhaust. Lights from a helicopter blink up above. Its propellers thump. Sirens howl from somewhere in the city. They clash with the news commentary from a nearby billboard screen.

One hand on my sternum, I scowl.

"Need a minute?"

"Or a few."

A couple of yards from the entrance, Darby helps me sit in the flattened grass sloping up toward the road. As she sinks down beside me, I bend over my knees and lace my fingers behind my head. Every breath aches.

My stomach lurches. What meager food I ate for dinner travels upward. I wrench to the side and vomit. *Here comes the contents of that lovely FudPak soured by stomach acid.* Good thing Cal isn't around. Her sympathetic gag reflex would have made us a miserable pair.

Thankfully, she's safe back at the garage.

At the end of it, I choke on a breath and drag a sleeve across my mouth. "Sorry."

"Doesn't bother me." Darby shrugs. "I clean up puke all the time. Comes with having an underground bunker that doubles as a nightclub. Felix's cleaning staff isn't always on point. He doesn't hire them for their skill."

I grin, then wipe my mouth a second time. "Sometimes I do the same thing for the girl who ran from the lab with me."

"Oh?" The word comes out funny, with a little hitch in the middle. "Is she your girlfriend?"

I let out a painful chuckle. "Nah, just the closest thing I've got to a little sister."

"Why'd you run? I mean…" She rolls her eyes and slides the black beanie off her head. Red hair spills out around her face, sticking to her neck and brushing her elbows. "I know the workhouses are supposed to be awful, but are they really worse than being on the street?

Worse than this?" She motions to my stomach.

Chin on my knees, I shut my eyes as if this will block out the horror stories I've heard. "Much worse. They're—" I cough, the taste of metal on my tongue. Bad sign. One I ignore. "They're not places where Designer Kids work. Not in the traditional sense. Workhouses are labs. Labs where they…do experiments. Designer Kids are the perfect test subjects. No physical defects."

Darby rubs her throat. "Don't the others, the ones who are…adopted? Sold? What's the right word?"

I shrug. Does it really matter what word we use? Cal would say it does. "Sold is more accurate."

Darby presses her lips together, eyes darkening, then says, "They all end up in affluent families. Rich ones. Don't they stand up for the ones who expire?"

A fair question, one I wrestle with all the time. I pick at a piece of gray-brown grass. It disintegrates between my fingers, and I flick it into the wind. "Most who don't expire are adopted real early. They don't remember what the labs are like, don't know the truth about the workhouses. I guess the others…I don't know, maybe they forget, or, or maybe they're scared of getting kicked out of their homes."

"Sick."

"Yeah." I cough again, this time into my hand. Blood spots my palm when I pull it away. I curse under my breath. Sign of potential internal bleeding. At best ruptured capillaries, at worst a broken rib. Fan-freaking-tastic.

Darby grabs my wrist, then meets my eyes. The space between her brows wrinkles.

"I need a—" I wince.

In a perfect world the word "doctor" would end that

sentence.

"I can treat this." She loops her arm under my armpits and pulls me to my feet. "Come on. My place isn't far."

Chapter Ten

Darby

Under normal circumstances, the trip to my apartment takes maybe fifteen minutes. With Sephrim's injury, though, we clock in at a little over half an hour. Shuffling along, clearly in pain, the poor kid keeps his hoodie up and head down the whole time. He doesn't need to worry—I know how to avoid cameras and cops alike.

We skirt the rim of Washington DC, trekking under overpasses and weaving around city parks. Vampiric fall sucks green from the leaves of the trees bordering black-painted fences. It leaves behind the fresh-blood reds and dried-blood browns.

At the street closest to my neighborhood, I guide Sephrim back inside city lines. Nestled in a modest, middle-class section of the city, my apartment is a place of stability, rest. Neither gaudy like Felix's club-inspired tunnel nor stark like Hellen's compound, my home overflows with secondhand things. Overstuffed armchairs and a matching couch bought at an estate sale, a sleek black kitchen set from a local online seller, and a flat-screen TV custom wired by a self-proclaimed "techno-genius." It's the home of my dreams.

It's just missing one thing. Or rather, one person. His drawings track across the fridge, intricate, detailed, colorful, all signed with the scribbled initials ML. I glance at them as we walk inside, the alarm whistling until I punch in the code. Longing spins through me like the cylinder on a revolver. That artwork has a way of making me simultaneously happy and sad. He should be here, with me.

And we should both be away, far away, from the rest of the family.

Once, I would have included Felix in a plan like that, a plan to run. Though never exactly sweet, or even all that nice, he didn't used to be so cruel. Then at nineteen—fed up with feeling powerless and rejected on so many levels—he asked Dad for money. With an overabundance of capital, he turned our simple weapons depot into the Cade complex. It didn't take long for his humor to shift from pleasant snark to painful cruelty, his passion to violence.

One arm around Sephrim's back, I help him ease onto the couch. As I straighten, he also squints at the drawings on the fridge.

"Who—" He coughs. "Who drew those?"

I frown at the rough, wet sound. Probably still coughing blood. Not good. Definitely not something I can treat. Hooking a thumb under the hem of Sephrim's hoodie, I throw a glance over my shoulder to look at the sketches again. One corner of my mouth twitches up. "My little brother." As gently as I can possibly manage, I help Sephrim get the sweatshirt over his head.

He groans.

As gingerly as possible, I work to get his T-shirt off next—a raggedy, yellow-stained thing that must've been white early in life—and grimace at the black bruise staining his ribs. Very, very not good. Especially if it's showing up on a Designer Kid's quick-healing skin. Maybe just a surface problem, but without a deeper look it's hard to tell.

"That's a good sign." He wrinkles his brow.

I blink, momentarily distracted by his bare torso. Do all Designer Kids have perfectly chiseled abs? Felix's guards all sport their fair share of muscle, but none of them look like this. Heat burns my cheeks. What the hell am I ogling him for right now? While he's injured and possibly bleeding internally?

A-plus timing, Darbs. Way to be a pro.

I clear my throat. "We'll see what's going on in there. One sec."

Damn. Why do I suddenly care so much? My stomach roils with concern. Some grand assassin. "Stay cold," my father always says. "Harden up inside, and you'll survive a hard world." I only recently noticed how my parents touched us with nothing but violence. The moment I put words to it, the lack of physical affection bit into my very body, gnawing like starvation.

So I took my father's advice, hardened up. I try and usually succeed. But right now, examining the damage done to Sephrim's ribs, feeling the absurd softness of his skin, I can't keep the protective wall in place, can't resist the longing for connection.

I pull a portable digital imager from a coffee table drawer. Though not as reliable as an X-ray machine, it's still pretty accurate. Before I use it, I set the device on the table and press my fingers into Sephrim's wrist, eyes shut. Nothing works quite as well as touch, a fact I learned from patching up the Cade guards after various and sundry altercations. I count out a full minute. A second later I nod and move my hands to his abdomen.

Tension embeds in my jaw at the give under my touch.

"Sorry in advance, this is going to hurt."

"I figured." He lets out a tempered breath as my fingers trace slowly across his damaged ribs. "Do this a lot?"

The words rake my nerves raw. "Too often." Sadness drags my lips into a frown. "I do it for Felix and his guards now and again, but…I also used to have to fix up Matty when…" I gnaw the inside corner of my mouth.

My fingers must've hit a particularly painful spot, because Sephrim sucks air in between his teeth. "So you get to see him at least?"

"Not anymore." I swallow a ball of frustration, gaze narrow. "But before my mom took him, he almost always needed some kind of mending."

"Ever tried to, I don't know, get him out?"

I glare at the black bruises, so painfully familiar. "Once."

Once. Only once. It hadn't ended well. Even if I had succeeded in getting Matty out, he wouldn't be any safer at Cade's. Unlike Sephrim and his semi-sister, we really don't have anywhere to run, not with our parents essentially in charge of the streets. In a way, we're as stuck as Designer Kids.

I work my way back to the top of his ribs. Every one sticks out beneath the skin. FudPaks apparently don't keep much meat on the bones. Again, my mind slips into ridiculous immaturity. How nice would it be to touch him like this under different circumstances? To run my hands up his chest, to cup his neck, to kiss him like a normal teenager.

Get it together, Darby! The kid is freaking damaged, and you're daydreaming like an idiot! Objectifying him like Felix.

I duck my head to hide a gag. "They don't feel broken. One might be cracked but not badly enough to be any real threat." Hot with embarrassment, I turn on the portable digital imager and hold it against his sternum. I frown. "Yup, one rib is busted but not totally broken. I'll just wrap it and keep an eye on you. Lots of times minor internal bleeding resolves itself."

He clears his throat. "I need to get back."

A laugh bursts from my throat. "You aren't going anywhere right now, buddy," I say, grabbing a roll of gauze. "Don't want you passing out on the sidewalk and getting eaten by feral cats."

"But Cal—"

"Will be just fine without you for one night. You said you leave her at the garage all the time, right?" Worry knots the muscles between my shoulders. He can't go out there on his own right now.

He frowns.

"Just accept the fact that I'm right." I grin. "If you try to make it back and do, in fact, collapse somewhere along the way, you might even put Cal in danger. Getting caught by a Slinger, especially in this condition, will make things worse."

He heaves a sigh. "Fine, so long as you don't have a problem with a homeless dude sleeping on your couch."

I smirk, relieved. "Doesn't bother me. If you want a shower, you're welcome to it. Felix crashes here when he's drunk and sad. You can borrow some of his clothes. In fact, you can take one of his shirts. This thing should be tossed into an incinerator." I hold up his old shirt, pinched between a forefinger and thumb.

Sephrim arches a brow. "You sure?"

"Positive. Shower. Please. I'm begging you, in fact. You stink." I wink.

Chapter Eleven

Cal

I picture Matt's garden as a sad little area lined with a small collection of potted plants and maybe a dusty skylight. As I follow him through the gray hallways, gaze zipping between exits and landing on every camera, I don't give any more thought to this assumption. More important stuff occupies my mind.

Does Hellen care that I'm roaming around with her son? She gave me permission to sleep in Matt's room and to eat, but going on jaunts to the garden? If she finds us, will she blow a gasket? Is Seph okay? Felix makes him so nervous with his stupid power trippy-ness. What if something goes wrong with his new job? I have to get out to protect him. He needs me.

I worry the end of my tongue between my teeth.

Halfway down the hall from Matt's room, Brunwick the guard stops us. She pauses in her march, stance wide, hand on the holster of her gun. Her upper lip hitches in a sneer. "What the hell are you doing wandering the halls?"

Matt shuffles forward, semi blocking me with his body. My pulse accelerates. I've seen Brunwick take people apart for Hellen, and I assume Matt's seen the same, but he just turned himself into a human shield, opening himself up to more violence.

"We—"

Brunwick shoves Matt sideways so he stumbles over his bare feet. "I wasn't talking to you." She jabs me in the chest with a finger. "Who gave you permission to be out here?"

Permission, noun, authorization granted to do something, formal consent. I gulp and lift my chin. When I open my mouth, Brunwick drives a fist into my face. Lights burst in shocked blackness, and a roar like a revving engine fills my ears. Pain cracks through my backside and up my spine when I hit the ground. I blink and, when the stars and loud confusion fade, look up at the guard.

Again, Matt stands between us, the tendons springing out along his jaw. "Don't touch her." He pauses between every teeth-clenched word.

"You have no authority over me, you little prick." She lifts a fist.

My chest seizes.

Matt shoves his mini-screen into her face. "No, but I do have eyes on your feeds."

Her chin hitches. Gray light spreads across her face as her pupils dilate. Matt moves forward, and she moves back the barest of inches.

"Leave us alone, or Hellen finds out," he says, voice rough. "Everything."

The guard swears, then swerves around us quick as her feet can move her. Shock rusts me to the floor as I gawk at Matt's shoulders. His muscles—wowza, how have I not noticed *them* before?—bunch together all the way down both arms. He doesn't move.

I shove myself up and grab his shoulder. He flinches, meets my eyes out of the corner of his one good one, then looks at the ground.

"Matt, you…that was…"

"Probably stupid."

"Definitely stupid. But brave too." I grin, then wince as the welt on my face pounds.

"I can't believe I did that, but when she hit you…" He finally unlocks and turns an inch toward me. His fingers brush my jaw. "You okay?"

Goose bumps spring out across my skin. The nice kind I don't mind much. "Sweet and dandy just like candy. Mostly in shock. Getting punched'll do that to you."

"It's how people talk around here. The one who hits hardest gets to be in charge."

A smile barrels its way onto my face. "And you figured out how to hit back in your own way. Pretty genius." I bump him with an elbow. "Now show me that garden of yours."

We trek a little farther to the farthest, darkest corner of the compound. With a slight smile, Matt presses a hand to a pad on the wall, and the door slides open. I gape at what I see beyond the gray metal barrier.

By fourteen, I shouldn't put so much stock in expectation. Reality usually surprises, often stuns me to silence, as it does now. Knuckles pressed into the bottoms of my overall pockets, I gawk at the high, vine-laced walls. Could I climb it and bust through that skylight?

Right. Like that wouldn't end in a quick death.

Flowers live at the very center of the room, a vibrant combination of colors and shapes and lengths and angles. Herbs squat along each wall bordered by beds of vegetables, melons, and a spiky fruit I don't recognize.

A smell filters into my nose. My head swims, and my mouth waters.

There are no other exits aside from the door we came through and that skylight, but I also don't see any cameras. Relief floods my veins. At least I'm not being watched anymore. Well, besides Matt, but he isn't so bad. Just the opposite, in fact.

"Breathtaking, adjective, thrillingly beautiful, remarkable, astonishing, exciting…" I turn in a circle, attempting to take it in all at once. How can something so beautiful exist in this compound of death? Like Matt, it doesn't belong but flourishes in spite of its surroundings. A flower poking through cement. I tug on the ends of my short hair, then meet Matt's gaze. "I've never seen anything like this before. How long have you been working on it?"

Pulling at the hem of his shirt, he shifts back and forth between his feet. "Since I was a kid. My mom set it up so she wouldn't have to buy produce from the grocery store. Something about unfair taxes. She'll do anything to avoid those." He shrugs.

I grin and follow the cement path through the plant life. Once, I read a book about fairies. A silly story. Illogical. Set aside quickly to make room for more challenging literature. But now, in this small, enclosed forest, the images from that book slip back into my mind. Maybe childish fantasies have their place after all.

I bend, sniff a flower, and wrinkle my nose. "*Bellis perennis*. A European species of daisy, of the Asteraceae family, often considered the archetypal species of that name."

Matt chuckles. "I usually just call them daisies. Mom says they're common, useless, but they're some of my favorites."

I turn, dragging my lower lip through my teeth. "Never had a favorite flower."

He looks down. Blood rushes to his cheeks. It makes the blue of his eye spring out, stark, beautiful, sad. "They're not very practical."

"Maybe not."

"But we need them." He says it too fast, like he's afraid I won't let him finish. "We need things that make us…stop."

A happy little rush swims through my chest. How adorably perfect. Things that make us stop sounds like poetry. "Interesting theory."

With a sigh, he looks up at the skylight. His good eye slides shut as starlight breaks through the clouds. Their pure light fills his entire face, bleaching out the bruises and scars, chasing away layers of pain and fear for one, shining moment.

"Feels different than sunlight, doesn't it? At least it does through the glass. Can't imagine what it's like outside."

Brow puckered, I frown, sadness stomping on that happy little moment. "You've never been outside?"

He sighs. "Not in a really long time. Dying to, though. Maybe one day."

Gently, I take his shoulders. The muscles and tendons go taut under my grasp. "One day soon. You…"

Words wither in my throat, straight back down into my chest as his face twists. In this light, even with his mouth and brows contorted, he somehow looks younger. But strong too. He could stand up to Hellen if he could just leap over his fear.

"Maybe." He opens his eye and meets mine. "Soon

as I figure out how to disable that bit."

"You really can't use another computer to do that?" The muscles tense along the back of my neck. Brilliant as he is, this sounds like an excuse.

Clouds drift back over the stars, hiding their light, and Matt bows his head, focus again on his bare toes. "I can't," he says, voice rough, teeth evidently clenched.

I scowl, the motion forcing blood back into the sore spot on my face. Stupid Brunwick. Does he mean that, or is he just too afraid to leave? Too afraid of Hellen? A reasonable fear, one I can't blame him for. But he has the power. The ability. He showed that when he stood up to Brunwick. With the right push…

I give his shoulders another squeeze but still can't find the words, not the right ones, anyway. They're all out of order, mixed up and too full of emotion. Misapply them, and Matt might break. Matt. Probably the sweetest person I've ever met, next to Seph. I pull him into a hug.

He tenses, solidifying like one of the broken tools I fix for Daniel. Except for the warmth. It radiates from his skin through his clothes, fueled by the thrum of his heart. It pulses against my body, rapid, frenetic, like it's driven by total terror. My tummy does a funny little dance, and I squeeze him tighter. It feels different than hugging Sephrim.

I comfort him with my touch in spite of every nerve in my body rebelling against it. They fight to push me away, to get my personal bubble restored to its original setting. I do it because I love Seph and he needs it. Now? Now my nerves relax. Maybe him hanging out in my bubble a while might not be so bad.

Matt never does hug me back, but when I let him go, he sniffs and offers me a twist of a smile. "Wait here."

Pulling a set of garden shears from his pocket, he squats next to a strange-looking plant by the wall. With a quick, diagonal snip, he cuts a flower off, then turns and hands it to me. "It's, um, *Ophrys apifera*. A bee orchid."

I spin it between my fingers. An appropriate name. Four purple petals surround a median lobe that looks very much like the abdomen of a bee. Fascination pulls a smile back onto my face.

"This is the coolest flower I've ever seen." I look up. "Matt—"

"I'm okay." He swipes at his eye with a fist. "Don't get all sappy on me."

"Hey." I point at his face. "You just gave me a flower and promised to save me from the mind-controlling chip in my head. I can do whatever I want." I swallow, gaze on his lips, then say in a quiet little voice, "Attraction, noun, a force by which one object attracts another, such as the gravitational or electrostatic force."

"Wha—"

Before he can finish the word—and I can talk myself out of it—I grab the collar of his shirt and pull him into a kiss.

This time, instead of freezing, Matt sways into me. On pure instinct, I hook an arm around his waist to pull him closer, the flower still hanging from my fingers. Inhaling sharply through his nose, he returns the kiss, and my stomach goes all happy and fluttery. As he gets steadier, I feel his arms loop around my waist. I grin and move my hand from his shirt collar to the back of his neck.

Goose bumps bubble up along his skin, but the strange stiffness is totally gone. We relax into the kiss, into each other, all the terror and tension redirected into something entirely other. Crazy? Maybe. But amidst the mind control and weird flowers and Hellen's machinations of revolution, I want a little normal, teenage crazy.

Chapter Twelve

Sephrim

I sit in the porcelain tub way longer than I should. Forehead braced against folded hands, I hunch under the stream of hot water, watching it run clean into the drain. Blood throbs against the bruised skin around my ribs and taints the inside of my mouth. Eyes squinted shut, I spit and rake fingers into my hair. Cal would be so jealous.

As much as I'd like to, I can't stay in here forever. I heave myself up, turn the water off, and climb out onto the plush, teal rug. I wince when I reach for the matching towel, barely able to lift my right arm high enough to yank it down.

While I towel off, I study the counter, curiosity a little too strong not to snoop. A straightening iron straddles the towel rack, and the handle of an immaculate round brush leans against two boxes of red hair dye. I grin a little. Guess Darby doesn't want to look like the rest of her family. I can't blame her with a brother like Felix and a dad like Marcus.

With more grimacing and stifled curses, I shimmy into the plaid pajama bottoms Darby gave me. The shirt, on the other hand, well, that's not going to happen. Instead, I take it by the collar, slide the striped shower curtain shut, and limp back into the living room.

On her knees in front of the coffee table, Darby

arranges two steaming bowls of soup on a set of dark-green placemats. Unlike the rubber ones Cal and I always used at the lab, these are soft, woven, frayed at the edges. Last time I ate on a placemat was the night we ran away. Dr. Gayle slipped us both an extra serving, one we hid in the pack I was supposed to take to the workhouse.

I ease onto the couch with a shiver. As I lay the T-shirt across a cushion, Darby pushes one of the bowls in my direction and hands me a spoon.

"Couldn't manage to get it on?" she asks, her gaze lingering a dash too long on my midsection.

Embarrassed heat flushes my face, though I can't say I mind her staring as much as I do everybody else. "Can't even get my arm over my head. Not without a lot of bitching anyway." I chuckle, which immediately produces a bloody cough.

Wiping my palm on a napkin, I slide onto the floor as carefully as possible to get closer to the bowl. A burst of complex flavor fills my mouth with that first bite, and pleasant heat rolls straight to my stomach. I let out a sigh, enjoying the feeling of someone taking care of me. Especially after Felix used me as a punching bag.

Darby grins. "If you're cold, there's a blanket over the back of the couch."

I shrug a shoulder. "Warmer here than I am most nights. Better food, too."

"Been living off FudPaks?"

Swallowing a mouthful of chicken and carrots, I nod. "When we can get them."

"Only ever had one of those at school."

I lift a brow.

"What?" She cocks her head to the side.

"Nothing, just figured you were an unsocialized

homeschooler is all." I wink.

She snorts a laugh. "We went to private schools until the family split. After that we got tutors." Tight-lipped, she waves a hand. "The salient point is that FudPaks are nasty."

"They are that." I slurp some broth. "Sometimes, if the garage is doing well or if Felix is feeling generous, we spring for a burger. My boss, well, my other boss, Daniel, knows a guy."

"He'd have to," she says. "Ground beef's hard to come by for anybody who doesn't live on Aaron Tuttleson's block." She chews a minute, then asks, "So why don't you live with him?"

"Aaron Tuttleson?"

Darby throws her napkin at me.

It hits me in the face. With a chuckle, I toss it back to her. "Kidding." I brush the hair off my forehead. "If Daniel got caught with us, he'd end up in jail for grand larceny. Technically, we belong to the lab since it's privatized. It's risky enough him giving us work. But we manage. One of the doctors from the clinic, Dr. Gayle, gave us as much as she could to get us started. Plus, the network's solid."

Darby arches a brow. "Network?"

"Sure. You don't think us Designer Kids just run around with no plan, do you?"

"Kinda did."

I grin and scoop the last bit of soup from the bottom of my bowl. "Dr. Gayle has people all over the city who help out: store owners, a few teachers, and one or two cops who work to throw off the Slingers."

One elbow propped on the coffee table, Darby purses her lips. "It sounds like the Designer Kids project needs overthrowing if you ask me. Ever think about rising up? Showing the world the truth?"

The muscles in my throat tighten. I've thought about that a lot, especially when Daniel and I help guide kids out of the tunnels and to their first safe house. But who am I? One dude who can barely watch a press conference without having a flipping panic attack. No. I'm not a revolutionary; I'm a scared kid just trying to keep from getting turned into a lab rat.

I rub my neck. "What brand of soup is this anyway?"

Darby shrugs, cheeks pink. "Not a brand. I made it from scratch."

"No way." I suck on the end of my spoon. Last time I had cooked carrots, they didn't taste nearly this good. Mushy and square, the orange objects designated as the aforementioned vegetable in the FudPaks taste faintly of plastic and aluminum. "Where'd you learn to cook like that? Not from your mom, I'm guessing."

She snorts and flicks a strand of hair out of her face. "Self-taught. My mom's idea of cooking is ordering someone else to do it. When we were kids, my little brother and I used to look up shows on the net. After we destroyed the kitchen with our creations, we'd…" Her eyes slide off to some distant memory. "We'd sit together on the counter and watch hacking videos. It entertained him more than cartoons ever did."

I grin. Hard to imagine the tough sister of Felix Cade cuddled up next to a little kid watching TV. Then again, she is afraid of heights. Everyone has their soft spots.

Curiosity pokes at my brain, sparked by the memory of her terror at the idea of climbing the fence. "So what was your other mission tonight? When you ran off before I went to get the egg?"

Rolling her shoulders back, Darby straightens, all the softness in her face hardening, and meets my gaze. "Taking care of Tuttleson."

"Taking care of…oh." Again, the muscles in my throat constrict.

She crosses her arms. "That's right. Felix wanted Tuttleson killed." She pinches her lips together.

"Why?"

"I don't ask questions. I obey orders."

I flinch. "That's what they always said at the lab." The words tumble from my mouth, unbidden, sharp.

"Don't you dare judge me. Don't you dare compare me to them."

Brow furrowed, I look up from my bowl. A thin layer of tears magnifies her eyes. Her lower lip trembles. A weird reaction coming from someone who just killed a guy. Then again, guilt does something to people, throws them out of alignment, emotions included. No matter how together Darby appears, her family has definitely screwed her up.

I shake my head, a short jerk right to left. "I'm not. You're just—"

"Just what?" The words snap from her mouth like sparks from an engine.

"Like me." I rub my nose. "We're doing what we have to do, but…"

She sniffs. "We shouldn't have to. It's all wrong."

"Yeah." I frown, resisting the urge to reach out, to squeeze her hand. She might not appreciate the gesture. "It's all wrong."

Flicking her braid over her shoulder, she leans forward on the coffee table, chin propped on a palm. "All hail the greater America."

I snort. "Sounds about right."
"You should get some sleep. I'll get some blankets."

Chapter Thirteen

Darby

Halfway through the night, a high-pitched sound jars me from sleep. Stifling my own strangled gasp, I sit up in bed, hand darting to the gun under my pillow. On light feet, I creep to the door and peek into the living room. Shards of moonlight scatter like broken glass across the floor, the walls, the thief on my couch.

I favor the balls of my feet as I sneak across the carpet. A few inches from Sephrim, I realize the source of the odd noise. Curled in tight on himself, the poor kid groans, a sound like someone trapped in a nightmare. I swallow, set the gun on the kitchen table, then step into the living room and sink in front of him.

His pale face twists like he's in pain.

"Hey." I elongate the quiet word. "It's okay, it's okay, you're safe." Chewing my lower lip, I smooth back his wild hair.

His eyes pop open, and he springs off the couch much faster than someone with cracked ribs should be able to. Both hands close around my throat, trapping a terrified scream. We tumble over the coffee table, him on top, then hit the floor. Yanking at the choke hold, breaking his grip, I flip our positions.

Pinning his wrists and ankles, I restrain him, wincing when he groans in pain and maybe fear. For three loud heartbeats he stares at me, brows low, mouth savage. Then, all at once, the tension drains from his face, followed by another shade of color.

"Darby. I'm sorry…I…" He lets out a shaky breath and shuts his eyes. "I'm so sorry."

I drop my head and slide off him onto the carpet. Sighing with relief, I lean back against the coffee table. Though it's still upright, most of the books and magazines now lie on the floor around it.

Running a thumb along the corner of a hardback, I watch Sephrim inhale through his nose and exhale out of his mouth a handful of times before I say, "You messed up my beautiful bandage job."

He laughs.

I push onto my knees and unwrap the gauze, grimacing at his bruised side. "Does that happen a lot?"

He keeps his gaze on the ceiling. "The nightmares or the unprovoked attacks?" A chuckle again morphs into a cough. "I don't make it through many nights without them, the dreams, not the attacks."

"How does, what's her name? The girl you ran with, how does she deal with them? I'm guessing you don't strangle her every night." I smooth the gauze back into place. Again, the skin-to-skin contact warms my entire body, tugs at my stomach. I clamp my teeth together until my jaw hurts.

"Not usually."

Outside, the sprinklers kick on. Though restrictions limit most neighborhoods' water usage, my complex falls into a similar category as Aaron Tuttleson's. Working for one of the biggest crime families in the city pays well. I didn't even think twice about choosing an apartment that can water its grass whenever it damn well pleases.

Fingers still smoothing the rough material wrapped around Sephrim's middle, I ask, "So what, then?"

A corner of his mouth twitches up. "She sings, well, hums."

I lift my brows. "Really?"

"Very off-key, but yeah."

"What songs?"

"Whatever pops into her head. Lots of commercial jingles she's heard on the garage TV, nursery rhymes." Again, he laughs and winces. He then places a hand over mine.

Cold and rough from constantly picking locks and working on cars, it sends a fluttering shiver through me. Felix says Designer Kids don't qualify as people. But touching one, feeling the effect of years on the street, tending to damaged bone, all this makes his statements sound absurdly stupid.

"I'll remember that if you wake me up again with your moaning." I try a grin, but it doesn't take. I loop an arm gently around his waist, haul him up, then steer him toward my room. He gives me a funny look, and I roll my eyes. "This way I don't have to get up to hum 'Twinkle, Twinkle, Little Star.' "

He doesn't argue, and a moment later we both lie under the covers of my queen-sized bed.

In the dark, red-tinged by my digital alarm clock, the thief finally looks at me. "Thanks."

"It's nothing."

"Sure it is."

"Don't get sappy on me." This time the smile comes without effort to my lips.

Sephrim turns on his uninjured side to face me. Felix

does have one thing right. Even too thin and beat up and exhausted, Sephrim is beautiful. That word doesn't even really cover it. He's almost otherworldly.

"Seriously, though," he says. "There's one more thing…"

I arch a brow. Does he have some other weird fetish or habit he needs to warn me about? Like, is he super into feet or something? Maybe I shouldn't let him sleep in my bed. "What?" I ask slowly.

For four blinks he stares at me, then he says, "I'd prefer if you didn't sing 'Twinkle, Twinkle Little Star.' I hate that song."

Laughing, I smack him lightly with the back of my hand. "Go to sleep, dork." I shut my eyes to emphasize the point.

He laughs too, and soon his breathing evens out. I open my eyes again to study his face. His lips have parted slightly. I lift my fingertips and flick a lock of hair away from his forehead, smiling a little. Maybe he'll turn out to be a good partner after all.

****

Matt

I tear the crust off one of my sandwiches, roll it between my fingers, and place it next to my plate. It sits next to a row of other bread balls, nice and neat spheres of brown and white. Like perfect lines of code. Cal sits across from me on the floor. She takes a massive bite of her own sandwich and munches with exaggerated movements. Peanut butter and jelly smears from the corners of her mouth like a smile overextended.

Laughter tumbles through my chest and into my throat. I press a fist to my lips to hold it in. Brows lifted into her blonde hair, she opens her still full mouth to reveal mostly chewed food and demands to know what I think is so funny. Giggles catch her too. She grabs a napkin from under her plate.

"Sorry," she says after swallowing. "Sephrim says I lost all my manners when we started living on the street, but the truth is I threw them away along with my ID chip. Who cares about manners anyway?"

I drop another ball of bread onto my plate. "Hellen does. She says they give people—" I squint. "—dignity? Or something like that."

Cal rolls her eyes. "Actions don't give people dignity. They just have it."

"But somebody has to give it, right?"

"Why?"

I open my mouth, but whatever my brain planned to say gets lost on the way to words. Does somebody have to give dignity? Based on the way people talk—the way Mom talks—beauty, ability, talent, all give humans their worth. Maybe that's wrong. Maybe dignity's preprogrammed into people's systems.

Nice thought.

One of my computers squawks, and I look up. Hellen's office. Though she hates "being spied on," she also wants her stuff protected and let me install a security camera in the corner on a magnetic trackpad built into the ceiling. Only Hellen's thumbprint can lock it in its place at the front of the office.

Cal makes a funny noise, similar to the sound of Hellen's chair screeching. "No offense, but your entertainment sucks."

On the screen, Hellen rakes her fingernails over the back of the beige leather office chair. My muscles freeze

99

up. On the wall opposite her desk, the recording of that press conference plays for the millionth time since it aired. Jumbled together behind the high, white fences, crowds wave at cameras, cheer at appropriate—and inappropriate—times, and push each other to get a better look at the stage.

The camera flips back to that doctor. Again, Hellen's gaze sharpens. She crushes more weight onto the chair. Its screws let out a high-pitched scream and, as Dr. Troy speaks, groans and shivers under her choke hold. Every few seconds she digs her nails farther into the seams.

I drop the rest of my half-eaten sandwich as my mouth dries out.

"Why do you watch her?"

Brow furrowed, I look back at Cal. Her mouth twists, and one of her fingers now stabs straight through the bread. Jelly rolls like blood along her skin. I look away, back to the security feed, back to Hellen.

"It's better to know where she is." The statement comes out like a preprogrammed response. "As long as she's in there…" My vocal cords wind up and cut off the end of my sentence.

"She's not in here," Cal says. "Smart. Friends close, enemies closer. Always in your sights."

On the feed, Hellen growls. "Screen off." She cuts around the big desk, high heels clacking on the gray cement floor as she walks to the safe in the far right wall.

She stabs the thumb pad, spitting curses when the device fails to recognize her print fast enough. My heart races. My back teeth clench. When the safe finally clicks open, I sigh. Shoving aside the various and sundry tools, Hellen claws out a small, steel box, then pries it open.

"What's in there?" Cal asks, whisper-quiet.

Because of the camera angle, we can't see, but after so many years of watching Hellen do this, I can describe it in perfect detail. "This old picture of her and these two women she went to med school with. I got a screenshot of it once. Hang on." I climb into my chair and pull up the image on my left monitor.

Inside the steel box lies an old photo. Yellowed by years, it shows three women. They smile at the camera, all young, all in white doctors' coats. One wears her dark hair short and curly, one lets hers flow free in the wind, and the last traps her platinum locks back in a tight bun. The strict style tugs at the corners of her eyes so they look narrow.

Cal gasps and grabs the back of my chair. "That's Dr. Gayle and Dr. Troy… I know them. They're—"

"Designer Kid scientists." I suck my lower lip and nod. "It's what Hellen wanted to be."

A rough crease severs the space between Hellen and Dr. Troy. Bits of white flake away. She's traced that line so many times. Every day for twenty years. I know. She told me once. Thousands of strokes.

"What happened? How'd she go all loony?"

"I don't know all of it," I say, still staring at the picture of the doctors. "But sometime after she started dating my dad, they had this huge falling out. Dr. Troy threw her under the bus for something and got her kicked out of their program. After that, she swore revenge."

Cal leans on my shoulder to get a better look at the two screens. I freeze up. Warmth spreads from her skin into mine. Wiry muscle coils in the forearm pressed against me. Thin but strong and—as she showed when springing off the operation table—real quick. Probably life on the street did all that. Kids have to be tough to survive out there.

"That can't be it."

I squint at her. "What do you mean?"

She waves a hand between the picture and Hellen's security feed. "That can't be the only reason she's doing all this. Shoving mind-controlling tech into people's heads like we're—what do you call them?—hard drives. Your mom is off, but she's not just crazy. She's gotta have a better motivation. A better plan. I mean, I don't even know what she wants me to do…"

This exact question has been bothering me since Hellen demanded I fix the chip. Small clues have helped me build a theory, but I haven't fully fleshed it out yet. Before Cal, I didn't really want to know, but I can't stay ignorant anymore.

With a sigh, I rub my eye with a knuckle. "All I know right now is that she wants you to attack someone powerful."

Cal squeaks. "Attack, verb, to set upon in a forceful, violent, hostile, or aggressive way, with or without a weapon, begin fighting with." She shoves both hands into her pockets and sways. "But who? And why? What is she hoping to accomplish?"

I turn to my third monitor and pull up another window. Tapping my computer keys lightly, I chew my bottom lip. Hellen will kill me if she finds out I'm looking at her personal files. Terminated like a bad webpage. I take a deep breath. I'm a technological superhero. I can cover my digital tracks. No problem for a computer wizard.

"I don't know," I say, "but I'm going to figure it out. Time for a little technological snooping."

Chapter Fourteen

Sephrim

I scowl at the railroad car, one hand pressed against my throbbing side.

Empty.

Purple morning light filters through the half-open door. It spreads across the flannel blankets tucked neatly across our foam mats. Our extra sets of clothes still lie folded on the scrap metal shelves, and Cal's stuffed monkey sits on top of one of the brown pillows, its eye missing so it appears to wink.

"Maybe she's still at the garage." Darby leans against the doorframe. "Isn't that where you said she'd be?"

As anxious as I was to get back to Cal, exhaustion knocked me out until halfway through the day. Darby made me eat lunch before even thinking of leaving. Over a meal of coffee and chicken and potatoes, she insisted on coming with me, arguing I shouldn't be wandering around alone with damaged ribs. I resisted for a good three rounds, but her stubborn refusal to let me go alone felt pretty friggin' awesome. It's one thing for Daniel and Cal to care about my well-being but quite another for a girl my age to worry about it.

I tug my hoodie back into place. "Yeah, this was on the way, so I thought I'd check. Sometimes she uses the sewers to come back in the morning because she misses her bed." I grab the hook for the door and pull it shut. No reason to think anything's wrong. But the pit of my stomach twists and writhes.

Paranoia.

Darby touches my arm, and my skin warms at the contact. "You okay?"

"Sure. Yeah. Guess I just need to check the garage."

"I'll go with you."

I lift a curious brow, and Darby crosses her arms.

"You might not have coughed up blood for a few hours, but I'm still not confident you won't collapse somewhere on the sidewalk."

I smirk.

"What?"

"You're worried about me." I grin wider and tell myself I don't care whether that's true or not.

"I reiterate, you were coughing up blood. I'm an assassin, not heartless."

We walk down the cracked street together, a stifled laugh stinging my ribs, worry squatting in my gut. Rays of rusty light seep between buildings as the sun sets, warming the winter air as we trek over gray rocks and oil stains.

Abandoned trains form a border, guarding us from the digital and physical eyes of the city. Billboard screens play an afternoon show, a very late afternoon show. Outside the protective circle of train cars, I lead the way to a small grate surrounded by flattened, brown grass. The one I used the night before to escape the Slingers.

I glance back at Darby. "Sorry for the smell. Safest way to avoid the cameras."

She grimaces. "I'll survive."

We climb down a ladder into the dripping tunnel. A thin layer of moisture covers every rung. My joints ache. It's harder with a busted rib, and balancing on the narrow walkway will be even worse. Worried or not, I have to force myself to go slow the same way I did last night. Cal is fine. She can take care of herself.

At the bottom of the ladder, I spit the taste of blood out of my mouth and place a hand on the slimy, cold wall for balance. I stop for a long, slow exhale, willing the worry in my stomach to untangle.

Again, Darby touches my arm. "Sure you're up for this?"

Warmth uncurls in my chest. Probably dumb, selfish even, considering my worry for Cal. "I'm sure. It's only about a ten-minute walk. Just, uh, watch your footing. If you fall in, we'll both be in trouble." I snicker and start forward.

Darby's hand hovers at my side as we shuffle through the dark. A few feet in, she speaks into the silence, her voice thick. "Feels like a crypt."

"Been in many of those?" I scrape my fingers along the damp cement wall.

She laughs. "One or two. Though they weren't quite so...wet. Sometimes Felix wants things retrieved from the dead. Weird how people bury valuable stuff. I wonder why we do that."

Shoes sliding on the wet cement, I let out a grunt. Darby's hand on my arm keeps me steady, but my chest throbs with the effort to stay upright. "No idea." I wince. "We don't define value very well, do we?"

"What do you mean?"

"Just something Dr. Gayle used to say." I sniff.

"Never really asked her what she meant."

"*Dr.* Gayle?"

I hear the grimace in her voice. "They're not all bad. Some of the doctors at the lab only joined because they want to free Designer Kids. Take care of them until they expire, then smuggle them out. I think one day they want to reform the whole system, but…that's kind of a massive task. In the meantime, those of us on the outside do what we can to help kids navigate the streets, try to find work and shelter." I point up. "There. That ladder leads to a grate close to the garage. Mind going up first? Not sure I can get it open right now."

Darby shimmies around me and climbs. She pauses halfway and, lips quirked to the side, says, "I know it's tempting, but don't look at my butt."

I laugh, but the pain in my ribs cuts it off. "Eyes averted," I say, only telling a half lie.

As she chuckles and continues the rest of the way, I flick my gaze upward for the barest of glances. With a single push, intense sunlight splashes into the sewer. It lights Darby's features, flushing the color from her eyes when she glances down at me so, for a brief moment, they resemble Felix's. I shiver and start up the ladder. At the top, she helps me out the rest of the way.

I sit a moment on the damp asphalt, feet dangling over the edge of the sewer, one arm wrapped around my side. Every breath pinches and burns. I need to get moving, to make sure Cal's okay and ease the ever-growing sense of foreboding. "Thanks," I say around a gasp.

"No problem. Need a minute?"

Damn, do I want one. Darby's hand on my shoulder sends goose bumps straight through me, and for a second the pain in my ribs shifts to the back of the queue. "Yeah, but we don't have one. There aren't any cameras in this alley, but I can't risk being seen by somebody taking out the trash." I grin. "Mind giving me a hand again?"

With a grunt, Darby pulls me to my feet and kicks the lid back into place. I lead the way to the end of the alley, tapping the back of my knuckles against a gray wooden door across from a blue-painted dumpster. It swings open to reveal a bright-eyed Daniel, who holds out two steaming cups of coffee. When he sees Darby, his brow puckers.

"Afternoon." He extends one of the mugs to me. "Who's your friend? Where's Cal?"

I almost drop the coffee as my stomach sinks. "Cal's not here?"

"I haven't seen her since last night." Daniel leans out the door. "Better talk inside. Come on."

He leads us into the garage and then through to the office. One arm still wrapped around my midsection, I sink into one of the chairs, stifling a cough. I wash down the taste of blood with coffee. Darby leans against the doorframe, a frown weighing down her features, while Daniel shoves aside a stack of papers and sits on the edge of his desk. He throws a glance at Darby, then looks back at me.

"This is Darby. We went on a job. Now…Cal…" I fail to stifle another cough.

"The last I saw her, she was on the roof," Daniel says. "Haven't had time to check on her yet today, but I will after you tell me what happened to you. Felix again?"

I grip the mug. "I'm fine. Just check."

Brows low, eyes dark, Daniel sets his coffee on the

desk. "Okay. But we're not done talking about this." He turns and heads to the back of the garage.

I watch his shoulders until he disappears up the roof-access stairs. Breath trapped painfully in my chest, I struggle to keep myself present rather than spiraling. Darby saying my name finally does the trick. "Huh?" I ask, gaze still on the half-open door.

"You need to breathe." She squats in front of me, elbows on her knees. "I know you're worried, but you've *got* to breathe. If she *is* in trouble, you won't be any good to her if you pass out."

"What if the Slingers got her?" I stare straight ahead, dazed, heart racing ahead of the seconds. "What if—"

"What-ifs are dumb." Darby's jaw hardens. "And so's panicking when you don't know if she's missing yet."

"But—"

"Stop it." She points into my face. "Look. I can't promise she's okay, but I can promise I'll help you. Got that?"

I nod. "Got it."

"She's not there."

Darby twists around, and I look up. Daniel stands at the doorway, gripping its frame. In spite of the calm on his face, yellow springs out across his knuckles, tension along his neck. This, even more than his statement, sends sharp fear through my gut. If Daniel's scared…

"Where else would she go?" Darby asks.

Fist pressed into the arm of the chair, I shake my head. "Nowhere. She'd only be here or-or at the train car."

"That's not true."

I look up at Daniel. "What?"

Frowning, Daniel adjusts his cap. "There's something you need to know."

Chapter Fifteen

Sephrim

Head in my hands, I squeeze my eyes shut. Hellen. Cal's been selling weapons to Felix *and* Hellen, two bloody halves of the city's criminal underground. And why? Because she thought it leveled the playing field. And now? The possibilities of what might have happened to her form a burning pile in my brain.

Darby's hands, now on my shoulders, tighten with every word of Daniel's story. They work like an anchor, a weight keeping me from spiraling into pure, untenable panic. She stays crouched in front of me, frozen in place.

"When the hell did she start working for her? How'd she even..." I shake my head and glare up at Daniel. "Why would you let her do something so stupid?"

"You really think I could've stopped her?"

"Could've tied her up or locked her in the trunk of a car and let me talk sense into her." I grumble my response, embarrassed by how much I sound like a moody teenager.

Daniel lifts his brows. "I think you know how that would've ended."

A fair point. "She'd probably figure out a way to break free." I scrub a hand over my face. No time to throw blame at the one guy who actually takes care of us. Better to spend my brain power on finding Cal. "Do you know how to get in contact with Hellen?"

Grip tightening all the more, Darby ekes out the barest whisper. "I might."

Shock stings my face and chest. "I'm sorry, what?"

Gazing at her shoes, she flares her nostrils. "Hellen Jacobs is my mother."

All the get up and go in my body gets up and gets out. I sink backward in the chair. Too many words try to make it out of my mouth. All of them fail. So Cal hasn't just been selling to twin criminal arms—she's been selling to two gory bits of a broken family. That makes things *so* much less complicated.

Daniel tugs off his hat and runs a hand over his head. "If you can find anything out…"

"I, uh," Darby stammers, nails digging into my arms. "Yeah, I know someone I can contact. Give me a minute."

She straightens and pulls a cell from her pocket. The pressure on my shoulders disappears as she does so. Without her support, I wobble. Oxygen fills my head, making me float. I have to focus, stay calm for Cal's sake.

Darby squints at the screen for two of my calming breaths before her eyes widen. Lips mashed into a solid hard line, she shuffles backward and runs into the desk. Her nostrils flare again. She mashes a fist into her mouth, swallows, types a quick message into the phone, then says, "Hellen has her."

Knots form in my stomach. I gawk. "She told you that?"

"Matty did." Darby shuts her eyes. "He wants to help her escape but—"

"But nothing." Instant irritation laced with

desperation sends the words out of my mouth before I can stop them. "If he wants to let her out, if he *can* get her out, then tell him to do it."

Red flushes Darby's neck, and she glares. "Hellen will kill him if he has anything to do with freeing Cal. I won't let that happen."

I pop up so fast the chair tumbles backward. "So I'm just supposed to let Hellen kill Cal? Or worse?"

"Yeah." Darby sweeps her braid off her shoulder and rolls her eyes. "Because that's exactly what I said." Her words snap, sharp from her lips. Her hands shake.

Daniel's arm cuts across my chest before I can take another step toward her. "Hey. Idle a sec and let her explain." He looks at Darby. "Because I assume she has a solution that won't involve either of them getting hurt."

Brows low, she lets out a painfully slow breath. "I do have another option."

"What?" I barely get the word past clenched teeth.

"For months now Hellen's been trying to get me to meet. I think it's because she either wants to recruit me or to try and get information about Felix." Her voice trembles. "Maybe we can get more info, figure out a way to trade something for Cal."

A small semblance of relief cools my chest, and I nod.

"I'll have to be careful so she doesn't know Matt told me about her." She rubs her temples, then meets my eyes again. "I'd tell you not to come with me, but I doubt it'll do any good, will it?"

Jaw locked, I cross my arms. "If your brother was the one missing, would you let anyone stop you from going?"

"Not a chance."

****

Near the edge of the city, close to my railroad sanctuary, sits a bar simply called Sam's. Built into an old warehouse during the 1990s by a woman named Peggy Sam, it serves all kinds of criminals and citizens who want to stay hidden from the law—including runaway Designer Kids. Wired internally into the building, the camera feeds from their security system never make it to the police or any other government entity. Only the current owner, Peggy's daughter Meg, ever sees the videos.

Though we knew about the bar, Cal and I have never gone inside. At least, I don't think Cal's ever been here, but I also didn't think she kept secrets from me, not secrets quite this big. Maybe she does hang out at Sam's. Sells guns to whoever wants them just to "level the playing field."

I brush away the anger. I still don't know the whole story. Better to wait and ask if, no, *when* we find her.

Wind warbles the aluminum walls as we climb the porch steps. I wince and curse. Dumb ribs. Apart from a handful of people in business suits nursing cups of coffee, very few patrons fill the bar this early. None of them look at us head on when we walk in the door. Instead, each performs their own manner of observation—peeks from the corners of their eyes, glances in the mirror above the liquor.

Paranoia creeps along my shoulders. I tug on my hood farther and slide into a corner booth with a groan, facing the front door. Air rushes from the plastic-covered seat. Darby sits next to me just as a woman with unruly curls approaches. The warm lights overhead glow through her hair, lighting up the threads of copper amidst strands of brown. She wears it tied back from her face with a neon-green bandana. A tattoo of Van Gogh's *Starry Night* covers her upper arm.

"Welcome to Sam's, my name's Meg, and I'll be your waitress this morning," she says, snagging a pen from her apron pocket. A slight Texas twang flavors her words, and asymmetrical dimples border her grin. "Who's your friend, Darby?"

Darby's gaze flicks to me.

I tuck a foot under me. "Sephrim," I say after another beat. "Darby and I work together."

"Ah, I was wondering." Meg smiles. "Well, you're always welcome here at Sam's. Dr. Gayle and I have been friends for a very long time. You new on the street? Haven't seen you pass through here yet."

"Been out a few years." I glance at the door, then back to Meg.

"It's okay." She twirls the pen between her fingers. "Glad you're here now. Let me know if you ever need anything. Can I get you two something to drink? Dinner?"

Darby orders two coffees, black—one for her and one for Hellen. When I hesitate, she insists on buying. Discomfort burning my ears, I order a latte, extra foam, a long-time favorite from the lab. Scribbling on her pad, Meg winks and spins toward the bar. Darby lets her head fall back.

Twisting in my seat, I face her. "Thanks for doing this. I know—"

"Don't mention it." She squeezes her eyes shut. "Seriously. If I think about it too much, I might run right out of this bar. Because Felix is scary, but he follows rules. My mom is unpredictable. Says as long as you keep people guessing, you've got control."

Without thinking it through, I take her hand. It shakes, then her fingers thread through mine. Calluses harden her palm. Though Cal and I worked with our hands in the lab, the techs took great pains to keep our skin smooth and soft. They removed the barest development of roughness with the same sort of immediacy as they treated sickness or "corrected" weight gain.

That all changed when we ran, but I still can't shake the small twinge of anxiety when imperfections inevitably show up on my body even if only for a moment. For the most part, no buyer wanted a Designer Kid with any sort of wear and tear, and years of conditioning make it difficult to avoid old thought patterns.

Darby returns the squeeze, the pressure only intensifying when the front door opens and a dark-haired woman walks inside. Her pointed features rob her face of any potential beauty, or maybe the set of her lips does that. She doesn't frown or scowl. In fact, I can't quite come up with the right word for her expression. Fear curls in my gut.

Hands in her trench coat pockets, Hellen pauses when she sees Darby and me. Both brows drop over her narrowed eyes, and everything else in the room fades into the background. Darby's body shakes against mine. Great sign when someone scares an assassin. If her mom opens fire, we've chosen a stupid place to sit. Maybe we could hide under the table.

Great plan. That won't make us easy targets.

Then Hellen applies what I'd loosely describe as a smile and approaches the table. "Darby, my dear, it's been far too long. I'd say I'm glad you finally agreed to meet, but the presence of your"—she arches a brow—"friend leads me to believe you have ulterior motives."

"Why don't you sit instead of looming like that?" Darby's grip on my hand tightens even more, but her face stays smooth, passive.

Head tilted to one side, Hellen slides into the booth across from us just as Meg comes back with a tray full of coffee. Steam streams in soft ribbons from the wide-mouthed mugs, distracting me from the tension at the table for a sliver of a second. My mouth waters.

After Meg sets the cups in place, she focuses a grin on Darby and rests a fist on her hip.

"Decide on something to eat?" she asks.

"We need another minute," Darby says.

"No problem. Our special today is fried chicken and waffles." Meg lifts her brows, as if she's asked a question rather than made a statement.

"With the spicy syrup?" Darby asks.

Meg nods. "Of course."

"We'll let you know."

With a final grin at Darby, Meg heads to the next table, tray under her arm.

I look at Hellen, nervous to move too much. Like a wild animal or cornered runaway, she might strike if startled. She hasn't so much as shifted since sitting, not even to take her hands from her pockets. Her eyes, however, flick between me, Darby, Meg, the patrons, and every exit. Paranoia? No. Preparation.

No wonder she has Darby scared.

I squeeze her hand again, nervousness twitching along my forearm.

"Now," Hellen says, her voice low but as sharp and

hard as her features. "What is it you want?"

Darby meets my eyes, then looks back at her mom. "The girl who's been supplying you with guns has gone missing. Do you—"

Hellen laughs over the end of Darby's sentence. "And I thought I'd found the perfect subject no one would miss." She levels her stare at me. "Tell me, did you grow in the lab together? Run to the streets hand in hand?"

I straighten. "So you have her?"

Hellen sips her coffee, studying me over the rim of the mug, then dabs her lips. "Yes. And I'm afraid you can't have her back. I need her more than you do."

Fury flushes out fear, and I flinch forward on pure instinct. Darby jams my hand into the plastic cushion to hold me in place. I swallow the rage, but the words still come out rough, slow. "Need her for what?"

With a flick of her wrist, Hellen dismisses my question. "I'm afraid I can't tell you that. Sorry, honey." She pouts—the expression odd on her sharp face—and takes another sip of her coffee. "Anything else I can do for you?"

Letting out a curse, I slide to the end of my seat, nails biting into the edge of the wooden table. "Let her go." Not part of the plan, but every last bit of rationality evaporated with Hellen's words.

"Seph…" Darby says under a shaking breath.

All semblance of politeness shrivels from Hellen's face. Her hand shoots out, fingers strangling my forearm as she pulls me halfway across the table. Faster than the snap of a Slinger's whip, she presses the tip of a needle-sharp blade against the large vein in my wrist. Then she leans close, her nose almost touching mine.

"Are you telling me what to do?" She slides the knife back and forth with just enough pressure to hurt. "Because if you are, you're making a very big mistake."

This should terrify me, but anger overrides all other emotions. "I'm not that stupid. I'm asking. Let Cal go. Use me instead."

"Seph, don't." Darby's hold on my other hand cuts off the circulation to my fingers. She no longer sounds like the confident, cool assassin who demanded Felix stop whaling on me. Fear weakens her voice, makes it tremble.

Hellen cocks a brow. "Now, now. Let him talk. Things just got interesting." She continues to trace my vein with the knife, leaving behind an irritated red line. "How's your aim with a gun?"

I press my tongue against the backs of my teeth. How's my aim? Bad. Real bad. Cal's tried to teach me way too many times but stopped after a stray bullet nearly blew up our train car. I could lie. Daniel could protect Cal, smuggle her out of the city. Maybe. But what if Hellen wants proof? Too much left to chance.

"Bad," I say, mouth dry with disappointment. "Can't hit the broadside of a Slinger van." I will Darby to offer up something else to trade like she promised earlier. Unfortunately, she stays completely silent.

The knife digs deeper, drawing a small river of blood. "Shame. I might have been willing to make a trade. But I need a good shot." She flips the knife and presses it to my throat, against a vein pulsing rapidly with fear and adrenaline. "And unfortunately, it seems you're going to remain troublesome."

I flinch at the sound of a heavy click. Meg stands next to the table, aiming a shotgun directly at Hellen's head, that dimpled smile fixed in place. "Maybe you're not aware of our service policy. Threatening other customers is frowned upon. Afraid I'm going to have to ask you to leave. Coffee's on the house for your trouble."

Hellen smirks. "An understandable policy. My question is whether or not you think you're fast enough to stop me from spilling this boy's blood."

"Hellen…please…" Darby's voice shakes.

Pulse throbbing against my throat, I glance at her out of the corner of my eye. Fear leaves little color in her face, just like it did when I'd suggested we climb the fence. Strange. Faced with Felix, Darby stands shoulders back, makes logical demands. But with her mother…

Rage boils away terror completely. With a twist of my fingers, I free my hand from Darby's grip, then rock back and grab Hellen's wrist in one, sharp movement. I redirect the knife sideways into the table.

Hellen's eyes twitch a bit wider, then she smiles. "My, my. Again, with the surprises. I must say you've impressed me. Still, I have no need of you, and I must be going. Seems I've violated Sam's rules."

She pulls her hand from my grip and slides out of the booth, still covered by Meg's shotgun. Before Hellen turns to the door, however, she leans in.

"Just remember, whatever happens next, I really am doing this for your kind, for all Designer Kids. You'll see. It might take some time, but you will see."

Chapter Sixteen

Sephrim

Halfway back to the garage, in the cold hard sewers I find weirdly comforting, Darby stalls out. Blank-eyed, she stares straight ahead, refusing to budge another step.

"What's wrong?" Maybe a dumb question will get her moving again.

Nothing. She simply keeps staring right through me.

Horrible time for her to have a breakdown. Every second we stand here, Cal stays Hellen's prisoner. How can I make her snap out of it? She has to get how I feel. After all, her brother's been in a similar spot for years.

I turn and take her shoulders. "Darby, we've got to get back to the garage. You can have your hissy fit there."

Gaze sharpening, she finally focuses. "Excuse me?" Her words come out low and deadly. "I just put my little brother at risk and—"

"Good. You're talking. That means you can move." I force a grin, latch on to her hand, and drag her along. "If you still want to yell at me, you're welcome to do it so long as you keep walking."

"Bold move. I about shoved you into the sewer water for that."

"I'm smarter than I look."

By the time we reach the sewer lid closest to the

garage, Darby's hand shakes in mine. Half carrying her up the ladder sends sharp pain through my ribs, and at the top she more or less collapses against me. She presses into my good side, warmer and softer than I might've expected of a hardened teen assassin. Guilt immediately slams down on my chest. How the hell can I think about *that* with Cal in the hands of a psycho?

Trying to not focus on the feeling of Darby against me—and failing miserably—I pound on the back door of the garage. Daniel answers almost immediately, face twisted with worry, one hand wringing the neck of a wrench. Beyond him, his legally employed mechanics tinker and tap under an assortment of cars. None of them look up when we stumble past the garage owner.

"What happened?" Daniel reaches out to help Darby inside, then kicks the door shut with his heel.

I let out a grunt and wince, half relieved, half disappointed to let her go. "We met with Hellen. She plans to use Cal for something but won't tell us what." I press a hand to my throbbing ribs, mopping sweat from my hairline with the sleeve of my hoodie.

"We can talk about it inside," Daniel says, supporting Darby.

We weave through the garage and into the office. Darby collapses into one of the chairs, head in her hands, hair cloaking her face. I pace, jaw set so tight it clicks. Right before Daniel shuts the blinds, I catch sight of the lobby.

At the front counter, Kaylee the receptionist—a young woman with black curls and freckles across her dark cheeks—types out orders while customers in the lobby stare at their devices. They jab at the screens, sometimes speak into them, but rarely make eye contact with each other. Behind their digital barriers they hide, protected from reality, from worry, at least for a few seconds.

Lucky them.

On my third trip pacing across the office, I wheel on the ball of one foot, tug at my hood, then hook both hands behind my neck. "If Hellen won't let her go, we'll just have to save her."

Daniel opens his mouth, but Darby chokes, speaking before he can. "Are you insane? After what she did to you at Sam's? Do you actually believe—"

"It's *because* of what she did to me." My words snap off the end of her sentence. "You know what she does to your brother. Can you imagine what she's done to Cal? What she plans to do?"

Images flick through my mind, potential scenarios in answer to my own question. Panic sends my heart into a sprint, and I reroute my thoughts from "maybes" to making a plan. And breathing. Breathing is good.

Darby claws the hair away from her face. "She sliced up your arm, nearly slit your throat. What do you think she'll do if you try to break into her compound? She'll chop a limb off just to make a point." She curses. "Why do you think I haven't tried to pull Matty out a second time?"

Heat rages up my neck and across the bottoms of my cheeks. "I can't leave her there, Darby." I get her fear— especially after meeting Hellen—but I have to convince her to help.

"You can if you don't know where Hellen's compound is." She crosses her arms. "If I tell Matt no, he'll listen."

"Darby—"

Daniel cuts me off. "Let's just slow down, now. Back to your respective corners. And let me take a look at that arm."

I shuffle to the other side of the office and slump against the door. Mouth clamped shut, I glare at Darby as Daniel pulls the emergency kit from a cabinet. I shove up my sleeve with fury-shaken fingers but stay quiet, narrowed gaze fixed on her.

Daniel takes my arm and runs a thumb along the edge of the thin, deep cut. Dried blood fans out across my skin and clots along the wound. Something about Hellen's restraint makes it all the more terrifying. So close to the vein. A taunt. A threat of potential, permanent violence. She has power to protect the young, but she uses them instead.

And she has Cal.

As Daniel cleans the wound, he says, "Before we try anything, we need to plan. No point in getting maimed or killed trying to save her. The fact is, though, Sephrim's right—we're not going to leave her, and you're the only one who can help us, Darby."

"Not the only one." My jaw aches as I clench my back teeth. "I bet Felix could negotiate to get us in."

Darby scoffs, rolling her bloodshot eyes. "Says the guy whose ribs Felix just smashed."

"But he'll listen to you." My voice shakes. "You proved that last night. If you're so scared of Hellen, then ask Felix. You might even be able to get Matty out too." I wince a little when Daniel blots my arm with rubbing alcohol. "Please. I have to save Cal from whatever Hellen wants to use her for."

Letting out a slow breath, Daniel smooths a bandage over my arm and tosses the leftover paper into the trash slot in the wall. He then turns back to Darby and crouches in front of her. When she finally looks away from me, she won't meet Daniel's gaze. Instead, she dips her head, hair falling over her face again, hiding.

Good, she should be ashamed. I grit my teeth.

A healthy dose of my own shame burns right through me the second the thought passes. After she told me about everything Hellen put her brother through, I get why facing her mom freaks her out so much. But this reality aggravates my own fear even more.

"I know you're scared," Daniel says to Darby. "Don't have to know your specific experience with Hellen to get that. She scares the hell out of me, too. But if there's a possibility we can get Cal out—"

"You don't understand." She looks up. "There's nothing we can do to get back something Hellen's taken. It's impossible. I took Sephrim to meet her because I figured a few minutes with her would make that clear. If Hellen has Cal, she won't be letting her go."

"Then we break her out," I say, breathing slow, trying to calm my frustration. "Your brother says he can do it—"

"I won't let him." Darby glares at the ground. "If Hellen finds out, she'll kill him."

Tension throbs against my temples. "I don't want to put him in danger, but you said he's a tech genius. Are you saying she'll catch him because it's true or because you're scared?"

She doesn't answer. I turn, open the door, and slam it behind me.

Chapter Seventeen

Sephrim

Cold gnaws into my hands as I grip the rough cinder blocks at the top of Daniel's garage. Dense clouds form a slow-moving wall at the other side of the city. Gray-blue and fat with rain, they shift across the apathetic winter sun, choking out its light. Anxiety hardens into a ball in my throat. Cal could be in that direction, at the edge of that high barrier, or she could be in a thousand other directions, a thousand other places.

And why?

Because in her genius brain, she decided to put herself in Hellen's line of fire. After everything I did to protect her, to keep her from Felix and his crew, she still ended up in enemy hands. If only…I kick the wall. Stupid thought. What good does "if only" ever do? It won't bring her back, won't save her.

Only Darby can help with that, and she's too scared of her mom. Scared like I am of Felix, of Dr. Troy. I bend forward, elbows on the cinder blocks, head in my hands. This thought curbs the anger burning in my chest. Like I've got any damn business judging someone for their anxiety and trauma.

Shame cools my anger, leaving me with fear. I mumble a curse at myself. Behind me, the door whines open. I don't have to look back to know it's Daniel.

Something about his presence steadies me.

The garage owner leans against the roof at my side, fists clenched against the gray surface. "How's your ribs?"

"Bad, but better than they were after initiation." I run a knuckle under my nose. "Better than Cal probably is."

"I'm sorry, man. I should've told you what she was doing, but she asked me not to. She didn't want you to worry."

"Not your fault. When Cal wants to do something…" I shake my head. "Back at the lab, whenever the techs or doctors told her something was off-limits, she just wanted to do it even more. And the more barriers they put in her way, the harder she worked to get it."

Daniel chuckles. "Sounds like Cal. Knowing her, that means she'll break out of Hellen's compound, or wherever she is, before we even come up with a solid plan. She's not the eight-year-old you ran with anymore. Even then she was brilliant, tough."

Grinning, I nod. I need to stop thinking of Cal as the scrawny little kid I used to steal the lab techs' cookies with. Even back then, she probably didn't need my help, just enjoyed the company. Though I've always been better at picking locks, Cal could have figured it out on her own if she needed to. Then again, getting taken by Hellen is a little different than trying to pilfer a box of Chocochips.

I shove the hair off my forehead. My hood falls back, letting the cold gust around my neck. "You're probably right. But we still need to come up with something." I glare at the horizon. The sun's movement counts the hours since Cal's kidnapping, the hours since a psychopath took her captive. I tug my hood back up. "Cal didn't happen to know where Hellen's hideout was, did she?"

"If she did, she never told me," Daniel says. "But I doubt it. They always met in the same place. It's possible their meeting spot is close to an entrance, but that's not necessarily the case."

"You're right." We turn at the sound of Darby's voice. "She'd never set up a meet near her compound."

She stands in the open doorway with her hands in her pockets. Though still pale, she clenches her jaw, eyes narrow, again looking like the girl who stood up to Felix less than twelve hours ago. Fierce.

And a little terrifying.

With a wince, I turn full around and lean against the cinder-block wall. "So where is it, then?"

"Better if you don't know, but I told Matty to do his thing, help her escape." Color fades from her lips. "He says he can cover his tracks. That he'll be safe. Once she's out, Felix can protect her."

Dread tugs a grimace onto my face. Felix. Great. If Felix does agree to protect Cal, he'll probably insist she go through initiation. But without his help, we have no hope of protecting her. We could run, sure, but I doubt we'd get far. Not with Hellen so bent on her plans. Whatever they are.

Better to have some form of insurance.

"Okay, then, let's get in contact with him." I lift a brow.

"I need to go to Felix first." She shakes her head. "I'm sure I can convince him to help. And it's best if I go alone. Doubt he's gotten over what happened last night." She spins back to the door.

"Darby."

She pauses.

"Thank you," I say. "I know Hellen scares you, that you want to protect your brother as much as I want to save Cal. And I'm sorry for losing my shit. She's got me pretty freaked out too."

Darby doesn't turn but bobs her head and slips back down the stairs.

****

I spend the next twelve hours pacing the roof. A cloud-encased sun gives way to hazy stars and a fat moon, then comes back around long before my feet hurt or my stomach grumbles. I ignore both, barely aware of the ache for food. What did I eat last? Darby's chicken and potatoes? My mouth waters. What about Cal? Has Hellen fed her? Has she been able to sleep? Is she hurt? I kick a wall, the pain another physical cue I ignore.

When dawn comes and Darby doesn't, I wander back down into the garage. I find a work order for a particularly tricky fix and roll myself under a car, hoping a complex problem will take my mind off Cal's captivity and Darby's meeting with Felix.

It doesn't.

Every tool I pull from my belt slips in my shaking fingers. My ears perk at every pop and groan of the pipes, and my muscles burn every time I strain to look at the door. I glare at the black underbelly of the car, at the patterns that so often calm my nerves and screw my head back into place. None of it makes sense like it usually does.

I growl, grip the bumper, and roll back out into the dim light.

Hugging my middle, I lie on the mechanic's creeper, eyes squeezed shut. Sweat prickles my brow and lower back. With these stupid cracked ribs, I won't be any good to Cal at all. Totally worthless.

A familiar ping from the office distracts me from self-loathing. With a groan, I roll onto my good side, then push myself up and shuffle to the small net board on Daniel's desk. The sour ball in my stomach jumps, both with excitement and dread. Dr. Gayle.

I love the rare occasions she manages to make an F2F call. The closest thing I've ever had to a mother, Dr. Gayle didn't just free Cal and me from the lab. She checks on us as often as possible, asking about what meager lives we've made for ourselves, gives us information about new Designer Kids on the street, and warns us about upcoming Slinger hunts.

I've never dreaded these calls before. But today I'll have to tell her what happened to Cal, how I failed to keep her safe. Slumping onto one of the office stools, I tap the green box to accept the call. Dr. Gayle's face appears on the screen. Blue-white light shines across her high cheekbones, but it's her smile that truly lights her face when the call comes through.

She sits in an overstuffed, floral armchair in her living room. Nestled between a small bookcase and a tall, rectangular window, the little nook is usually cluttered with stacks of folders and files and always contains a chipped, ceramic tea kettle with its matching mug.

"Sephrim! I was hoping you'd be there. I feared I might have to get Daniel to hunt you down or deliver my message."

A Jamaican accent spices her words, carries her

cadence along in a smooth wave. It always calls to mind pictures she once showed me of her hometown. I've dreamed of visiting, of seeing a beach in real life, of sticking my toes in the cool of the ocean. Maybe one day.

In spite of my dread, I grin. "Glad I was in the garage. I spent the night on the roof."

Dr. Gayle's brow puckers. "It doesn't look like you've slept much. More nightmares?"

I fiddle with one of the drawstrings on my hoodie. "Sort of." More like a nightmare come to life. "Someone took Cal." The shame of the confession clogs at the back of my throat. I glare at my feet, dreading the disappointment bound to appear on her face.

"Taken? By who?" Fear sharpens the soft edges of her tone, and I wince.

"Hellen Jacobs," I say in a mumble. "I was out and…I really don't know how it happened. I'm sorry."

"Sephrim, look at me."

Head still bowed, I obey.

Brows now low over her eyes, she leans closer to the screen. "Remember what I told you about false guilt? Own what you're responsible for but don't waste time on things you have no control over. Now, tell me exactly what happened."

Worrying the knot at the end of my drawstring, I explain the last terrifying twenty-four hours. Dr. Gayle listens without comment. She frowns at the end, leans back in her chair, and presses clasped hands to her forehead.

I pick at a rough spot on the desk. As the events play slowly back through my mind, now removed from their immediacy, the fear I should've felt piles onto my chest. It aches under a suffocating weight, and the air in the office thins.

"I don't know what else to do."

"I know, it's difficult to wait, but it sounds like that's the only thing you can do at the moment." She drops her hands into her lap. "Perhaps a distraction while you wait for your friend to return?"

"New wave of kids coming?" I ask, hoping that focusing on Designer Kid refugees will help redirect my worry.

"Tomorrow at 1400. The new location's on the east side of the city this time. Full count should be three."

Flicking hair from my eyes, I nod. "I'll tell Daniel. We'll have the checkpoint ready."

Dr. Gayle frowns. "I should warn you. Dr. Troy is leading a movement to lift the ban on using Designer Kids as donors and child soldiers. Some in the medical community are against it but not nearly enough."

I grimace. At the lab, Dr. Troy used to muse aloud about her ideas for the expired Designer Kids "problem." Once, when taking a blood sample for my records, she pondered the concept of using the "leftover" teens as test subjects for the latest surgeries and medicines. Disgust crawls through me.

"We've got to stop her." I rub my temples. "End the whole system or fix it or I don't know."

A corner of Dr. Gayle's mouth lifts. "Sounds revolutionary. I always said you were a leader."

Heat stings my ears and the back of my neck. Yeah, she'd said that many times throughout my youth. Frankly, I don't see it. "If I was such a great leader, I never would've lost Cal."

"Only great leaders feel this kind of loss so painfully. Trust me, you are far more than you imagine."

"She's right, you know," Darby says from behind.

I whip around and stuff down a wince. She stands at the door. Backlit by the low light of the garage, hands on her hips, she resembles a superhero.

"Darby. Did you—"

"It's all set." She cocks her head. "Cal should be back soon and under Felix's protection."

"Sephrim, is that your friend?" Dr. Gayle asks.

I wave Darby over. Tucking her hair behind her ears, she steps up to the desk, then bends forward, hands on her knees.

"Darby, this is Dr. Gayle. She's the one who got Cal and me out of the lab. Dr. Gayle, this is Darby. She's trying to help us save Cal."

"It's very nice to meet you, Darby," Dr. Gayle says. "Thank you for your efforts, so far."

Darby snorts a little. "Don't thank me yet."

With the shadows bleeding into the worry lines around her mouth, she looks old, almost ancient, as if she's seen millennia. Being a seventeen-year-old assassin, terrified for the well-being of a younger sibling, would do that to a person—if it didn't snap a spark plug in their brain first. Hopefully, helping Cal won't cause a misfire that finally gets her a one-way ticket on the crazy train.

"We still don't even know what Hellen's done to her," Darby continues. "Somehow, I doubt her escape will be the end of it. From what my source says, we still have a lot to worry about."

I clench the stool, my fingers biting into the bottom. Doesn't matter what Hellen's done to Cal—whatever she needs, whatever it takes to protect her, I'll do it. I won't fail her again.

Chapter Eighteen

Cal

Five minutes.

In five minutes, I can run. That's when Matt will do some kind of "techno-magic," cause a distraction to divert all the guards away from my exit, risk his life to get me out.

Four minutes and twenty-eight seconds.

Sitting on top of the metal operating table, I stare at the blinking red light next to the door, stroking the petals of the flower Matt gave me. Flattened by the canvas of my overalls' pocket, it looks a little sad, beaten up, but I still love it. Hopefully, it won't fall completely apart too soon.

I look down at the small, transparent screen nestled in my palm, pulse pounding in my throat. A layout of the compound appears when I tap it with a thumb. Never great at directions, I repeat them over and over again. Anticipation pokes my stomach. *Two rights, one left, and out through the sewers. Two rights, one left, and out through the sewers.* Matt blanched at the idea, but they don't bother me, not when Seph and I use them nearly every day. A little scum won't kill me.

Leaving Matt with Hellen might.

I tried to convince him to come along, to run, but he insisted on staying with his precious computers. These apparently hold the key to my salvation—my true freedom—and his. And somehow, to many others. Even with my ingenious mind, I can't figure how he might free these "others." When Matt refused to expound, I accepted the explanation, albeit with a huff and a pout.

Meantime, I watch the red blinking light.

Blink.

Blink.

Buzz.

I spring off the table, stuff the screen into an overall pocket, and shove the door. It swings open. Only red flashing lights fill the hallway. I want to wait another minute, to listen for the pound of shoes on cement, but with just under four minutes to get to the sewer door, I need to run. Heaving in a deep breath to calm my nerves, I dive into the hall and sprint right, skid around the second right, then scrape left past the final turn.

A yellow light flashes over a gray door at the end of the hall. It stands slightly ajar, letting in weak winter sunlight. With a grin, I sprint forward. I don't have much time. As soon as the system resets, the door will suck shut. Because of the type of malfunction Matt programmed, the whole compound will lock down immediately after.

No second chances.

"Hey, you! Stop right there!"

Cold fear needles its way through my ribs at the voice behind me, but I don't stop. Lungs burning, I dig the balls of my feet into the ground and pump my arms. So close. My fingers touch the side of the door. Something hot and jittering pierces my shoulder.

A thousand bands of electricity snap through my body as I careen out into the open. Choking, jerking, shivering, and in full-on panic mode, I land on damp grass. Seconds later, the door slams shut, locking my pursuer in the compound.

I squint, blurry-eyed, at the sewer grate a few feet away. *Tasered. Disrupted connection…brain not communicating with muscles…numb…* I need to get moving…before…before… *Tase, verb meaning to electrically stun a living target using a Taser or similar stun gun.*

I blink. Though I won't be able to move, with the new advancements in technology, I'll also stay conscious. That way, law enforcement can read detainees their rights and question them fast. I guess Hellen hadn't thought of that with her chip. If someone tases me, it won't matter how good a shot I am…

Another jolt courses through my body directly from the chip. It starts at the base of my head, at the incision site, and flushes feeling back into my limbs. I stand corrected. Maybe Hellen *did* think of everything. What's the point in having a weapon that can be so easily disabled? She must have had Matt program the chip to restart my system after a tase.

Relieved, I shove up from the cold ground, pull out the prongs from the Taser, and crawl to the grate. One hand on the cold metal, I glance back at the door.

Leaving Matt behind makes sense, but I still hate it. I pull the lid up and slide one foot onto the top rung of the ladder. As I climb down into darkness, I swear on my one-eyed monkey I will come back for him with a better plan, reinforcements, whatever it takes. He won't be Hellen's prisoner forever.

In the sewer, I grab a pipe—a wonderful, familiar feeling against my skin—and shut my eyes. The rush of water inside the cold metal shivers under my hand as it heads away from the compound still at my back.

Good, I have no desire to travel under my former prison. Sucking in a breath of damp, smelly air, I move forward at a fast-paced walk. Though I'm wearing rubber-soled shoes, the algae-slicked concrete makes for unsure footing. I probably look like one of those weirdo mega-mall walkers I've seen on TV, hips swaying like an off-balance engine with a defunct stabilizer.

Even though I slip a few times along the way, I don't take a dip in the city's putrid water. I reach the manhole closest to the railroad tracks, scramble up the ladder, and nudge the lid open a crack.

Adrenaline pulsing through me, I glance around, then roll out onto the cold grass and crawl to the railroad car, anxious for my bed. No sign of Sephrim. I frown. He must be at the garage. Or maybe Cade's? I grimace and hope he's not with that power-hungry putz.

A familiar snap cracks the atmosphere, and I jump like a piston. I spin to face a small cluster of Slingers. From hilt to tip, their whips crackle blue. Light from the city reflects off their dome-shaped helmets as they charge forward without preamble. No. Nope. This is stupid. I didn't just get away from the grand high priestess of crime only to get taken back into the hands of the evil mother brain, Dr. Troy.

Fists clenched, I let out the most unhinged, furious scream and sprint toward the Slingers *a la* Han Solo. The soldier at the front of the group lifts her whip. As it reaches toward me, the woman shouts, "Freeze! You are suspected of being one of the Expired—"

A ringing sound pierces my ears as electricity pulses from the chip's incision site at the back of my head. It charges through me, numbing all emotion, all feeling. Energy races down my spine and into every muscle. It hooks into my nerves, then drives my body in the opposite direction I originally intended.

I duck under the tail of the whip and rip the gun from the closest Slinger's holster. As I kick a soldier in the hamstring, I aim the weapon at another and pull the trigger. Blood sprays the air. I throw an elbow into an attacker's face. Before the Slinger even hits the ground, I spin and bury a bullet in the man's neck. A fourth rears her whip back. I blow her hand off, then put a hole in her head. I wheel on the first Slinger, the only one left alive.

"Who…what are you?" The helmet muffles the woman's quaking voice.

"A Trojan Horse."

Those little fibers of electricity wind through my fingers. The gun goes off. In that final burst of blood, when the last heartbeat comes to an irrevocable stop, tension melts from my muscles along with the foreign current. Feeling slams back into me. With a gasp, I drop my traitorous hand and clap the other over my mouth. I turn in a jerky circle.

Dead.

All four dead. *Dead, adjective, no longer living, deprived of life.*

Crumpling to my knees, I gasp for air, then lean back and let out another, primal scream. I don't care if the sound brings every Slinger in the city to this very spot. I pour all my pain into it, all my sorrow. Dead. All dead.

Chapter Nineteen

Cal

Patches of memory get lost during my trek back to the garage. One second I'm at the railroad car—no Sephrim, he has to be with Daniel—and the next, I stumble out of the sewer and into the alley behind the garage. I immediately catch sight of Daniel, a bag of trash in hand.

Shouldn't I feel something? Relief? Joy? It all hovers outside my reach. Like the potential parents I used to watch through the glass of the observation room back at the lab. Close but far, present but absent all at the same time. Wrong. They always told me I was wrong.

"Wrong, adjective, not suitable or appropriate."

Daniel looks up, and his jaw drops. "Cal."

Coated in dirt and dripping wet, hair plastered to my neck, overalls torn, I feel like someone tried to drown me. Did I fall in the sewers? Did it rain? Why can't I remember? In spite of the smell, Daniel drops his bag and grabs my arms. They shake under his touch. I try to meet his eyes but can't drag my gaze from the space over his left shoulder.

"Where did that blood come from?"

I scowl. What the what is he going on about? "Blood...I don't..." I try to blink.

It doesn't work. Somebody needs to fix my internal

wiring and make my body start obeying my commands again. Stubborn thing's got a glitch.

Daniel grimaces. "Get inside." He cradles my shoulders and pulls me through the door.

Comfort. Verb. To soothe, console, or reassure, bring cheer to. Whatever the definition of that word, I can't make myself feel it, though I figure I should.

"Sewer travel. Gotta love it." I sneeze, squeaking at the end. "Cold and smelly. Cold, adjective, the relevant absence of heat…" Another sneeze. "Also, a respiratory disorder characterized by sneezing, sore throat, coughing…caused by an allergic reaction or by a viral, bacterial, or mixed infection."

Last time I had a cold was when we escaped the lab. Piss-poor timing trapped me and Sephrim in the sewers a full week before we could surface. Miserable. Totally miserable.

"Don't worry." Daniel steers me toward his office. "You know I got all the drugs."

I give him a double thumbs-up.

"And bandages. Are you bleeding from somewhere? Is that…"

"No. I'm not…" My lips quiver. I feel half awake. Maybe I'm dreaming. Still lying on Matt's hide-a-bed. Poor Matt. Why did I leave him behind with the mother from hell? "I don't remember anything after the empty railroad car… Seph, where's Sephrim? Is he okay?"

"Been worried sick about you. You know how he does. He's in here. Hasn't slept since we realized you were missing."

We find Sephrim in the office on the couch, an arm thrown over his face, mouth half open. A redhead slumps across the desk, the side of her head resting on her folded arms, probably leaking drool all over Daniel's papers. Gross. Who the heck is she? Doesn't look like a Designer Kid, not with that nose.

Daniel nudges Sephrim's foot with the toe of his boot. Seph sits up with a yelp, and I dive-bomb him. After letting out an odd cross between a groan and a gasp, he gets with the program and wraps his arms around me.

The redheaded stranger jerks awake too. She jumps from the office chair, fists in front of her face, gaze narrow. "What happened?"

Seph clears his throat. "Cal's back. Your brother did it."

"Works pretty fast, it seems." Daniel grins.

I untangle myself from Sephrim's arms, then sink against the side of the couch and pull a towel from the basket on the floor. Shivering, I clamp it between my fingers and press it tight under my chin. Brow quirked, eyes narrow, I stare the other girl up and down.

"Your brother? You mean Matt? Are you the sister he can't shut up about? You look like him." The family resemblance hits me the second I say it. Same eye shape, similar jaw.

The girl blinks, shakes her head, then blinks again.

As she tries to catch up, Daniel gets the first aid kit from the cabinet, fishes out a small packet of pills, then tosses them to me. "That should help. Tea?"

Dumping the two blue pills onto my tongue, I nod. "Uh-huh."

"Matt," the strange girl finally says. "Yeah, how was he?"

"Bruised. Sweet." One corner of my mouth twitches, but the smile fails. "Your mom's a tyrant. I tried to convince him to leave with me, but he wouldn't. And what happened to you, Seph? You're in pain." I point at him, glaring. Emotion finally pokes through. If Felix hurt him again, I'll dismantle the guy and dump his bits in the sewer.

"Doesn't matter," he says.

"But—"

"We're just glad you're back." Daniel hits the power button on the electric kettle. "What did Hellen do to you?"

Towel balled in my free hand, I analyze my fingers as I explain. "She put a chip in my head to make me her mindless little robot or whatever. It does what the chips in the workhouses are supposed to do. Turns me into some kind of assassin…noun, a murderer"—my voice breaks on that word—"especially one who kills a politically prominent person for fanatical or monetary reasons."

I shove terror back with the definition. Glimpses of images flip through my brain. A scream. The snap of a whip. Bullets and blood and brutality…

I clear my throat and look at the redhead. Darleen? No. Darby. "Matt said he was going to fix it… He's as good as he says, right?"

Darby sinks onto the office stool, pressing her nails into her knees. She meets Seph's gaze, then Daniel's. "He's a tech genius, yeah. If anybody can figure it out, he can." She digs her fingers in harder so her skin yellows at the tips. "In the meantime, we need to go see Felix. He won't agree to protect you unless you meet him, and soon."

The teapot dings, and Daniel pulls out a stack of cups. "You can all go see him after you get some sleep

and something to eat…and Cal gets a change of clothes.
That's an order, not a request."

Chapter Twenty

Darby

It's a calculated risk, but Daniel lets us stay at the garage another night. Though it requires some convincing—and a lot of help from Cal—I finally convince Sephrim to take the couch. That kid is so damn stubborn. Logic and solid reasoning, however, finally win out. I now lie next to Cal on a large army mat Daniel apparently keeps on hand for emergencies. Smart man. Well-trained man. Former marine if I'm reading him right.

We lie near the couch, Cal closest to Sephrim. Both fists clenched beneath her chin, thumbs tucked in, she breathes through her mouth, nose bright red. Poor kid. I frown, guilt like a stranglehold on my chest. Hopefully, the meds Daniel gave her will knock her out. She's been through enough without having to deal with a fever and mucus.

I lie on my back, head propped on an arm, eyes shifting between Sephrim, Cal, the door, the roof-access stairs. After a few minutes, I arch a brow at the couch, just barely suppressing an amused grin. Every time I catch him looking at me, he flushes and pretends he wasn't doing it in the first place. Adorable.

"Stop staring, creepster." *Ugh*. Why'd I have to call him a creepster? He probably doesn't interact with girls his own age much. Not that I interact with guys my age much either. At least none I care to interact with...or think about snuggling up to like we did a few nights ago...

Stop it! Now is so not the time.

Sephrim grimaces, blushing again. "Sorry."

"Can't sleep?" I roll to my side. "Still worried?"

"There's a chip in Cal's head that'll put her on autopilot, with Hellen in charge. Even if Felix can keep her from getting kidnapped again, he can't stop that." He rubs his temples. "Unless your brother can figure out how to disarm it."

Looping my fingers into the holes of the afghan, I shut my eyes. "What *can* you fix?"

"Not much. I can get her to Felix. It's just that damn initiation. It took nearly three weeks for me to recover after mine."

Unpleasant thought. A second wave of guilt sours my stomach. "I remember."

"You do?"

"Watched from the sidelines." I twist my fingers as memory echoes back into my brain, the smack of fists against bone, of blood splattering the concrete floor. Sephrim himself didn't make a sound. I'd witnessed countless initiations, but none left quite as intense an impression as his. "Felix didn't used to be like this, so hard, so mean. I'm not making excuses for him or anything. Just...I don't know."

For a long time, Sephrim doesn't say anything, then finally he clears his throat. "Can I ask you a question?"

"Might not answer."

"I'll try anyway." He sniffs. "If Matty is so good at what he does, if he can so easily spring Cal, and your mom is so abusive, why won't he just leave? Get Felix's protection?"

Eyes still shut, I spit the answer out like it burns my tongue. "Matty won't leave."

"Won't."

"Won't." I nod. "He makes excuses, finds ways to explain why he needs to stay, but the reality is, he's smart enough to do it."

"But he's too afraid to leave."

"Terrified."

"Understandable. Hellen is terrifying."

I squint up at him. "She didn't seem to scare you." My heart hitches in fear at the memory of my mom pressing the knife to his throat.

Rolling his eyes, Sephrim tugs a hand through his hair. "No. She definitely scared me."

I lift my brows. "Sure didn't seem like it. Especially not when you defended yourself."

"I was too angry," he says. "It made me stupid."

"A little. Though I think even if Meg hadn't come over, you would've been just fine." I grin. "Which is particularly impressive after seeing how you react to Felix."

A quiver shakes Sephrim's body. He rolls onto his back. "When it comes down to it, Felix has really only ever threatened me." He sighs. "I can't let Cal go through that initiation. Felix is already pissed at me, so maybe he'll let me take her place."

He *would* suggest that. Even after I warned him just how dangerous my brother is. Damn bleeding heart. Stomach knotted, I push myself upright. The mat wheezes as I stand, step over Cal, then sink onto the edge of the couch, near Sephrim's feet. Frowning, I grip my braid in one hand.

"He probably won't go for that. Everybody's got to pay their way." I try a confident smile on him. "Besides, Cal seems a lot stronger than you give her credit for. It'll be okay."

Chapter Twenty-One

Sephrim

A green tinge sickens the clouds over Cade's. Plane lights fill the small pockets with blips of white. Wind comes in sharp, uneven gusts full of tiny raindrops, screeching sometimes, mourning at others. Though neither Slingers nor cops ever come near Cade's, I glance over my shoulder every few feet, anxiety heavy on my lungs.

Cal sticks so close she bumps my elbow. Focus distant, arms tight across her chest, she hasn't said much since last night. She still can't remember a good chunk of her escape. Scared and scarred and implanted with a weird device that might go off at any time. What activates it anyway? If Hellen has some kind of remote, she could activate it whenever she feels like it, or make Cal run right back to the compound. Is there a timer? A trigger word?

A few paces ahead, Darby stops at the gate and turns to Cal and me, hands in her pockets. She meets Cal's eyes. "You ready?"

Cal doesn't answer. I pull her into a hug. Stiff and unmoving, she lets out a shudder that grinds right into my body, shoving away the last bit of relief I've felt after getting her back. Because now I'm taking her to another crazy crime lord. From one danger to the next.

Finally, Cal nods and eases out of my arms. "All I have to do is, like, kneel, right?" She glances between Darby and me. "Right?"

We could run. We could run right now and leave the city, and she will never have to face Felix's initiation. I tug at one of the drawstrings on my sweatshirt, then rub the space between her shoulder blades. Seriously. We can survive on the road. Cal's strong, way stronger than I am. She'd be okay.

Again, I steel myself because really, who can hide from Hellen Jacobs? "Yeah, yeah, you'll be fine."

With a nod, Darby opens the gate. We walk in silence down to the center of Cade's. In the main room, Cal clenches my hand so tightly it chokes the feeling out of my fingers. I return the pressure and duck my head.

Only a handful of people fill the massive room tonight. Most hang out along the wall or congregate in corners. Though the music pounds in my ears, I appreciate the lack of crowd noise.

Even Felix's circle lacks some of its typical members. Two layers of the hierarchical rings are completely empty, while the rest only have one or two people, max. Good. The less people who know about Cal, the better. It also means Felix doesn't have a large audience to impress, which might make the beating less brutal.

The three of us stop at the empty outer ring. Cal doesn't let go of my hand, so I gently untangle our fingers and mouth *sorry*. Wide-eyed, she nods, glances at my open palms, then does the same, fingers trembling. She mumbles something so low I almost miss it entirely, another definition.

"Sorry, feeling regret, compunction, sympathy,

pity…"

During the pat down, she continues to mutter but doesn't squirm or raise her voice. Every so often, she glances from Felix to Marcus, then looks back at her feet. At one point, the guard pulls a crayon out of the front pocket of her overalls and arches a brow. Cal shrugs. The guard puts it back, then turns and returns to Felix's side. Darby leads us forward. She stops, and I sink to my knees. I nudge Cal. She flinches, then kneels too.

Felix's shoes squeak on the cement floor. He doesn't say anything until he pulls Cal to her feet, one finger under her chin. I clench my jaw and watch out of the corner of my eye, wanting to pummel Felix into blood and bone dust. The crime lord tilts his head. His gaze drifts over Cal's face, then he smiles.

"As lovely as Sephrim." Felix presses his hand onto my head and leaves it there, applying more pressure than usual. "I'm gratified to finally meet you. I understand you need protection?"

"Gratified, to satisfy, indulge, humor, as one's desires or appetites."

I tense, fear and anger both pulsing in my skull.

Cal clears her throat. "Yes. Protection. I need it."

"Of course," Felix says. "I'd be delighted. Though you must pass the initiation. I'm sure Sephrim has told you about it."

The pressure from Felix's hand intensifies. Pain cramps down my neck. "If I could make a request—"

"No." Felix digs his fingers into my scalp. "While you remain on the payroll, thanks to my sister's unfailing logic, you are still out of my good graces. You have no voice in my court. Now, Cal. I understand you've had a trying few days, but for my protection, initiation is

149

required."

"It's fine." Her voice wavers. "Better than getting taken by Hellen again."

"Excellent." Felix throws up an arm with flourish. "Alura. If you would?" With a final shove at my head, he strolls back to his chair as the female guard marches forward.

Now free of Felix's grip, I spring in front of Cal. A stupid move, one driven by sheer panic. "Please, let me go through initiation for her."

Alura swings a fist at my jaw. Shock roars in my ears. I stumble sideways, caught by the other bodyguard. The man pins my arms tight to my sides, holding me so I have a front-row seat to Cal's oncoming beating. Though I kick and struggle, I can't get free.

Alura sneers at me. "Stay out of the way, or you're next." She turns back to Cal.

Sweat slicks Cal's brow. She takes a breath through her nose, lets it out through her mouth, then meets my eyes. "I'll be fine. You'll take care of me."

Alura backhands her. "Damn Designer Kids." She sneers, walking a circle around the other girl. "Think you're so much better than the rest of us, even though nobody wanted you. Even though you expired."

In one sharp move, Cal plants a foot to stop her fall. The pupils of her eyes shrink to pinpoints. Alura throws a punch. Cal catches her fist and twists it to an unnatural angle. I stare, slack-jawed, as she grabs the bodyguard's gun, presses it against Alura's temple, and fires. Blood and brains litter the air. She lets Alura drop and takes aim at the bodyguard restraining me.

"Cal, what the hell are you doing? Stop." Horror boils in my stomach. I throw an elbow backward twice, once into the bodyguard's stomach, and once upward into his chin. The man falls, and I step in front of the gun, so close the muzzle touches my chest. "Put it down."

Felix shouts something.

I ignore him, terror buzzing across my skin.

Cal's narrowed eyes shimmer with a strange glowing haze, a color similar to the whips Slingers use. Under the blood and brain matter, red blossoms out across her jaw where Alura hit her. "You are not a threat," she says to me, voice odd, robotic.

She tries to redirect the gun toward Felix, but I grab the barrel and shove it forward. Before I can grip the back side and disarm her, she lets her hand drop and twists around me, throwing off my defense. She springs sideways, taking aim at Felix again. I regain balance, jump into the line of fire again, and grab her shoulders.

Panic clouds my vision. "Cal, this isn't you! Stop. Please, stop! You're safe. There-there is no threat." A lie, but one I have to tell.

Cal's gun hand shakes. The muscles in her wrist and forearm stand out under the skin. Sweat beads along her brow. Her pinpoint pupils grow, shrink, then grow again, widening to normal size. She blinks and gasps, then lets out a yelp.

"No, not again, not again. No, no, no." Crumpling, Cal collapses. Tears soak her cheeks as she grips the gun to her chest.

Again? What does she mean again? I drop with her, pull the weapon away, then take her shoulders. Tense with fear, I study her face. "Cal—"

Hands clamp around my arms and haul me back. A third guard steps around me, pressing a gun to Cal's head. "What are your orders, sir?"

"Don't, please." I struggle. "This has to be because of the chip in her head. Alura must've said the trigger word or…"

The guard holding me shoves me to the ground and levels a kick to my gut. Pain shatters through the already cracked ribs. A snap fills my ears, and I shudder. Definitely broken now.

Still in his chair, Felix narrows his gaze. "Kill her."

"No." Marcus Cade's voice stomps down on the command.

Shock runs through my body as the older man slips from his seat. Marcus waves the guard to one side, then squats in front of Cal. She doesn't meet his gaze but continues to sob and rock, bloody hands clenched in her lap. Behind her, Felix balks but pinches his lips together. Again, though Marcus has no official authority, no one challenges the money.

One arm wrapped around my waist, I stare. I've never seen Marcus leave his chair, much less stoop to anybody's level. Not once. Just beyond them, I catch sight of Darby. She stands in a fighting stance, tawny eyes wide, lips parted. When her father kneels next to Cal, she straightens and folds her arms like a soldier, tendons standing out along her neck. I look back at Cal.

Marcus rests both elbows on his knees. "Now, it's my understanding that my Hellen has a chip inserted into your noggin because she wants to use you as some kind of assassin. That right?" He points to his own temple.

Cal offers the barest of nods.

"A chip my Matthew helped program?"

Another nod.

"And it turns on with the right code word?"

"Yes," she says in a whisper.

"And you have no idea what that code word is?"

"I have an idea." For the first time, Cal looks up at him.

"Do tell."

She grimaces and curls her fingers around each other. Her lips move, then stop, then move again as her eyes slide shut.

Marcus runs a thumb and forefinger along his jaw but doesn't rush her.

After another moment of mumbling, she says, "I'm scared to say it. I don't want to…" She chokes. "Right after Matt helped me escape, I ran into Slingers. They said it, and I killed them all."

My eyes bug. That explains the blood when she showed up at the garage. Daniel said he thought she had some kind of PTSD that messed up her memory. Unintentionally murdering someone definitely qualifies as that kind of disorder.

Again, Marcus strokes the stubble on his chin. "Let's try something else. The code word was something Alura said, yes?"

Cal sniffs and nods.

"Cal," I say, my voice a croak. "What's the definition of the word?"

Her eyes brighten. "Verb. Meaning to come to an end, terminate, as a contract, guarantee, or offer."

Come to an end, terminate…the last thing Alura said was "expire." Good. Now we just need to figure out how to switch it off. Hopeful, I ease up onto an elbow but stay quiet until Marcus nods at me.

"Cal, what shut the chip off when the Slingers attacked you?" I ask.

Swallowing a sob, she says, "When I killed the last

153

one, when the threat was gone."

"Cal, you didn't…" I rub the back of my neck. Time for that later. "What shut it down tonight?"

She draws a shuddering breath and meets my gaze. "You."

I blink. "Me? I said one of the code words?"

"No. Just you." Her gaze drops back to her fingers. Her mouth twists, and she shuts her eyes again.

Just me. I frown.

"Well now, this is all very interesting," Marcus says. "Felix, we need to consider how to handle things. Seems to me that chip makes you quite a warrior. I have a new deal. In exchange for the Cades' protection, you will be our secret weapon. Only when strictly necessary, of course."

My stomach clenches. I open my mouth to protest, but Cal speaks first. "It doesn't seem like I have much choice." She glares at her bloody hands.

So much blood. I grimace, disgusted. All our running and hiding and working and she still ends up with one of those damn chips in her head.

"Then we have ourselves a deal," Marcus says. "For your safety, you and your…brother can stay here. Too much of a risk for you to be wandering about with my Hellen around. Meantime, Darby can get in touch with my Matthew, see if we can't figure out how to control this chip."

Chapter Twenty-Two

Matt

I yawn and ball a small piece of bread between my fingers. If I have to comb through another one of Hellen's files, my brain will one hundred percent dribble out the corner of my eye. I grimace. Time to pause. I need my brains to stay where they are.

A few clicks pulls up the Designer Kid lab security feed. Too small for the cameras spying on me to pick up, my screens help me keep watch over the kids I help save. One day I'll use my techno-powers against the whole project. Expose evil Dr. Troy.

Like a technological superhero. I snort. Childish idea, but still a fun thought. Trapped in this tiny room, I indulge in fantasy to keep myself just this side of sane, especially when working on something illegal for Hellen. Monitoring the Designer Kids lab feeds my dreams of grandeur.

On the screen I pull up, Dr. Gayle stands next to a hospital bassinet, staring down at a new baby just pushed out of a surrogate machine. Its skin is green. Green. Seriously, green. Like Designer Kids don't have it hard enough, a bunch of crazies have to make some look like aliens!

I roll my eye so hard I can see the back of my head. Well, I could if it wasn't so dark in there.

On the other side of the glass case, lying on a blue mat and dressed in a duckling-covered onesie, the new Designer Baby gurgles and grins up at Dr. Gayle. Spit bubbles form on his lower lip. He kicks fat legs. Dr. Gayle smiles. She tickles the bottom of his foot with a gloved hand through a hole in the case. The baby squeals, then shoves a hand into his mouth.

Dr. Gayle looks up at the ceiling, probably thinking the same thing I am. At least Designer Kids like this don't usually expire. Too hard to hide on the street, weird-colored kids get picked up by Slingers real easy.

Dr. Gayle glances at the door to the lab, then she hits a button at the bottom of the pod. The lid slides back, and she picks up the baby. Bouncing, she whispers a soft song.

Another voice comes from the other end of the room. "You know the lab techs can do that."

I jump in my seat. Dr. Gayle shuts her eyes at Dr. Troy's stupid statement. My stomach gains ten pounds of dread and then sinks to my toes. Troy doesn't get kids. Or humans in general. Not that I do either, but she doesn't even *try*. I bet she's a cyborg. Every kid cringes away from her, like they know the doctor sees them as products, not little people.

Nostrils flaring, Dr. Gayle turns to her colleague. Like usual, Dr. Troy wears her blonde hair in a tight bun, her mouth in a sneer. It tightens her face so much it cuts lines into her pallid skin. I grimace as Dr. Gayle asks, "What brings you to the infant ward this morning?"

Dr. Troy strolls to one of the pods. "The nurses informed me I'd find you here." She wipes her glasses on her lab coat. "I wanted to discuss our lost product."

Bile rushes up my throat. Product. She doesn't even

pretend to see them as anything else.

"You mean the runaways." Dr. Gayle's face twists.

Still reading the baby's diagnostics, Dr. Troy waves a hand. "The expiration date for a handful is coming up shortly. I wanted to discuss strategies for ensuring their retention. Every month we lose between seven and ten percent of our expired product to the streets. This is unacceptable. The men and women who sell us their gametes expect them not to be wasted."

I sneer. "Sure. Because throwing them into labs and testing mind-control tech on them is a great use of people."

The green baby blows a raspberry.

"You got that right, little dude. And don't worry, one day I'm going to figure out how to hack into that lab too."

As the infant grabs at Dr. Gayle's chin, she asks, "Shouldn't you be speaking with the head of security?"

"Oh, that's been taken care of." Dr. Troy taps something on her net board. "I merely wanted to ask for your assistance. Clearly, the safeguards currently in place are not effective. We've had multiple visits from IT, and none of them seem able to identify the problem."

Dr. Gayle runs a thumb across the baby's chubby cheek. "And how can I help ensure the safety of the children? I have suggested an extension of the expiration date multiple times—"

"A foolish idea. They're a drain on the state."

Even from this end of the screen, I can see the tension build in Dr. Gayle's shoulders. I can guess her thought process, complete with word choice. She's ranted about it enough times. "A drain on the state, indeed. So many options apart from the workhouses, so many solutions other than turning them into lab subjects, discarding them as if they were somehow...non-people."

Dr. Gayle petitions to limit the number of "orders" for Designer Babies and to increase the penalty for rejecting the child requested at least once a week. I watch as each one shoots from her email to the higher ups. They all totally dismiss her suggestions. Claim it puts "unnecessary restraints on commerce."

Commerce. Seriously?

Dr. Gayle stiffens her face, clearly fighting a grimace. "Have you another idea? One that does not involve the workhouses?"

"Of course." Dr. Troy's lips turn up in what she must think is a smile. "As you know, I have been working to lift the bans on using Designer Children as donors and soldiers and have been getting some excellent traction. However, I believe there is more we can do."

I grind my back teeth.

"I am afraid I cannot support this." Dr. Gayle bounces the baby as he fusses. "Designed in a lab or not, they are still children. They deserve to be protected."

Dr. Troy continues to tap on her screen. "My dear Dr. Gayle. Designer Children would not even exist if it wasn't for us. When they fail to please our customers, they become a drain on the lab. The deposits only cover so much."

"Then why not charge for rejection? I cannot understand—"

Another dismissive wave of her hand. "How can we charge customers for something they don't benefit from?" Dr. Troy says. "No, their deposit is penalty enough. The workhouses are a fine solution but only a temporary one. When the chips drive them mad, they again become a drain, and unfortunately, the law still stubbornly refuses to allow their merciful disposal.

"My proposal to remove the donor ban will remedy that," Dr. Troy continues. "If we are not allowed to euthanize them, then we should at least be allowed to use their vital organs. The question is, how do we put an end to the runaways?"

I dig my fingers into the arms of my chair. Getting Dr. Troy out of the way would be so easy. I could get her fired. Hellen has me frame people all the time. But I can't guarantee Dr. Gayle would take her place, and if I can't guarantee that, they might just fill her vacancy with someone worse. Besides, Dr. Troy isn't the root of the problem. The system is. And until I can come up with a way to fix that, I plan to stick with saving as many kids as I possibly can.

"If they had a better option than the workhouses, the children would not run." Dr. Gayle shifts the baby to her shoulder to rub his back. "There are many parents in the general population who are unable to conceive. If we extended to them the opportunity to adopt those who have expired, they would neither be a drain on society nor desire to run away."

That they don't already offer this makes zero sense. Dr. Gayle tells me this all the time. Even with a discounted rate, general adoption would help the lab way more than the workhouses. Solve the "loss of product" as Dr. Troy labels it.

For a third time, Dr. Troy waves her hand. "Those who run from the lab when they expire clearly have a propensity for rebellion. Otherwise, they wouldn't have expired in the first place."

"Or perhaps we have perpetuated the false

assumption that they are worth only the money they bring in," Dr. Gayle says.

The green baby sighs. The monitor around his little wrist beeps in time with his breath. I want to hold him. Make him laugh. Keep him away from evil Dr. Troy. Who could put a price tag on a kid?

"Ever the idealist, aren't you? But I suppose after the rebellion against, and subsequent termination of, the project in your home country, this shouldn't surprise me."

Dr. Troy crosses to the large screen on the wall and swipes information from the net board in her hands. Digital files scatter into their folders. Each turns blue as it downloads.

"I will personally be monitoring the product that is about to expire for the next few months, to ensure they don't run. If you would join me, I'm certain together we can protect them. After all, they are in danger on the street. At the mercy of crime lords and disease. Surely we can agree on this."

Dr. Gayle takes a slow breath, and her face remains calm, smooth, neutral. But I don't have to maintain *my* calm. Not in my little cave with nobody watching me. My heart hits super speed. I glare at Dr. Troy. She doesn't care about the kids' safety, only about lost product. Losing my temper won't stop her plans or help her victims. Hacking will. With my mad coding skills, more kids will go free and be safe from her evil plans.

"Of course," Dr. Gayle says. "Anything for the children's safety."

In my little cave, I nod in agreement. For the safety of Designer Kids.

Chapter Twenty-Three

Cal

Prisoner, noun, a person confined in prison or kept in custody, especially as the result of legal process, prisoner of war, or a person or thing that is deprived of liberty or kept in restraint.

Marcus gives me a single rule—*don't leave your room*. Room, however, doesn't quite do the place justice. Really, it's three rooms. Oriental rugs hang over the steel walls, two blanket-covered beds stand on either side of a love seat, and a small light shines over a rectangular table next to a stove in the kitchenette.

And miracle of miracles, the third room has a real, functioning bathroom.

Darby leads me inside. I resist the urge to race to the shower, rinse away the blood and other body bits. Instead, I turn back to Seph. He rests against the doorframe, arms wrapped around his battered midsection, lips mashed together.

How's he still standing after a beating like that? And what does he think of me now? After I killed people? Guilt grinds in my gut like worn-out gears.

I stare at him. So many things I want to say. The words stick in my throat, barely tumbling out. "S-Seph, I'm sorry."

Both of his brows lift into his hair. "Sorry? For

what? The chip made you kill those people. That wasn't you."

"But they're still dead." My throat thickens. "And it's my fault."

He pushes himself off the wall. Face contorting, he wraps an arm around me as if I'm not splattered with carnage. "It's not your fault."

"I should have told you about Hellen."

"It's okay." He shifts, clearly trying to find a more comfortable position. "It's okay."

I press my forehead against the soft material of his hoodie. It smells like Daniel's economy detergent and garage grease. All the pain and terror of the last few days wraps around my throat, choking off oxygen, but I shove it back down. Here, in his arms, nothing can hurt me. An illogical thought, but one that holds me together.

Then Seph coughs. Something warm and wet sprays across my shoulder, and the smell of blood intensifies.

I back away and choke on a gasp. Red coats his pale lips. He wipes it away, but it smears across his hand. Before I can react, Darby steps forward, takes him by the shoulders, and steers him to the couch.

My body goes rigid. I'm the one who takes care of him. But I can't fix innards. At least not squishy ones. Give me a broken appliance with metal insides any day. I'll have to leave organs to someone who knows them.

As Darby helps Seph lie down, she glances back at me. "Why don't you go wash up? I'll take care of him. There are some clean clothes in the bag I brought."

Rubbing my arms and shifting the weight between my feet, I stare at Seph, broken because he tried to protect me. Like he always tries to protect me. Tugging the ends of my hair, I turn and head to the bathroom.

Inside, I peel off the sticky clothes, then catch my reflection in the mirror. Red clumps cling to my jaw, blood drops dot my temples, and something indefinable sticks in my lashes. Images dart through my head: the Slingers, each face contorted in terror, that bodyguard...

With a shiver, I climb into the shower and let the water beat it all away.

As soon as it runs clear of suds and blood, I dry off and wriggle into the scrub-style clothes from Darby's bag. Before I leave, I dig out Matt's flower. I find it wilted, smashed. My lips tremble. Some things can't be saved. I slip it into a scrub pocket.

I avoid the mirror this time as I walk back into the bedroom. Seph still lies on the couch with one arm draped over his face. Darby's pulled a kitchen chair next to him and sits perched on its edge, smoothing the bandages across his ribs. Frowning, she looks up at me.

After a moment, she works her lips into neutrality before she asks, "Better?"

"I've still got a mind-controlling chip in my brain, but I'm not sticky anymore, so that's a win." I lift my shoulders then let them drop. They weigh more than normal. Maybe they'll drag me into the earth. I could join with the dirt, disappear, never hurt anybody again. "How're the ribs, Seph?"

He swallows and peeks out from under his arm. "They're fine."

"Pretty sure they're broken." Darby digs into her bag and pulls out a white, unlabeled bottle, then tosses it to Sephrim. "Take two."

"All of them are broken?" I ask, sitting on the arm of the couch.

Darby shakes her head. "Probably just one, but it's

still bad. He really needs a hospital—"

"No hospitals." I flinch at the sound of my own voice. High-pitched and too loud, it hurts my ears on the way out. A gut reaction. She probably doesn't frequent too many hospitals herself.

"I know." Darby lifts her hands. "It's okay, Cal. Trust me, I get it. Besides, all the doctor would do anyway is keep him for observation, so long as his lung isn't punctured."

"Punctured? Is that why he's coughing up blood?"

"I'm fine. My chest wall's probably just bruised," Seph says, arm still over his eyes. "But we need to talk about how you agreed to stay here and work for Marcus and Felix."

Picking at loose threads on the couch, I nod. "I know. It's bad. But it was the best plan out of a bunch of really, really crappy ones. At least here, most people'll know what word to avoid. I'm hoping Matt'll figure out how to disarm this thing before they ask me to kill anybody. Besides, I'm safer in here than out there."

Seph lets out a slow breath. "Right, I know you're right."

"In the meantime…" I twist my fingers together. "Maybe we can test my theory."

Darby squints. "Theory?"

"Yeah, that Sephrim's the one who can stop me. That he overrides the bit's protocol."

"No." This time, Darby's voice hits a pitch higher than it should. "I mean, what if…what if you're wrong and you kill him?"

"That's why you should be there," I say. "You could knock me out. It makes the most logical sense."

Seph stays quiet for so long I wonder if he's fallen

asleep from the drugs Darby gave him. In the silence of the room, his wheezing breath sounds loud, painful. I wince. How many beatings can a guy take in one week? What will happen if he takes a third? The kind that really, genuinely needs a hospital or a healing tube? I yank the ends of my hair until my scalp stings.

Finally, Seph slides his arm to his forehead. "It's a good plan. Mind if we wait until tomorrow night?"

"You got a deal, buddy." I look at Darby. "Could you—do you mind staying with us tonight? Just in case?"

For the first time, she smiles, something real and solid. "Let me go check in with Marcus."

****

While we wait for Darby to get back, I try talking to Seph, but as the drugs kick in, his conversation quickly becomes nonsensical, bordering on absurd. Eventually, I tug a blanket off one of the beds—an achingly soft blanket—and tuck it around him. He groans but doesn't wake up. I sit on the arm of the couch, eyes locked on to him. If I can't fix his insides, I can at least protect him, make him comfy.

If I can help it, I'll never let him out of my sight again. And the next time Felix tries to break him, I'll return the favor, even if I have to use the stupid chip to do it. I wrench my fingers together until the pain distracts me from my hatred.

I plot Felix's demise until Darby opens the door, her arms full of familiar odds and ends.

"You got our stuff." I slide off the couch and meet the redhead halfway.

Frayed, blunted, and holy, our shabby possessions relax the tense muscles in my chest. A small slice of the

165

home I built with Seph. Real home. Not a lab, not a garage rooftop—a home.

Tears of joy sting the backs of my eyes when my fingers ghost over my one-eyed monkey. "Thanks."

"Brought this too." Darby slides a mini net board across the table. "It's so Marcus can contact you."

I clench the stuffed animal a little tighter and force a swallow past the knot of dread in my throat. Maybe I'll give it to Seph. Better for him to be in charge of it anyway.

Together, we sit at the narrow table to sort through the flotsam of our lives. I cling to my stuffed monkey. One half of my mind latches on to the vague memory of a blurry-faced someone extending the long-tailed creature to me. No matter how often I try, or how hard I focus, I never can remember any details of the person's face. Some smells drag me back sometimes, but they don't clarify anything, just a warm sensation, the kind I feel around Seph.

Only half conscious of it, I pull a crayon from my pocket and roll it between my fingers. At some unidentifiable point, I tore most of the blue wrapping away. A few ragged pieces cling to the flat end, dark from grease and rust.

"Out of curiosity, what's with the crayons?" Darby asks, walking to the kitchenette to grab a bottle out of a cabinet.

"Nostalgia." I grin. "They stopped giving me pens and pencils at the lab after I kept turning them into weapons. Made me mad at first. Threw a fit like you wouldn't believe."

Filling two glasses with something that sure as heck doesn't smell like water, Darby lifts a brow but doesn't say anything.

"I know, right? Can't imagine why nobody wanted to buy me." I spin the crayon again, watching it twirl. "When I realized I could draw things besides guns, I kinda liked them more, so I kept them. I can't draw with anything else anymore."

Darby sits hard enough for the chair to creak, then pushes a glass in my direction. "Trust me, you need it. Just go slow."

I sniff the drink and wrinkle my nose. "Smells like rubbing alcohol." I glance back at Seph, then shrug. "Eh, what he doesn't know." Heat blooms in my mouth with that first sip. I relax back in my chair as it spreads through my chest and down under my belly button. "You and your brother know how to take care of people. Matt anyway. Full disclosure? I don't like Felix. He's a creepy creepster lug nut."

"I don't know how Matty ended up so sweet, so different from the rest of us." A strand of hair falls across her eyes, and she flicks it out of the way. "Both our parents tried to…beat it out of him. They did it to all of us. I hardened up quick. Felix got…twisted, but it had the opposite effect on Matty."

Threading the monkey's tail through my fingers, I frown. "Hellen's going to know he helped me escape, won't she?"

Her face contorts. "Maybe, but he's been tricking the Designer Kid security systems for a long time, so maybe not."

I straighten, curious. Fooling the Designer Kid security systems? Dr. Gayle mentioned an outside hacker who created glitches or blackouts that helped her free expired kids, but can it really be Matt?

What a joke. Of course, it's Matt. Sweet, computer-genius, flower-growing Matt. Who else would work so hard to save kids from abuse? I grin.

"That doesn't surprise me." I unfold a blanket, then refold it, the monkey still pinned under one arm. "He might be scared of Hellen, but not enough to stop him from doing what's right."

Darby swallows another swig of alcohol. "True, just wish he'd do the right thing for himself."

I tap a fingernail against my glass. "What if we tried to get him out? You, me, Sephrim. We go in, use the code word. I fight Hellen and her cronies while you two grab Matt. Then Sephrim can shut me down. Bam." I clap my hands. "The perfect plan. And then he could stay with you."

A genius plan, actually, if I say so myself. Use Hellen's own weapon against her. Lovely thought. She might have an extra code word to shut me down, but we can plan for that. With a little strategy, we can account for most eventualities. Besides, with Darby on our side we'd—

"No," she says, interrupting my train of thought. "It's too risky. You might get captured, and you'd never get Matty out of there. He'd never leave."

Valid concerns. Not impossible to overcome. I sit a little straighter in my chair, fist clamped around the monkey tail. "What if we went in when Hellen's not around? And if Matt won't come, we can just knock him out. He'll thank us later." I grin, quite certain of my plan.

Darby's fingernails bite into the table. She throws back the last of her drink and sighs. Tension crawls up her neck so the veins stand out. "How 'bout we talk to Seph when he wakes up? We'll see what he says. If we can all come up with a good enough plan, I'll pitch it to my dad. Deal?"

Oh yeah, Marcus. Mr. Moneybags basically holds sway over my entire existence now. Like a rental car, I can only go where he says. How far does that leash extend? After killing one of his bodyguards, I might be stuck on blocks for a while.

In the meantime, maybe he'll let me train, figure out exactly how the chip in my head works. Training makes sense if he wants me as an assassin. Hopefully, I'm right about Seph's ability to shut me down.

Chapter Twenty-Four

Matt

My head snaps sideways as the back of Hellen's hand collides with my cheek. Stumbling, I ram into a wall.

My skull bounces.

My vision doubles.

Whatever curses Hellen spits out fail to compute with my brain.

Silence stuffs my ears like cotton. Only the soft hum of the computers lies under it, barely loud enough to chase away quiet terror. Hellen glares down at me, pure fury hardening her muscles. It rages under the surface, a virus ready to attack, kill, destroy.

Bare toes jammed into the ground, I use my other superpower to smother every emotion besides pain and fake confusion. I've got more than enough practice. As the sting fades, I brace myself on the back of the desk chair. "I don't know what happened. But—"

"How can you not know?" She strains the words through clenched teeth. "Your computers run the entire system."

Blood pulses under my permanently damaged eye, and beads of sweat roll down my back. "I just started running diagnostics. I'll know more when they're done. The system just came back up after the malfunction a few minutes ago."

Hellen's nostrils flare. Terror vibrates through me. To my relief, she doesn't move from her spot again. Not yet, anyway.

"How long will it take?"

"Five, ten minutes." I glance at the status bar on my computer to confirm my guess.

"And the malfunction knocked out all the cameras and the damn doors?"

"Yes, ma'am." I nod too fast. "I'll rework it so they're not all connected to each other. The new cord should help too."

Not a total lie. The old cord *did* leave the entire system at risk. Its replacement makes things more secure. Since I didn't change them out until after Cal escaped, it's the perfect excuse for computer failure. Easy enough to pretend Uncle Wally didn't give it to me before then. Hellen won't question it or blame her brother. The perfect firewall.

She glares at me. The status bar inches forward. I watch it out of the corner of my good eye. Count the seconds with each gained centimeter. Fifteen minutes until Dr. Gayle needs her blackout. Enough time to appease Hellen. Enough time to finish diagnostics. Enough time to set up the malfunction for the Designer Baby lab.

A growl turns into the word "fine" followed by a command to fix it. "And when you do, turn on the GPS in that chip and find her."

****

While I wait for the last computer to finish rebooting, I press my fingertips to the side of my face. It stings. At least she wasn't wearing her ring this time. The large, green stone sticks out past its setting in jagged, sharp edges. I trace the scar under my left eye. A few inches higher and I might've had to wear an eye patch. Like a pirate. I grin. A blind pirate.

A monitor dings. 14:00. Blackout time. Exhilaration zings through my muscles like tiny crackles of static electricity. Popping my knuckles, I lean toward computer number one. As the newest in the bunch, it runs fastest. I don't trust the older ones for this job.

My gaze darts to the door, then back to the coding. Can't use the back door from last time. Somebody might have eyes on it. Not that anybody has my mad skills. But I won't risk it. Too many kids' lives at stake.

I first read about the leftover Designer Kids when I was five and immediately wanted to help them. I'd never met one, but I identified with rejects. The out of place. The "not good enough." I told my dad I wanted to save them. Marcus just laughed, patted me on the head, and sent me back to hacking.

In the middle of wiggling my way into the DMV, local court, and post office—simultaneously, like the digital genius I am—I stumbled across something called "Slingers." This rabbit-trailed quickly into the Designer Kids lab. I met Dr. Gayle, and the rest, as they say, was—

Ping!

I fist-bump the air. Perfect back door. And different from any I've used before. This time, with the great and evil Dr. Troy hovering like a deranged, maniacal hawk, I have to take extra precautions. A final few strokes set my virus in motion. Grinning, I lean back and cross my arms.

Computer number four dings. My stomach makes a panicked escape attempt. Diagnostics complete. Time to find Cal. I turn the GPS back on. If my stomach fought for freedom before, it practically shreds my chest when the digital flag drops to indicate Cal's location.

Cade's.

As a kid, I couldn't work out my last name. Between two parents who never married, no one ever told me. Darby and Felix always went by Cade, but I could never decide.

Cade.

Jacobs.

Did it matter? Instead, I usually signed my first and middle name, Matthew Lucas.

I type in another code, then tuck both hands under my arms, proud of my work. There. One more kid under the cover of my digital mastery. Now to dig back into Hellen's records.

Chapter Twenty-Five

Sephrim

Broken ribs complicate things. Cal insisting we save
Matt? Much more sticky. I sidestep the whole issue by
convincing her we need to learn how to control the chip
first. She figures out my game—her dramatic eye roll
makes this pretty damn obvious—but doesn't fight me
on it. Not with such a logical suggestion.

Full of a breakfast that doesn't consist of FudPaks,
stale bagels, or leftover hamburger, Darby and Cal haul
the kitchen table into a corner. Darby stands on the edge
of the carpet at the center of the room opposite me.
Hands twitching in the pockets of my hoodie, I stare at
Cal, who stands in between us.

She sucks her bottom lip. She's still wearing the
scrubs. About three times too big for her, the extra
material pools around her bare feet, and the sleeves hang
to her elbows. Overnight, the shiner on her chin shifted
from red to an ugly blue-black. When she smiles, only
one half of her mouth hitches up, her swollen jaw getting
in the way.

Anger winds up the back of my neck, crackling and
burning inside me.

Cal lists her head in Darby's direction. "Ready?"

Cracking her knuckles, she nods. "If this doesn't
work, it'll be lights out. Don't worry, I won't let you hurt

him."

"Good, but don't let yourself get hurt either, huh? Not in a hurry to get…brain bits on my nice, new, mental-patient clothes."

A grimace twists the uninjured half of Cal's face. She shakes her head and fights it off with a grin.

"We don't have to do this right now," I say. "We can wait, take it easy today. Get some rest."

After the last twenty-four hours, she deserves a break. But if I know her at all, she won't take the bait. Sitting around will only give her time to remember. She didn't sleep at all last night. I know because I found her at the table this morning, coloring the rough surface with the crayon saved from her overall pockets. Blood stains the paper wrapping, a disturbing mark on childish things.

As expected, she waves both hands. "I'm sweet and dandy, just like candy."

I smirk. "Okay then, here goes." Drumming my fingers, I take a deep breath. "Expired."

Fear prickles my face and chest as Cal's pupils shrink. She throws an elbow at Darby. It goes wide as Darby ducks. Cal twists and kicks out. Her bare toe clocks Darby in the thigh. She winces and grabs Cal's leg. Losing her balance, Cal hits the floor and slaps it with her hands to absorb the shock. She lifts her hips and thrusts a heel into Darby's chest. The other girl grunts but hangs on tight.

I step forward. "Darby—"

"It's fine." She curses as another blow lands, this one on her jaw. She shoves Cal's legs out of the way, dives forward, and straddles her. Panting, Darby pins her arms and legs.

It looks like a clear victory. Then Cal bucks her hips

again. Darby shoots up and falls forward. The second she loses her grip, Cal drives a knee in between Darby's legs. Another kick sends Darby backward, and she collides with the stove. Cal pounces. Both hands wrapped around Darby's throat.

Enough.

Though Darby can probably save herself, if she can't get free, it will only take about three seconds for her to lose consciousness. I bolt forward. Pain stops me halfway across the carpet. Air whooshes from my lungs as the movement sends razors through my ribs. Under Cal's grip, Darby's face shifts to a scary shade of blue.

I cough. "Cal! Cal, look at me!"

She doesn't move.

Fear amplifies my voice. "You're safe, you're okay. There's no threat!"

Cal's muscles twitch. She gasps, lets go of Darby, and falls onto her backside. I stumble past her. Blue recedes from Darby's face as I sink to her side. She gives a single thumbs-up.

"Guess we know the shut-off word," Darby says with a croak.

I nod. "Think you're right. Threat. Yeah, Cal?" I look over my shoulder.

She wraps both arms around her knees, eyes still wide, pupils back to normal size. She stares through us and says, "Threat. Noun. An indication or warning of probable trouble." Rocking herself, she repeats the definition over and over, barreling forward and back.

Worry clutching my chest, ribs aching, I take her shoulders. "Cal, look at me."

She keeps rocking, gaze vacant, focused on horrors unseen as if the room doesn't exist anymore.

I cup her face. "Hey, come on, Cal, you're okay. Darby's okay."

"He's right, I'm fine, Cal." Darby crawls to my side. "You did just what you're supposed to do, and now we know for sure how to help you, right? You're okay."

Cal exhales a shaky breath, repeats the definition again, then shuts her eyes. "Sweet and dandy, just like candy." The words bump and tremble, but when she opens her eyes again, they focus on me. "I don't like being on cruise control."

"More like autopilot," Darby mumbles.

Sorrow and anger roil inside me, but I keep my face neutral. Cal needs me strong and steady. In this state of precariousness, I have to be her stabilizer. I rest my forehead on hers. Keeping my voice as even as possible, I say, "We don't have to do that again."

Her staccato breath fans out across my hands. "No, it's okay. Just shut me down before I start choking somebody next time, huh?"

"I second that," Darby says, rubbing her throat.

Though still skeptical about trying again, I agree, with that caveat, at least. I sit on my heels and glance at the digital clock on the wall, then back at Cal. White-lipped and baggy-eyed, she presses a fist to her mouth like she's about to be sick. Maybe she is. She needs rest, and I need to go touch base with Daniel and Dr. Gayle. Maybe I can convince Cal to take a nap.

"Listen, I've got to run back to the garage," I say, rubbing my jaw. "Why don't you try to get some sleep? Seeing as how you stayed up all night graffitiing the kitchen table."

Before Cal can protest, Darby cuts in. "That's a really good idea. And how about this? If you lie down at least for an hour, I'll get you some new crayons…maybe even a weapon to work on. I know Felix has some guns that are on the fritz."

Cal screws her face into a scowl, and her eyes drop to her fingers. "Sure, yeah, as long as they're not loaded."

My insides twist up, and Darby rushes to respond. "Of course not. Definitely empty."

Still concentrating on the floor, Cal pushes herself upright, then extends a hand to haul me to my feet. "Okay, fine, Mom and Dad. I'll take a nap."

As I stand, I bite back a wince. A nap would probably do me good, too, but it'll have to wait until later. "I'll be back soon. Promise."

****

No one looks at me when I leave Cade's back room, but still I pull my hood up anyway and stick to the edge of the crowd. In spite of my efforts, however, someone steps into my path. Shock strangles my windpipe. Marcus Cade stares down at me, arms folded over his chest.

"Mornin', Sephrim. Where you off to?"

Though I'd rather keep my eyes on him, I drop my gaze out of necessary deference. "Running back to the garage. Cal's taking a nap. Or should be."

"I see. How's that side of yours? Took two pretty intense beatings over the last few days."

"It'll heal."

"My Darby fix you up?" He steps closer.

Unlike Felix, he doesn't bathe in cologne. Smells of gunpowder and sweat. Both preferable to the former. At least I won't suffocate at this proximity. But what does he want? Aside from the incident last night, Marcus never talks to me. Does this have something to do with Cal? My current attempt to leave? No matter what, I need to answer.

"Yes, sir."

"Sir. So polite." He clamps a hand on my shoulder.

I crumple an inch, ribs smarting under the pressure, fear pumping through my veins.

"Now here's the deal, son. I know you got in bad with my Felix a few nights ago, and I know your position's a little precarious 'round here. But I heard how you stood up to my Hellen. Takes a lot of balls to do that. I want you to know, so long as you can keep that…friend of yours under control, your position here's firm."

Tentative relief calms my pulse. In theory, this is a very good thing. Marcus probably has ulterior motives. The good thing about those? I can use them to protect Cal. I have to be careful. Watch out for a double-cross and hope Matt can figure out how to disable that chip.

I meet Marcus' eyes. "Thanks. I just want what's best for Cal. And so long as what's best for her helps you, I'm in."

A bold move. A risky move. But it'll pay off if I've gambled right.

A grin breaks out across Marcus' face. He claps my other shoulder. "Like I said, you got some brass ones, kid. Just know same goes for the Cades. Second you two become more trouble than you're worth…"

Risk number two. I lift my chin and reach out.

His grin widens, and he shakes my hand. "Looks like we got ourselves an understanding."

Chapter Twenty-Six

Sephrim

Needle-like pain stabs my side as Daniel and I power walk through the cold, foggy city. He'd probably press me with a lot more questions and objections if we weren't in a rush. It's only been a few hours since the hacker—Matt, apparently—sabotaged the Designer Kid security system, which means the runaways should be in the tunnels by now. All the Cal craziness has set us back about thirty minutes. We need to move fast if we want to get to the checkpoint on time.

With my hood up and Daniel close, I don't worry too much about cameras. Walking alone, head down, I look suspicious; walking with a registered citizen and highly respected businessman, I look like any other apprentice. Still, I avoid eye contact with the other pedestrians and tuck my chin.

Daniel takes precautions, choosing sidewalks far from rich or middle-class areas in which security cameras mark nearly every door of every building, and keeping his voice down. We have to cut through one higher-end neighborhood to get to the docks, though, and this short trip has me resisting the urge to run.

Instead, I keep my focus on the slick gray concrete and try to catch glimpses through large dining room windows with my peripheral vision. Families gather around tables or TVs. Some laugh. Others yell. Many play video games, and one couple even knocks a ping-pong ball back and forth between them. Longing pulls at my insides.

Is this what normal people do? What family looks like?

"Cade hit you again?" Daniel asks through gritted teeth.

"Not exactly." I lift my shoulders. "I might've gotten kicked after stopping Cal from shooting Felix. Ungrateful jerk."

I grin.

Daniel doesn't. "You sure it's the best plan to hide there with Cal? Sounds like you traded one crime lord for another equally bad crime lord. Way you tell it, he wants to use her as much as Hellen does."

I run a thumb over my calloused knuckles. Freaking Daniel and his logic. Thankfully, I already have a response. "I know. Actually talked with Marcus Cade before I came to the garage."

"Marcus? Not Felix?"

"Yeah. Good old Moneybags." I crush my chin to my chest as we pass a group of giggling girls standing in front of a brightly lit store.

One glances up from her cell to give me the side-eye. She winks.

Heat rushes to my face. I tug on my hood. "We have an understanding. Right now, I'm counting on Matt, Darby's younger brother, to disable the chip. If he can free Designer Kids, chances are he can free Cal."

"Hold up." Not slowing down, he lifts his hands. "Matt? The youngest kid of Hellen Jacobs and Marcus Cade is the one who's been disabling the security system?"

Stepping over a crack in the sidewalk, I nod. "Same kid. Apparently, he's a tech genius."

"He'd have to be to pull something like that."

We walk in silence for a few blocks. Interviews with world leaders play on the billboard screens. Reporters flash cameras and toss questions to various representatives. Most every nation plans to attend the upcoming summit. Images of the delegates scroll across the large screens. Some wear business suits, others brightly colored robes, a few simper, one smirks, but all hide pent-up tension behind their expressions of choice. Dread, hope, anticipation, anger all gather under political facades. Each understands the perils and possibilities of what might come next.

I glance at the current dignitary on display. Prime Minister of India, Apurva Laghari, doesn't smile, not with her mouth, anyway. Soft at the corners, her eyes exude warmth as she answers reasonable questions or weaves out of the way of ridiculous ones. She looks kind. Maybe she needs a mediocre mechanic/incredible thief. I roll my eyes, irritated by the stupid, far-reaching idea of finding a family of my own.

Too late for that.

The interviews and speeches fade as we reach the outer limits of the city, replaced by an increase in sirens, train horns, and the occasional snap of a Slinger's whip. Rats sniff through trash that consists mostly of discarded FudPaks. One of them hisses as we pass. Daniel kicks an empty beer can at it, and the rodent scuttles into the shadows. I frown, almost feeling sorry for the disease-infested little guy.

At the farthest end of the farthest alley in the city,

near the docks, we find the sewer flanked by Slingers. We shrink back behind a dumpster. The air sparks with electricity from their whips. Static mixes with voices on the radios hooked to their shoulders, but the soldiers themselves keep silent watch over the sewer lid.

I curse. Perfect. How are we supposed to get rid of them? A diversion might make them split up. With busted ribs, though, I'd probably get myself caught. Too bad Darby's not around with her nifty little knockout device. If Cal was here… I cringe and shove the thought away, disgusted with the idea. If I start thinking like that, I won't be any better than the Cades—or Hellen. We need a plan.

Then I see it on the other side of the dumpster. An old, rusted motorcycle. Now *that* could create a diversion. If I can get it going fast enough, that is. I pull a few tools from my belt.

"Soon as I'm clear, get those kids out, huh?" Before Daniel can argue, I trot to the bike. With a twist and a spark, it roars to life. I slide onto the seat, rev the engine, and ride out into the middle of the Slingers. "Hey, guys, looking for runaway Designer Kids?"

All shouting at once, the Slingers lift their signature weapons. I wink and gun it. Over my right shoulder, the air crackles. It stings my back but doesn't latch on. Waves of electricity wiggle down my spine. Not nearly close enough for lights out, but enough to hurt. The second whip snaps the air next to my ear. I take a corner at top speed. Before I clear it, a whip snaps again. This time, the electric current jitters through the bike. The engine sputters and spits and dies.

Teeth clenched, I wait for the bike to slow, then jump off. Against the ache in my side, I sprint through the alley toward the docks. A fourth snap wraps liquid fire around my torso. I let out a strangled grunt. Neck seizing, I collapse. My body convulses, and my head bounces against the damp asphalt. The Slingers catch up, and one crouches next to me, turning off the whip's electric pulse.

"You are suspected of being one of the Expired. You will now be searched for official documentation. If you do not have it, you will be returned to your lab and assessed from there."

"Be honest. You just want to touch my butt, don't you?" I ask through still-clenched teeth.

I will my muscles to fight the paralyzing numbness. They ignore me. Maybe the lab exaggerated the horrors of the workhouses to scare kids into obedience. Rumors are always worse than reality, right? I gulp. Somehow, I doubt that.

The Slinger quirks a brow. "You know you have the right to be silent, ri—"

My eyes widen as the two Slingers freeze, shake violently, then collapse where they stand.

Darby walks up and blows on the ends of two guns in Taser mode, a full grin on her face. "Thought you might need a little help."

"My hero," I say, relief loosening the muscles in my chest. "How'd you know I was here?"

She squats and loosens the whip from around my middle. "Matty's tapped into the feeds. There aren't many out here, but he's got control of the ones that are, and I take a glance at them now and again. Saw the Slingers, then you and Daniel. Good thing I decided to follow you. You seem to attract trouble." One hand between my shoulder blades, she helps me sit up.

Pain crackles across my ribs. "Whoever I pissed off up there needs to get over it." I rub the back of my head. "Don't know if I can handle another beating, choking, or electrocution. Maybe just to get it out of the way, you should try to drown me."

"Oh, stop and stay still."

She threads her fingers through my hair to check the damage. Their warmth spreads out across my skull. One small spot stings at her touch.

"A minor bump. I think you'll live. Can you stand?"

Stand? After getting electrocuted and slamming my head into the ground, I'd like to sit a minute and enjoy the feeling of a friend making sure my brain isn't leaking from my head like oil. But we've got runaway Designer Kids to move before the Slingers come to or more show up to check on their oddly silent buddies. With Darby gripping my forearm, I get to my feet and hobble back toward the sewer.

"Was Cal actually asleep when you left?"

"Pretending to be," she says. "She still seems pretty jarred after trying to squeeze my head off on top of everything else."

I wipe cold moisture off my forehead with a sleeve. "Hope she can get some rest. Losing control of your own body is…" Shivering, I shove aside the screams of the past.

The bedraggled group we find with Daniel reacts when Darby and I turn the corner. One flinches back toward the still open sewer while another freezes where he stands. The third pales but clenches her fists.

She narrows her pink eyes, then furrows her brow. "Is he the one who distracted the Slingers?"

Daniel lets out a pent-up breath and laces both hands

behind his neck. "Thank goodness. What happened? Where *are* the Slingers?"

"Writhing." Darby spins her guns around her pointer fingers. "Well, unconscious now, but they were writhing. It was beautiful."

One shoulder pressed against the dumpster, I readjust my hood. "After I spent a few minutes writhing myself. That really ruined how cool I looked when I stole the motorcycle." I grin, then reach out to help the kid still standing on the top rung of the sewer ladder.

The runaway stares until the girl says, "It's okay, Gabe. I think he's the one Dr. G's always talking about. Seraphim?"

Darby laughs. "Aww, Seraphim. You're our little angel."

I laugh and pull the kid out of the manhole. "It's Sephrim, but yeah, that's where they got my name from or the idea for my name anyway." I rub my side. "We need to get moving before more Slingers show."

Chapter Twenty-Seven

Cal

Elegant hands lower a plush, smiling monkey toward me. It smells like mint…not the monkey, the owner of the hands. I wrap one chubby arm around the stuffed animal and reach with the other. A face appears now. She places a finger over her smiling lips, and giggles bubble in my chest. Then her features and coloring shift. Blood blackens her skin. Alura. The guard I killed. She aims her faraway eyes at me.

"You did this, did what you were always meant to do, what you were created to do."

A wail snags in my throat. I slap a hand over my mouth to trap it. Air charges in and out through my nose as I stare unseeing at the ceiling. The vision of Alura continues to stare down at me. A scream ebbs and flows against my palm. The image from my dream refuses to fade. I bite the side of my hand until it bleeds, and the cinder-block ceiling replaces Alura's face.

Even after her face finally fades, I lie as still as a dysfunctional weapon. The pain anchors me to the present moment, chases the second memory—and its dumb emotional baggage—away. I claw at the first, but it slithers through my fingers. I punch the mattress.

"Dream, noun, a succession of images, thoughts, or emotions passing through the mind during sleep…" I spit bloody saliva onto the floor, then punch the mattress again. "Memory, noun, a particular recollection of an event, person... Come back." I say the last phrase between my teeth with a growl.

Wiping my mouth with a forearm, I fling one leg over the side of the bed, then the other. A toe touches something sticky. Probably my bloody spit. I tap it a few times and grimace. Gross. I roll off the bed and stagger to the bathroom. Ignoring my reflection, I wash the blood away.

Now what?

No going outside unless I want to risk some idiot tripping over my trigger word. Trigger word. Great. Fists on hips, I glare at the door, the couch, the table. Nice little safe space to protect the crazy girl. I cringe. No. To protect everybody else from *me*.

Options?

Coloring the table, taking another nap with nightmare potential, or pacing aimlessly. I blow a raspberry. Nope, nope, nope. I could dismantle the oven and make a new gun. On a scale of one to nuclear, how pissed would the Cades be if I did that?

After killing one of their security guards? Hiroshima, probably.

I turn in a circle. My hands need something to do. Maybe I can make something with one of the forks... I take a step, then freeze. A see-through version of Matt stands about a foot away, or at least half of him does. The table cuts off the majority of his legs at the knees, and one chair obscures his left arm. An ugly bruise stains the side of his jaw, swelling it big time.

I slap a hand over my mouth, again stifling a scream of surprise. The teeth marks sting.

Matt holds up his palms. "Sorry. Meant to give you a little warning before I showed up but thought maybe having a voice in your head would be worse."

"How are you doing that?" I ask, my words still muffled.

Matt's mouth twists into a half smile, and his brows buckle together. "The bit. I programmed it so it could project a hologram through your eyes."

"So you turned me into a projector?"

"Kind of. If the projection had the ability to see its surroundings."

I stare for a moment.

"Sorry about that. Just figured it would be the best way to communicate with you," he says.

"You are seriously a genius."

His cheeks flush. "You might take that back in a second after I tell you about my progress."

I let my hand drop. "Progress? Have you made any?"

"Not exactly." Matt frowns. He looks off to one side, as if over my shoulder, but I figure it's actually toward his own little door. The pupil of his good eye shrinks, then expands again as he sighs. "Sorry. Anyway, the only update I have so far is that I scrambled the GPS attached to it. I'm still working on a command to disable the chip from here. I have to be careful, though. Don't want to set off the kill switch."

I half fall, half slump onto the floor. "The who-da-what-now?"

He grimaces. "It's a fail-safe. Mom wanted it put in."

"And when did she plan on using this fail-safe?" I ask.

"She was only going to use it if you got taken by a Slinger...or if you threatened not to follow orders. She hasn't used it yet because I promised to get you back." Gaze aimed down, he tugs his collar away from his throat. "I'm sorry. Should've told you."

Isn't that just sweet and dandy? Not only has Hellen turned me into a mindless assassin, but she can also shut me down, decommissioned like an unreliable car. Wonderful. At least she has fairly narrow parameters for the circumstances under which she'll flip this particular switch.

"But I'm going to shut it down," he says in a rush. The skin between his brows puckers, and his good eye widens. "I promise. I'm getting closer. I just need a little more time."

"That's right. You will." I grin. "If it wasn't for your technological magic, I'd still be stuck in the compound..." I tap my temple. "So I know you'll figure out how to disable this thing. Also, I'm going to rescue you from the big, bad witch. And there's nothing you can do about it."

I puff out my chest. Hellen and Marcus want an assassin, Daniel and Sephrim and Dr. Gayle want me safe, and Darby wants me to be able to defend myself. A thousand strings yanking me in a thousand directions.

What do I want? Matt. He can't stay Hellen's prisoner. More than that, Hellen can't get her way.

I grin wider. I'm going to save him, but I won't tell him when it's going down. It will be a surprise. Plus, then he won't be able to argue with me or try to lie to Hellen. In the meantime, I need more information. In particular, about one little factoid in that long list of wants that just ran through my brain.

"Matt, what exactly does Hellen want to make me do?" I ask.

All the confidence that lifted his soft features when he explained flowers and coding hardens into immovable fear. "I can't tell you that. Hellen will kill me if she finds out I told you."

I rub the backs of my arms, sorting through my words, defining each rapidly before I choose them. "She won't. You're smarter than she is. And I know you'll do the right thing. Just like you always do."

"I can't." An odd jitter runs through his voice.

"Matt." I keep my voice soft the way I do when I sing to Sephrim sometimes. "I know you're scared, but I've already killed people because of this thing in my head."

His eye snaps up to meet mine as color fades from his face. "Someone said your trigger word?"

I drop my gaze, following my stomach's downward dip. "I've heard it three times now."

"How—" His voice cracks. "How many…"

"Casualties? Five."

"Cal…I'm sorry. I'm so sorry."

I smile, appreciating the sentiment. Though I doubt sweet, soft Matt ever killed anyone, he's been made to do things he hates. Empathy binds us in many ways, threads I don't much mind having.

"And it shut off? How? Let me run a diagnostic."

I scratch a rough spot on the chair as revulsion tightens my throat. "I doubt you need to do that. The first time, I was attacked by Slingers. It shut down when I killed the last one." Metal fills my mouth and sticks to my fingers. "The second time was different. Sephrim stopped me. He and Darby both think it's a word, 'threat,' but I think it's him."

"Cal, there's only one code word," he says. "It's supposed to shut off when the threat's over. So it makes sense it would power down if the Slingers were the only ones around, but with Sephrim? Until you were alone, you should've kept killing."

Excitement sparks through my chest. "So if there's no trigger word to shut it off…"

He shrugs. "I guess your emotional connection helped you snap out of it. I'm not surprised. Hellen wouldn't think much about family bonds. She'd never expect it to get in the way of what she wants."

"Ha! I told Sephrim he made me stop, and I was right!" I grin, most proud.

"Seems like a common occurrence."

"The longer you know me, the more you'll realize how true that is."

Matt laughs. A glorious, free sound, absent of fear. It bounces off the walls around him, the prison disguised as a computer room. My eyes twitch to the bruise on his jaw and the remnants of the one darkening his right cheekbone. Resolve tightens my hands into fists. If I have to knock him upside the head, then drag him out of the compound cavewoman style, I'll get him away from Hellen. Even if I need to use the demon chip in my head to do it.

He meets my gaze, that smile still lighting his entire face. I want to reach out again, to touch the bruised spot on his jaw, to brush the hair from his forehead, to tell him in gestures what words can't communicate: he's wanted, he's loved, he doesn't deserve the pain his mom puts him through.

All at once, he sobers, swallows, and says, "She

wants you to assassinate the members of the New United Nations."

My vision doubles at his statement, and I nearly topple out of my chair. "She what?"

Swallowing, he looks over my left shoulder again, then back at me. "I don't know exactly why, but she wants to take out as many as she can. She wants to start some kind of revolution, Cal, and she wants to use a Designer Kid to do it."

Chapter Twenty-Eight

Sephrim

Maybe, sometime soon, I'll enjoy the luxury of not being punched or choked or electrocuted for a full twenty-four hours, but that time is clearly not this week. As we lead the runaways along the outskirts of the city, I resist a limp. Wind shunts along the clouds overhead. It leaves behind piles of bright, white stars and a fat, red moon. Is that significant? What's the phrase? Red sky in the morning? No, that's something else.

I veer toward Daniel. "Where we headed?"

"Sam's."

Darby gawks. "Seriously? Criminal Central Sam's?"

"The one and only. Just when you think we'll get a short break from the underworld, they pull you back in." I laugh.

"Meg's been part of the chain for a while," Daniel says with a grin. "The criminals she lets in make police nervous, so Sam's is a safe place for just about anybody who wants to stay under the radar. Even Slingers won't go in there. Though they did try on the last rotation. Didn't last long. The Sams have always had…a way with people."

I snort. A way with people. Anybody who holds a gun to Hellen Jacobs' head and gets away with it has guts of iron. Or a death wish. Doubtful the second is accurate.

Fifteen or so minutes later, we reach the docks closest to Sam's. Red light from the bar's sign stains its walls, the cracked sidewalk around it, the parked cars. Two women stand near the entrance, one dressed in a typical black business suit, the other all in white. I assume it's white anyway. Like the rest of the parking lot, the sign soaks the fabric in its gory glow.

They both look up when our small group approaches. Their focus drifts along the kids, to Daniel, to Darby, and finally lands on me. Unflinching, the women's eyes stay on me as I pull open the front door. I let the runaways and Daniel inside first. Embarrassed heat billows to the surface of my face. My stupid, flawless, way-too-symmetrical face. After so many years, I should be used to people staring.

I'm not.

Darby glares at the women. Without a single word, her gaze frightens them away. Their heels clack on the concrete. The dark closes behind them, and she turns back to me, brow buckled.

"Get that a lot? I mean, outside of Cade's?"

"Why do you think I wear the hood?"

"Because that works so well." She chuckles.

As we walk into Sam's together, I pull the hood farther down. The new runaways bunch together in a back booth and bend over plates, flanked by Daniel and Meg. Shotgun strapped to her back, the latter watches the occupants of the bar, guarding the kids like a reverse Slinger. She grins when Darby and I push through the crowd.

"Well, if it isn't the kid with brass guts." Meg gives me a slow clap.

A smirk tugs at my mouth. I step up to the table. Gabe and the girl with pink eyes—Lailah—both look up. The third kid, Zad, continues to spoon soup into his mouth.

I cross my arms. "Feel better with some food?"

Lailah nods. Strands of black hair slip across her forehead. "We ran out of supplies pretty fast in the tunnels. Would've been fine if Dr. Evil hadn't made the techs dig through our packs before we left."

Cold worry hardens my guts, then snakes up to clog my throat. "Wait, what? Dr. Troy searched your packs?"

"Yeah." Gabe sucks the tip of his fork. "Took most of the extra food Dr. Gayle gave us for the road."

"Can I see them?" I ask.

Daniel frowns. "Think she put something inside?"

"Maybe." The three kids hand me their backpacks. "That could explain why the Slingers showed when they did."

When Cal and I ran from the lab, we dug out our identity chips to remove the GPS tracking. Based on their bandaged arms, these kids did the same. But what if Dr. Troy took extra precautions? The SkinTech doesn't work as a GPS, so what if she added an extra device to the packs they were given to take to the workhouses? I find nothing floating around in their sparse belongings. Then my fingers bump across something hard in the lining.

I pull a pocket knife out of my tool belt, then cut out a small, black square of fabric. Like the bits placed in our skin for ID, it blinks green on one end. I curse. As I scramble for the other two backpacks, a crackle snaps through the room. Electricity burns the air. Before I can react, Meg and Darby both step around me.

"Get them to the basement, Dan," Meg says in a

hiss. "We'll take care of this."

A dull roar fills my ears. With shaking hands, I tear out the other two trackers and stomp them to pieces with the heel of my boot. Then, with a stiff breath trapped in my lungs, I help Daniel herd the kids out of the booth. We round the bar, and the panicked roar ebbs away, replaced by shouts from the crowd.

Then Meg's voice rises above the rest. "Can it!"

As Daniel pries open a door in the floor close to the kitchen, I crouch behind the bar, curiosity overriding my instinct to hide. After the story about why Sam's is such a great safe house for the runaways, I've got to know why they'd risk coming back. Besides, if they saw us come inside, they might already know she's hiding the runaways. If I need to, I can be a distraction again.

I gnaw the inside corner of my cheek, so not excited about *that* prospect. But more than that, the idea of not knowing what's going on freaks me out. A factory for anxiety-induced worst-case scenarios, my mind will come up with images that might send me into a full-on panic attack. Then I'll be totally worthless.

I peek out at the scene.

Meg stands with one elbow against a pillar, the shotgun still strapped to her back, chin tilted up as if the Slingers are no more than regular rowdy customers. To her left, hidden among the actual regulars, Darby hovers, one hand in her jacket.

At Meg's command, the crowd falls into quiet murmurs. The bar owner looks around the room, and the volume decreases more. Even the Slingers keep quiet until she turns her attention again to them. Before they can start their spiel, Meg lifts a free hand.

"Warrants, if you please," she says.

"We have reasonable cause, ma'am." The Slinger says the last word like a curse.

Daniel tugs on the hem of my hoodie. "Come on, man, we've got to get these kids out of here."

"Go on without me," I say under my breath. "If I need to, I'll create another diversion."

"Seph—"

"Just go. It's okay." I finally look back at him.

One hand on the half-open door to the basement and one foot inside, Daniel frowns. Then he glances over the bar and grimaces. "Be careful. Don't be the distraction unless you got to."

The instant the door shuts, I turn back to the scene on the other side of the bar. Meg hasn't moved. She taps the butt of her shotgun. I catch the tail end of her sentence. "…article four A. Which means that, unless you have a witness, this probable cause you've imagined is nonexistent. Try again."

In spite of my nerves, I grin, impressed.

"Oh, but we do have a witness." A woman steps through the line of soldiers, the woman in white, from before.

The witness smiles and taps the side of her face. My world dives into a panicked tailspin as glowing blue lines cut across her skin. They fade, and the bone structure and coloring shift into their proper place—into the face of Dr. June Troy.

All feeling leaves my hands and feet. Had I not already been squatting, I definitely would've toppled over as my chest muscles pinch my lungs. I take a painfully slow breath. She saw me at the door. Knows I'm here. If I pass out now, I won't stand a chance.

I let the breath out carefully.

Meg speaks again. "Am I supposed to be impressed? We've got plenty around here with fancy tech."

Dr. Troy smirks. "Impressed or not, I witnessed four Designer Children I personally helped create enter this establishment not twenty minutes ago, one of whom I've been attempting to find for years. Now, if you would be so good as to call off your lovely—and I'm sure law-abiding—patrons, we'll do our search and leave you to your business."

Energy evaporates from my muscles. I tip onto my ass and reach for the basement door. Then my hand freezes. Closed, it disappears into the floor, leaving no sign of the room below. If I pull it open at the wrong time, I'll give away the kids' hiding place. Not acceptable.

Choking on the thickness in my throat, I scoot back against the counter, now watching through a crack in the wood. The kitchen might have an exit. Even with my various and sundry injuries, I could outrun them. Meg and Darby said they'd take care of it, but that was before Dr. Troy showed up as a witness. Or at least before we recognized her. I shiver at the thought of her lingering stare, at the memory of…

I gag and clamp a hand over my mouth.

"Well, I guess if you have probable cause. Here's the thing, though." Meg slips the shotgun around and braces it against her shoulder. "Only rules we play by here are my rules."

A blast shatters the tense quiet. Electricity burns the air around me as the Slingers react, scalding my exposed skin. The counter throbs against my shoulder and the side of my head. Black spots grow in my vision as I whip around, focusing on the door to the kitchen. I lurch forward.

A hand clamps down on my upper arm when I'm only inches away. It pulls me back with so much force my feet kick into the air. Chin tucked into my chest, I slam my free arm against the ground to absorb the impact. A Slinger straddles my midsection and pins my arms. I buck my hips, and the soldier lurches forward onto her hands.

Before I can make my next move, electricity sears through my body. The shock locks my limbs to the floor. For the second time that night, I jerk against an unforgiving ground. Then the weight lifts away from me. In the blur, I see Darby tackle the Slinger and drag her away. A face moves into my line of vision, and terror seizes my chest.

Dr. Troy runs a finger along my cheek and smiles.

"Thank you, my sweet angel. I always knew you'd lead me where I wanted to go." She smooths the hair away from my forehead, hooks an arm under mine, and drags me away from Darby and the fighting to rest against a wall. "Now, where is my missing product?"

My windpipe closes. Childhood terror tears its way through my guts with frigid claws. I can't move, can't speak, can't even force my thoughts back into their proper order. Anxiety tips to panic. The ground disintegrates under me, and black bubbles expand in my vision.

Great. If I pass out, no one can interrogate me. Solid plan.

Dr. Troy's smile broadens. She grips the back of my head, fingers digging into my hair, exactly the way she did in the lab. "I see not much has changed. Perhaps a little motivation will unlock that tongue of yours."

Motivation.

More bubbles grow and shrink in front of my eyes as Dr. Troy lifts a syringe and jams its point into my neck. The thick drug crawls inside me. Pleasant heat follows, soothing the ache in my ribs, the sting of electricity, dampening the sounds of chaos around us. My throat and chest muscles relax, and the bubbles dissipate. I still float but now on a comfortable cloud. Why had I been so scared before?

"That's right. Just relax." Dr. Troy's voice slips through my ears, its sound growing and fading. "Now, where are those runaways?"

"Runaways?" I mumble the word. I shouldn't tell her, but I can't remember why. It twists away from me like a wisp of car exhaust caught between fast-moving traffic.

Car exhaust.

The garage.

Cal.

I blink slowly, then grin. "Go to hell." Not the most original response, but it feels damn good.

Dr. Troy's eyes darken as they narrow. "I should have taken you myself the day you expired, you worthless boy."

"Well, it's not going to happen today either. Sorry to disappoint."

I look past Dr. Troy. Daniel stands about a foot away, his pistol—a Cal special—aimed at her head.

No. He can't show himself. If they find out he helps Designer Kids, he'll go to jail or worse. I try to make my mouth work, but the muscles along my throat tense, and my tongue weighs too much. None of my limbs want to move. Probably a combination of multiple instances of electrocution and the mystery drug.

"Ah, Daniel Todd," Dr. Troy says. "We thought you might be part of the conspiracy to steal my product but never had any proof. So nice to finally meet you."

"Wish I could say the same," he says. "Now, back off."

"Or what, Mr. Todd? Will you paint the walls with my blood? Adding murder to the long litany of charges already in your ledger?" She frowns. "Somehow I doubt you have the stomach for it after all the death you saw in combat."

Daniel glares. "You're right. I don't have the stomach for it anymore. But I've got a hell of a weapons designer. Creative one too." He pulls the trigger, and a charge bursts from the barrel.

It arches through the air, sending volts of energy through Dr. Troy's body. She jerks, twitches, then collapses. The chaos quiets. Through a new wave of black bubbles, I squint at the still bodies of the Slingers. Meg and her crew made quick work of them.

Now what? Those words finally make it past my sluggish lips. I say them again, "Now what…they know…"

"Don't worry." Daniel squats, then pulls me upright. "Leave it to Meg and her crew. They'll take care of it. Let's go check on the kids."

"Where…where are we gonna take them?" My feet tangle together as we walk to the basement door.

"I'll show you."

Chapter Twenty-Nine

Sephrim

This close to the shore, I don't expect much from the basement beneath Sam's. Maybe a single dark room, dusty boards, rickety chairs, but nothing fancy. At the bottom of the stairs, though, I find something really different.

Six cots line the far end of the room next to a worn, plaid couch, and a thick wooden table with matching chairs crowd a small kitchen. Gabe, Lailah, and Zad sit around its rough surface, flinching when we come down the stairs.

Lailah stands. "What happened?"

I sink into a free chair. "All good…don't worry…" I sound wigged out, drunk. What the heck kind of drug did Dr. Troy give me? I rub my eyes.

"We took care of the Slingers." Daniel squeezes my shoulder. "Meg and her crew will make sure they're off our trail. At least long enough for y'all to get a good night's rest here and then head off to the next checkpoint."

His voice comes to me from high above and far away. Everything in the room lies behind a barrier of glass, cutting me off from the reality of its nearness. Part of my mind knows I can touch it, but the other part can't grasp this concept. Even the pain in my side only registers peripherally.

Lailah sits again, her gaze focused on me. "Did Dr. Evil use the truth serum on you?"

"Truth serum?" My words blend together.

"Yeah," Zad says. "She uses it on us when she knows we break one of her rules but we won't tell. Makes you forget why you weren't going to tell her in the first place. You're acting that way. Weird. Foggy."

Fingers pressed into my eyes, I nod. "Makes sense. Almost told her...then didn't."

"Wait, you didn't tell her?" Gabe asks. "How?"

I shake my head, regretting it when the room sways. "Cal...then Daniel tased Dr. Evil, I mean, Dr. Troy."

Gabe's eyes bug. "Wow, no wonder Dr. Gayle fangirls all over you. Says one of these days you're going to lead a revolution or something."

With this statement, the glass between me and the rest of the room shatters. Adrenaline brings back some mental clarity. A revolution? Me? The kid who has a freakin' panic attack every time I face Dr. Troy? Brilliant plan. I'm definitely the top pick for the Designer Kids' champion. Dr. Gayle needs to stop reading dystopian fiction.

"Speaking of Dr. Gayle." Daniel pulls a net board from his pocket. "We're supposed to check in now that things are settled, or as settled as they can be."

He sits next to me and props the screen against a metal napkin holder. It dings almost immediately. Daniel taps the answer button. The screen fills with Dr. Gayle's face. Her brows furrow.

Then she lets out a sharp breath. "Oh, thank goodness you're all there. Did you run into trouble?"

I pinch an inch of space between my pointer finger

and thumb. "Slingers, Slingers, more Slingers, and Troy with truth serum."

Dr. Gayle's eyes widen. "June was there? And she drugged you? Oh, Sephrim, I'm so sorry. I've tried to convince them to discontinue that serum, ban it from use entirely, but as you know, Dr. Troy is extremely persuasive."

Adjusting his hat, Daniel grimaces. "It sounds like things are getting worse."

"Way worse," I say in a mumble.

"I'm afraid they are." Dr. Gayle laces her fingers together as if in prayer. "Under different circumstances, I would encourage the younger members of the group to leave. What I'm going to tell you is…disturbing. Then again, none of you are strangers to such things. Things are indeed getting much worse. A handful of scientists from around the globe share Dr. Troy's attitudes toward the Designer Baby project. The bit testing was only phase one. There is much support to lift the ban on child soldiers as well as the donor program. Troy is also increasing security."

"We found tracking things…" I shake my head, annoyed at the sluggish stream of my thoughts. "In the lining of their packs a few minutes before they came. The Slingers." I knead my forehead.

"Of course." Dr. Gayle frowns. "Again, I'm so sorry."

"What do we do?" Lailah asks. "We can't just let this happen, keep happening. We gotta do something, Dr. G. Don't we?"

The doctor nods slowly. "We're doing everything we can to battle this politically, but there is more that can be done. If the Designer Children come together as a united front, make a demonstration at the event…"

Whatever Dr. Gayle says next gets lost in the static in my ears. The event. The first meeting of the United Nations in fifteen years. Where politicians and doctors and all kinds of other influential people plan to come together to make decisions for the entire world. Decisions for children stuck in a lab. Do they only see the ads put out by Dr. Troy and the rest? The happy adopted ones? Or do they know the dark truth of the Expired?

"Sephrim, Seph, you okay, man?"

Some of the fog from before thins, and my head clears as I look up at Daniel. "I need to go. Cal's been alone too long, and I don't trust the Cades."

"You found Cal?" Dr. Gayle asks.

"Long story." Yanking a hand through my hair, I clear my throat. "One I'll explain later. But I need to get back to her."

Dr. Gayle smiles. "Be careful."

Chapter Thirty

Sephrim

Back at the top of the stairs, I find Darby in the bar with Meg and a mysterious lack of Slingers. In fact, I don't see any sign of invasion at all. Every chair sits in its upright position, and every piece of glass now lies in piles near a heap of black trash bags. They've even cleaned the scorch marks from the Slingers' whips off the floor.

After a quick sweep of the room, I climb the rest of the way up the basement stairs, relief loosening the muscles in my chest.

One hand in a stranglehold around her braid, Darby turns to me and heaves a heavy sigh. "He lives! How many lives do you have?"

"Think I'm down to five," I say. "Let's get back to Cade's, huh? Maybe take the tunnels this time. I don't want to risk the other four."

"Is Daniel coming with us?" Darby asks.

"Nah, he'll stay the night here with the kids, then help them get to the next checkpoint." I want to ask what they did with Dr. Troy but figure it might be best if I don't know.

We thank Meg for her help, then step out into the red-soaked night, power walking to the nearest tunnel in mutual quiet. Frogs and pigeons and crickets sing an anthem. The sewer lid silences them, but their song continues through my still-foggy mind, along with Dr. Gayle's insistence on a Designer Kid rebellion.

Darby brushes the back of my hand with her fingers, her touch chasing away some of the sliminess Dr. Troy's left behind. "Okay, buddy, two zaps and an understandable panic attack in one night is a lot to take, even for somebody with nine lives. You're not going to fall apart on me anytime soon, are you?"

"Hell no."

"Don't give me that macho BS. It doesn't suit you."

For a few paces along the algae-covered ledge, I consider a better answer. What's the point in lying anyway?

"Fine, not feeling stable at all," I say. "Especially after what Dr. Gayle said."

She lifts a brow in question.

"She thinks I should lead some kind of revolution…" I rub my nose and step over a break in the cement. "Unite the Designer Kids. Which is terrifying, but at the same time, if we don't do something, the UN will probably bring a lot of bad along with the good."

"It's the way of the world. Bad's never absent where good hangs around. They seem to be…eternal bedmates." Her short laugh snaps across the walls.

"I have to do something to, I don't know, encourage the good and stop the bad." I drag a hand over my face, frustrated at my inability to communicate. "I just don't know what."

Darby's fingers slide around my wrist. Warmth chases some of the cold away. One of my feet slips on the slick ground, and she keeps me steady. We walk a little farther along without a word. The rush of water fills our silence, an oddly calming sound. It stinks, but the noise is still nice.

"Why does it have to be you?"

I suck my lower lip. "Because I'm one of them. And they need a voice."

"I reiterate." Her grip tightens. "Why does it have to be you? Aren't there other runaways? You have Cal to worry about. Isn't that enough?"

Irritated, I roll my eyes and kick a wad of trash into the water. "Why do people ask that? Enough? By what standard?"

"What do you mean?"

I run my hand along the cold, wet grain of the wall. It numbs the tips of my fingers and anchors me to the present as I think about the question. By what standard? Whose standard? "I don't know." I shrug. "I just don't think that's the right question."

We walk to the end of the tunnel in stifled silence. Her grip slips to my hand and stays there the rest of the journey. Even when we climb back out onto the sidewalk, into the bloody, unobstructed moonlight, she holds on.

With Cade's in the distance, I pause and look up at the dust of stars overhead. I focus on Darby's touch. Her fingers tighten around mine until they ache, but it keeps me on the ground, stops me from floating away on the last dregs of Dr. Troy's drug.

Gaze still skyward, I ask, "How's your neck?"

She lets out a faint laugh. "It hurts. Cal's a lot stronger than she looks. Unless of course the chip has the ability to give you superhuman strength."

"Oh no, she is freakishly strong." I chew my lower lip again. A flock of geese treks across the sky. "Heard from Matt?"

Her hand on mine tightens to a choke hold. "For a few minutes."

I look at her. Even with her head bowed and the shadows cloaking her eyes, the anger hardening lines along her face is clear. This she doesn't try to hide. Fury comes easy for her, works like a fresh coat of paint obscuring scratches on a car. Sorrow? Fear? These she keeps under that protective finish.

"Is he okay?" It's one of those dumb questions people ask, the kind where they know the answer but ask anyway. The response that follows proves the level of intimacy shared. Or at least that's what Daniel says.

Her upper lip curls, and her jaw tightens. "No. Hellen didn't even know he was the one that let Cal out and still...still..." She trails off, then shakes her head. "I have to get him out of there, Seph. I know you don't like the idea, but Cal—"

"If Cal wants to do it, if she wants to try and free Matt, okay. And if she doesn't, I'll still do what I can," I say, heaving a heavy sigh. "So long as your dad doesn't get in the way. He is a scary, scary man."

"Seriously?" Emotion thickens Darby's voice.

"Matt risked a lot to save Cal. He deserves to have someone save him too."

She throws her arms around my neck, pulling me impossibly close, so close it actually hurts. My ribs throb, a feeling I've grown used to, but I fold my arms around her waist anyway. Chin resting on her shoulder, I suppress the tense fear running up my chest.

A few breaths later, we break apart and walk the rest of the way, hand in hand, to Cade's. We cut through the thick crowd toward the back. Halfway across the room, a man who typically sits in the lower levels of Felix's circle steps into our path. Taller than Darby and me, he looms over us like a living sentinel-droid.

"Out of the way, Erik," Darby says through her teeth.

"Happy to get out of your way, little Cade, but not this one." Erik jabs a finger into my sternum.

His voice rumbles from deep in his chest. It matches his massive form, strong and heavy and thick. A beard covers his chin, making up for the lack of hair on his head. He looks at me the way Felix often does, the way Dr. Troy always did, like I'm fascinating, but…not quite human.

"What do you want?" I cross my arms and lift my chin.

He inches forward, muscling out the oxygen with the smell of body odor. I can't decide which is worse, sweat-induced stench or the overapplication of cologne. I choke on my own bile, a reaction I've gotten very good at hiding. Still, my nose wrinkles. Not enough self-control in the world to stop that reaction.

A sneer twists Erik's features. "What do I want? I want you and that other freak to watch yourselves. Why Felix ever let you in, why Marcus stuck up for you, doesn't make sense. You're unnatural, dangerous. If somebody else dies, don't expect Daddy Cade to protect that science experiment in there."

I tilt my head. "That a threat?"

"I don't make threats, I make—"

"Promises. Sure, sure." I wave a hand.

Everything that's happened tonight dwarfs threats from a dude like Erik, a man so far on the outer circle neither Marcus nor Felix probably even knows his first name. Big and burly and suffering from a low production of brain cells, Erik's the kind of guy Felix and Marcus use as a human shield, a battering ram, an expendable first wave in times of war. Yeah, he has the strength to turn me into a tiny ball of broken bones, but he'd never make a move without the Cades' consent.

When I dismiss his "promise," his face reddens. He lifts a fist. Before it ever reaches its intended destination, I catch it. Wrenching the meaty wrist around, I twist it behind his back and force him into the wall. I shove the arm up until the angle elicits a cry of pain. In this position, bulk and strength don't matter. For once, I have all the control.

Riding high on adrenaline and no longer dizzy from Dr. Troy's drug, I lean in close to his ear. "I appreciate the warning. Now, let me return the favor. If you ever even *consider* touching Cal, I'll dismantle you, limb by limb, and scatter the spare parts in the sewers. We clear?"

His arm tenses as he tries to push away from the wall.

I shove Erik's hand farther up his back and repeat, "Are we clear?"

"Clear," he says between gasps of pain. "We're clear. Now get off me, freak."

With a final shove, I let him go. Erik winces as his arm returns to its proper place. He then turns and scuttles off. Hands clenched into fists, I watch until the crowd closes around him. I flinch when Darby touches my elbow.

"That was pretty badass, Seph," she says. "Didn't know you had a little serial killer in you."

A laugh jitters up my throat. "Think the dismantling thing was a little overboard?"

"Nah, he deserved it." Darby gives me a squeeze.

I shrug. Tit for tat. If Erik wants to play his crazy chips, I've got a stack of psycho and zero qualms about going all in. "Yeah, maybe it wasn't the highest of high roads…or any kind of high road, but damn, it felt good."

"That jerk said some pretty awful things…"

I shrug again. "Heard worse."

We hug the wall the rest of the way to Cal's room. Thankfully, no more goons cause trouble. Again, dressed in freshly cleaned overalls and goggles, Cal lies on the kitchen table, holding two metal planes in the air. As she swoops and dives them toward each other, she makes exploding noises with her mouth. Bits of the oven lie scattered on the floor, material for her creations.

"Hey, Cal, planning on taking apart the entire room while you're here?" I step over pieces of metal and lean against the wall next to the table.

Eyes still on her toys, Cal grins. "Until I'm otherwise occupied."

I snag one of the planes and study the craftsmanship. In spite of the minimal tools at her disposal, the model looks like she bought it at a shop. "How about a covert mission? Would that be enough of a distraction for you?"

"Covert, adjective. Concealed, secret, disguised." She makes another exploding sound. "Does Marcus have somebody he wants…gone?" She crashes the plane into one of her knees, face stiff like she's fighting off panic.

"No." Darby drops into a chair. "Actually, Sephrim agreed to our plan to rescue Matty."

The plane slips from Cal's fingers. It bounces off the side of the table and clatters to the ground as she sits up to grab my shoulders. "Really? You agreed?" Brows lifted almost to her hairline, she stares at me in gaping, open-mouthed shock.

I grin over a wince. If I'd been her actual blood brother, I couldn't be more proud. Even after everything, after the chip made her kill multiple people, after it nearly got her killed, she still wants to use it to help somebody. It doesn't matter that our plan involves using her trigger word or that it will probably leave further mental and emotional scars.

But that's Cal.

Funky, word-defining, gun-making Cal. I push the fear of losing her away. I can find a way to keep that from happening. What I can't do is leave that kid stuck with Hellen. Especially after he helped free Cal. Who she really seems to care for. I doubt I could lead a Designer Kids rebellion, but I might be able to rescue one kid.

"Yeah, I agreed," I say. "Let's go save Matt."

Cal beams, then lifts a finger. "I'm glad you agree. Because we're going to need him if we're going to stop Hellen's evil plan."

That's when Cal drops a bomb that makes me wish I could have another dose of Dr. Evil's calming truth serum. Hellen wants to use her in the exact same way the "workhouses" want to use every expired kid they can get their hands on—as a mindless soldier who can't fight back.

Chapter Thirty-One

Cal

I almost didn't tell him. Seph will probably freak, might change his mind about saving Matt, but the key to a good strategy is having as much information as possible. I'll just have to do a little extra work to make sure Hellen doesn't catch me. After I calm any and all of Sephrim's fears.

He takes a funny step back, bumping into Darby, then runs both sets of fingers through his hair. Gently, she nudges him forward and into one of the chairs next to the table. As he sits and breathes and processes, I retrieve my plane off the floor, tracing the wing to distract myself. Counting each pass.

Rushing him will only make things worse.

I've made it to fifteen before he finally unstalls. "I guess this doesn't really change all that much, does it?"

"Logically, no." I shake my head. "At least not in relation to saving Matt. Except for the fact that if he's in Hellen's hands, she'll probably make him be part of her plans to take down the United Nations."

Sephrim looks up at me.

"But we'll talk about foiling that plan later." I turn the plane over between my fingers, eyes on the designs I carved over the last hour. "One foot in front of the other. Only way not to fall off the edge."

"Right." He clears his throat. "Right. One rescue mission at a time."

After a few hours of planning, we shuffle to the bedroom. I lie on top of my sheets and watch Sephrim and Darby argue about who'll sleep on the bed or the couch. It takes a lot of impressive maneuvering, but finally, she convinces him to use the bed on account of his busted side. She slumps on the couch, her head close to mine, gaze on Sephrim.

Following the stitched lines of the blankets with my fingers, I listen to the sounds of the pipes sigh and creak. When Sephrim starts to snore lightly, I rest my chin on a forearm. "Darby," I say in a whisper. "You awake?"

She doesn't turn but responds with a quiet, "Mmhmm."

"Is he okay? Seph? He doesn't look okay." My fingers continue their path along the threads, over and over until she finally answers.

"I need to do another scan."

"But is he okay?"

She cranes her head to look at me. The skin between her brow wrinkles. "He needs more help than I can give him, Cal."

More help than she can give.

I stuff the worry rising in my chest back down and out of sight where it belongs. "After Sephrim's initiation, I thought for sure he would die. Daniel did a lot. Iced bruises, stitched up cuts, bandaged broken bones, but then we had to wait. I sat beside Sephrim in the railroad car for so long. Checking his breathing, pinching myself when I got sleepy, trying to keep up with his Slinger tracking on the wall…

"Every three thousand six hundredth tick of my

watch, I'd prop him up, try to get water into his mouth. He coughed up most of it. All red. Whenever he got too still, I had to talk myself out of dragging him to the nearest healing tube... But even if I could've gotten him there without being seen by Slingers, any place with a healing tube would have too many cameras. I couldn't let that doctor get him again..."

Now, in the tiny bedroom at the back of Cade's, the desperate temptation tugs me again. A healing tube would put his broken pieces all back together so fast. Seal up his lung, numb his pain, but it might also throw him back into Dr. Troy's hands. A fate worse than drowning in blood.

Across the room, Sephrim tosses in his sleep. His face contorts, and I sit up.

"There has to be something. In all his years of criminaling, your father never stole a healing tube, did he?"

Darby grins.

"What?"

"Nothing. It's just funny to hear a girl who defines everything make up words." She chuckles.

"When you know the rules, you can break them."

"Makes sense."

"So about a healing tube—"

"No." She shakes her head. "At least, not that I know of. But I can ask tomorrow. Because you're right, he needs one." She looks at Sephrim, then crawls to the other side of the couch and brushes the hair from his damp brow. Blood flushes his cheeks.

"Would Hellen have one?"

A loony idea considering her complete lack of care for the health and welfare of others. But since Hellen plans for everything, it might not be totally out of the realm of possibility.

One of Darby's hands curls into a fist. "Maybe. Matty would know. Even if she does, there's no way we could use it. For one thing, it takes a few hours for them to heal broken bones, not to mention the fact that my mother would never voluntarily allow him to use it. We're just going to have to wait for him to heal. And he will. I promise." She purses her lips, then says, "Better get to bed. We've got a lot to do tomorrow."

I dread sleep. Nightmares wait behind closed lids. But the need to shut down weighs on me like thick car exhaust. I curl around a pillow, squeezing my eyes shut and tucking my thumbs into my fists. This might keep memories at bay.

It doesn't.

As before, the hands lower the stuffed animal through fog. Again, that spicy, sweet smell tickles my nose, again I reach, and again I fail. Blood comes next, the new memory splattering across the old one, horror driving away comfort: Alura, the Slingers, Darby…all people the chip made me hurt.

****

Darby

Finally.

After so many years of waiting seized up in fear, I have a solid plan to save Matty. Countless times I've argued with my father and Felix about getting him away from Hellen, and countless times they've brushed me off, saying it might start an unnecessary street war. Three years ago, I got fed up with their excuses and made a rescue attempt alone. Hellen caught me and made me watch her punish Matty for my infraction.

I've been too terrified to try again. Now, with Sephrim and Cal's help, I might stand a chance. *Might*. That chip is unpredictable. Yes, we think we know how to shut it down, but Hellen never leaves anything to chance. What if she turns Cal against us? Or worse?

I stab my fingers into my ponytail. Every time Sephrim groans or whimpers or grimaces, I wince. Long after Cal mumbles herself into unconsciousness— defining words with astonishing accuracy considering her exhaustion—I sit on the arm of the couch watching both Designer Kids sleep. One curls tightly in on herself, still as a corpse. The other never settles.

Almost imperceptibly, Sephrim twitches and adjusts and lets out soft grunts when his ribs ache. The more he shifts, the more sweat litters his brow and soaks the collar of his shirt. But in spite of his pain, he never wakes up. He continues to toss, unable to still for longer than a few moments.

But Felix is right. Sephrim really is beautiful, eerily so.

Tension strangles my lungs. Carefully, I crawl onto the bed behind him. As gently as I can, I wrap an arm around his middle to hold him steady. Maybe I can give him a few hours' peace.

He flinches. Every muscle along his back balls up against my chest and stomach. "Darby?" he asks quietly. Fearfully?

"You okay?"

He sniffs and relaxes. "Better now. Thanks." Blood stains the back of his neck as he blushes.

"Sure." I pull him closer. "I used to do the same thing for Matt when he had nightmares. Doubt anyone does that for him anymore."

Sadness pulls at the corners of my mouth, and my throat constricts.

Images from childhood, from the short time our family lived under the same roof, flit through my head. Through our shared wall, I often heard Matty whimpering after a rough encounter with either one of our parents. I'd creep down the hallway and into his room, holding him until he finally stopped shaking.

"When did your mom take him?" Sephrim asks. The question comes out light and halting, like an afterthought delayed by exhaustion.

I rub his bare arm, surprised at the softness of his skin considering his time spent on the street. "Matty was six. I was nine. One night, she and my dad had this fight to end all fights. Something about the way they wanted to run things, I think." I chew the side of my tongue. "Matty and I were hiding at the top of the stairs. I'd tried to get him to go back to his room, but he wouldn't budge. Just kept holding on to the banister. Finally, my mom said she'd had enough and was going to…'accomplish her vision' on her own. Or something like that. She stormed up to the second floor and…" Again, my throat muscles crush the words as I relive the memory.

As Hellen's boots rattle the staircase, I grip Matty under the armpits, trying to drag him back. In white-knuckled fear, he clings to the railing. Hellen reaches the top. He lets out a whimper. Our mother glares down at us both, then seizes Matty's wrist and wrenches him to his feet. The whimper morphs into a strangled cry.

"Mom, please." I scramble forward. "Leave—"

The back of Hellen's hand makes contact with the side of my face. Her ring slices into my cheek. I stumble blindly into the wall. One hand pressed into the floor, I fist away tears and squint down the hallway at my mother's retreating back. Matty stumbles along at her side. His socked feet slip on the slick floor.

With a gulp, I stand, but a hand on my shoulder holds me in place. I look up to meet Felix's then-hazel eyes.

Brow furrowed, he shakes his head. "Leave it. If she wants him, let her take him. You can't win against her. Even Dad can't."

"I just stood there," I say. "Watched my mom make him pack his little blue backpack and haul him out the front door. He was too scared to even say anything." Thick saliva coats my words. I swallow, but it sticks in my throat.

"Did your dad not try to stop her?"

"No. He just stood there, watching, drinking his bourbon."

Sephrim's fingers thread through mine, rough and clammy but pleasant just the same. "Your dad should've done something."

"He was just as bad." I wrinkle my nose. "Hit Matty as often as Mom did, called him weak and worthless… I should've run away with him when I had the chance."

"You were just a kid."

"How old were you when you and Cal ran?"

His grip tightens. "Ten. Cal was eight."

I trace his knuckles with my thumb. "*You* were just a kid."

"It's not the same."

"Isn't it?"

He doesn't answer. Instead, he presses a soft kiss to my knuckles, then rests our intertwined hands back on the bed. Warmth spreads through my stomach at his tender touch. I long for more. How would it feel to have him kiss my arm? My cheek? My lips? Heat rushes to my face.

Thank the universe he can't see into my head.

A shiver jitters through his body, and I give his shoulder a little tug. Gingerly, he rolls over. In this small space, nose to nose, our breath mingles together. After two encounters with Slingers, he smells faintly of singed hair. Just under this hovers the scent of government-grade soap, fresh grass, and car grease. I inhale deeply, pulling the scent into my lungs.

It burns there, soaking my senses, reminding me of all the different parts of this beautiful, broken boy. Like Matty, he deserves to be taken care of, not tossed around and used like a lifeless machine. No matter what they do, people stay the same. Nobody changes. The world's screwy, and time races on and keeps slipping away, and we might die facing Hellen or worse and…

And to hell with decorum. Lifting my chin, I brush my lips against his. Soft and warm and a little chapped, they don't move at first. Fear freezes my insides. What if he doesn't want this? What if I misread all of the things? What if—

He kisses me back.

Hesitant, careful, slow, and everything I would've expected from him. All the stars in existence march together in perfect sync. Something hot and obscenely pleasant burns through my gut and right on downward. It forces a funny low sound out of the back of my throat. I brush the tips of my fingers along his jaw and scoot closer. When he laces an arm around my waist, I about turn to complete and utter nonsensical mush.

Should I… What the hell, why not? Slowly, gently, I part his lips with the very tip of my tongue and find his. It flinches back, then brushes forward to meet mine, oddly sweet. And absolutely perfect. I arch into him.

Then he breaks contact and presses his forehead to mine. His breath comes out all shaky and shallow, and he chuckles. "Sorry, I…" He sighs through his nose. "Sorry…"

I run a thumb over his cheek. "It's okay. Really, it's okay."

"That bad, huh? To be fair I don't have much experience."

I laugh. "Stop that. You were perfect." I wrap my arms around his waist and snuggle my head under his chin. "And you'll get better with practice."

He snorts. "Maybe we'll have time for that after we save Matt."

"Yeah. After we save Matty." I smile against his neck, then quietly sing, "Twinkle, twinkle little star…"

Chapter Thirty-Two

Cal

I thrash awake. Biting into my forearm to stifle a terrified scream, I stare across the room at the other bed.

Empty.

I glance at my arm. Teeth marks imprint themselves into my skin, but no blood wells from the indentations. Progress. Sliding off the bed, I pad into the second room. Sephrim lies on a blanket on the floor, one arm draped over his eyes, mouth twisted in pain as Darby scans his bruised ribs with her portable digital imager.

I pause to watch the screen on the tiny machine. Though I don't know much about reading digital images, Darby's pursed lips make the results pretty clear.

Worry winds tight around my throat, but I still plaster on a make-believe smile. "Seph, you need to stop ramming your ribs into people's fists and feet."

Under the shadow of his arm, he grins. "I knew I was doing something wrong with my life." A cough produces a thin layer of blood on his lips. "Not gonna make me sit out of the mission, are you? Don't know if you noticed, but I'm pretty good at picking locks."

I want to tie him to the bed and never let him go anywhere ever again. If he doesn't face sadistic lunatics, logic dictates he won't get beat up anymore. Do I think he'll listen if I try to put him up on blocks?

Nope.

Hands on my knees, I blow a raspberry. "You're as stubborn as a rusty gear shift. Doubt I could talk you out of it if I tried."

A *bing* at his side makes us all jump. Arm still over his face, he pulls the mini net board from his tool belt and hands it to me. "News alert."

I drag the blinking icon up so the image spreads across the wall above the kitchen table. A podium appears with Dr. Troy behind it. I rock and land on my backside. My lips move without sound. *Evil. Adjective, morally wrong or bad, immoral, wicked.*

New lines sprout from the corners of Dr. Troy's eyes, and when she speaks, I can't help but want to clear my own throat.

"Last night, in an effort to retrieve three of our runaway Designer Children, a taskforce of Slingers and I were attacked. Our aggressor, a runaway Designer Child himself, has taken up with criminals. He is proof of the corrupting power of the streets and of the desperate need for the reforms I advocate."

Sephrim gags and pulls his arm farther over his face.

"Soon," Dr. Troy continues, "world scientists will meet once again. This new phase in our nation's history is an opportunity. An opportunity to change our society for the better. That is why I am asking you, the citizens of this great nation, to vote yes on propositions six, twenty-two, and fifteen in the coming days. Thank you."

A police alert follows the broadcast. Sephrim's face pops up on the screen, and I splutter. "Where the heck did they get that picture?"

Though in the grainy image he wears his hood, whatever camera caught him snagged just the right angle. It looks recent. As if Dr. Troy's evil plans aren't enough, now my best friend's face is all over the news. I drag my lower lip between my teeth, worry gnawing my gut. Terrible timing just before our super-secret mission.

Sephrim peeks out from under his elbow and grimaces. "Looks like some terrible security camera still. Wonder where I messed up."

"Can't tell much from the background." Darby rubs his shoulder. "But don't feel bad. You were already an outlaw. It's just official now."

Hugging my knees, I study the picture. "I bet Matt could wipe that from the public record. Like he did for your parents."

"You're right. He definitely could." Darby tugs at the end of her braid.

"He can't erase me from public memory. Besides, right now his priority should be disabling that chip," Sephrim says. "And we need—"

Lifting a hand, I cut him off. "We need you to rest because in a few days you're going to have to help us break into Hellen's and save Matt." I grin and push up onto the balls of my feet. "Time for some breakfast, huh?"

A knock shatters my calm, and I wobble. I frown at Seph and Darby, then straighten. Darby grabs my wrist. A digital screen on the door lights up. Felix's face appears, and my stomach cranks. I swallow. How bad would it be if I ignored him? I could pretend to be asleep.

Darby makes the decision for me. Hand still closed around my wrist, she stands. "Wait here. I'll see what he wants. Stay with Sephrim." With a squeeze, she crosses to the door. She doesn't even open it a full inch. "Can we help you with something, big brother?"

Through the tiny crack, I see Felix smirk. Who would want white eyes? Honestly. And he calls us freaks. What's that old saying? Something about boards and dust? Planks and crumbs? People who rage the most about the weirdness of others usually have heaps of their own weirdness hidden in a dark corner somewhere.

I press the bottom of one foot into the top of the other as Felix finally speaks. "Indeed you can, Sister dear." He tilts a little to aim an eye past her shoulder. "We have a job that requires chip girl's unique skills. Might I come in?"

He says it like a request, but I know better. Felix Cade doesn't make requests.

"As long as you promise to behave," Darby says. "Remember, Sephrim and Cal are under Father's protection."

The smirk widens. "So long as they hold up their end of the bargain, that is."

One boot pinned to the corner of the door, Darby crosses her arms. "Worry about your own damn self. Do you promise or not?"

"If it makes you feel better, then of course. You have my word."

Behind me, Sephrim makes a funny noise. A cross between a choke and a laugh.

I sink down next to him. "Okay, Sephy?" I ask as loud as I dare.

As Felix steps past Darby, Sephrim peeks at me from under the arm still over his eyes. "Sure. So long as he doesn't decide to tap dance on my sternum, this should go pretty well."

I giggle.

Then a shadow falls across us, and creepy-crawlies

inch up my back.

"Creepy," I say in a whisper. "Adjective. Having or causing a creeping sensation of the skin, as from horror or fear." I sweep my hands wide for Felix. "Welcome to our humble abode. How can we help you today?"

Felix's smirk broadens into a full-on grin. "I see you share…Sephrim's wit."

"Nah, she's way funnier than me." Seph lets his arm fall back over his eyes. "Smarter, too."

Heat rushes to my face. Like a normal older brother, he thinks too much of me and too little of himself. One thing's for sure, though. I won't let Felix wound him anymore. I stand and roll both shoulders back. At my full height, I don't even sort of reach Felix's shoulder, but I lift my chin to better meet his gaze, fists on my hips.

"Marcus said you'd only use me if—" I cock my head. "Strictly necessary. What world-ender do you need me for?"

"So bold." Felix sinks into a crouch next to us. "Considering…" He lets the sentence hang, trailing a finger along Seph's jaw.

Tension coils up Sephrim's arm. He pinches his lips together until every last drop of color bleeds out. I grind my back teeth, digging my nails into my palms as two words echo in my brain, danger and *kill*. I'll cut his hand off and feed it to sewer rats. Or maybe one finger at a time and make him watch them make a meal of it.

Still by the door, Darby lets out a quiet growl, a sound like an engine revving. Her upper lip curls into a sneer as both hands ball into fists. A corner of Felix's mouth hitches up, and he grazes his knuckle down Sephrim's neck.

Logic tackles my brain. I take a breath, then let it out

slow. "Considering the fact that you apparently need me and that I can turn myself into a brutal assassin with a single word? Yeah. I'm going with bold. Unless this comes straight from Marcus, I'm out."

Bold. Adjective. Not hesitating or fearful in the face of actual or possible danger or rebuff, courageous and daring. A bead of sweat slides down my spine. I'll destroy Felix. Tear him into a million tiny parts even a healing tube couldn't screw back together.

Felix's smile jerks, then solidifies. "I knew I liked you." Hands up, he stands and steps back. "A request, then?"

"I'll think about it." *For two seconds, then ignore it, you asshat.*

Felix glances at Darby. "This does not come directly from our father, but it does relate to him." He rubs his chin. "Marcus is perfectly happy with how things are and doesn't care what happens with the reconfiguration of the United Nations. Quite frankly, he doesn't believe it will change much. I, however, do not share his…optimism. Idealism? Either way."

"Do get to the point, Brother." Darby's eyes darken with anger, and she moves away from the door and places herself between Sephrim and Felix.

"Surely, you've seen the press conferences." Felix's gaze drifts from me back to Sephrim. They have a tendency to always return there. Hungry.

I want to dig those cursed white eyes out of his skull.

"Yes, they're horrifying," I say. "What's your point? You want me up on a roof with a sniper rifle? Murdering all those dignitaries?"

"Of course not." Felix waves a hand, still focused on Sephrim. "The doctors are the ones truly causing problems. On that, I'm sure we can agree. My request"—his upper lip curls on the word—"is that you cut the problem off at the source."

"You mean…" I glance down at Sephrim. "You mean kill the doctors?"

Though the idea makes me sick, I've definitely thought about it before. As a kid, when the doctors and lab techs alike poked and prodded and stared, I thought about how glorious it would be if they weren't around. How freeing it would be to no longer have their eyes like X-rays on me.

I never really considered killing them, but I knew life would be easier if they stopped existing. Now I wonder how much easier many lives would be without them, not just my own. Is that the answer?

"Not all of them," Felix says. "Only the ones you know will perpetuate the most damage. The most dangerous leaders. Consider it. You could be a revolutionary, free others like yourself, like him." He gestures to Sephrim, who snorts at the end of Felix's speech.

"Right," Sephrim says. "That'll solve all our problems. Because nothing says, 'Hey, we're not dangerous; we deserve to be treated with equality and respect,' like murder."

I scratch my chin. "Seph's got a point. Murdering them will only make things worse. Especially if it's done violently, which is the only kind of killing the chip knows anything about."

"Not if it's pinned on someone else," Felix says. "Diverting blame is an easy thing. We're quite good at it."

Pressing my tongue against the backs of my teeth, I

turn this over in my head. With Dr. Troy out of the way, Dr. Gayle could take charge, influence the scientists of the world in favor of the Designer Kids. And she could protect the ones whose time runs out. Change the system for good.

But.

But why does Felix care about any of this? From the little I know about him, he only cares about one thing—expanding his empire. How does killing Designer Kid doctors come into play? A few days ago, he ordered my execution. Now he wants my help? That doesn't make sense. I need more information.

I glare. "Why do you want them dead, anyway?"

"I've read a great majority of the propositions the doctors wish to pass," Felix says, an odd glimmer in his eye. "Each will, in one way or another, interrupt our business. While we can certainly adapt, it's far more ideal that things remain as they are. You understand."

Of course, it has something to do with that. In spite of his vagueness, it makes a certain amount of sense. To a point, Designer Kids are property, product. If that's tampered with, it might interrupt some aspect of the many lines of Felix's trade. What that means exactly, I don't know, but I will find out.

Later.

For now, I need to delay, if at all possible. "No, that would just turn them into martyrs. There has to be a better way to stop them."

Felix's nostrils flare, and for the first time in a while, he tears his gaze from Sephrim to meet mine. "Don't give me your answer now," he says, jaw tight around the words. "Give it some consideration. I'll be back tomorrow when you've had time to think about the consequences." With a final glance at Sephrim, he shoulders between me and Darby and slips back through the door.

All my energy fizzles, and I sink down next to Seph. Forehead on my knees, I let out a groan. "Is he crazy? I thought I was supposed to be the crazy one. Only enough room for one of us around here. His plan is loony-patoony. Right?"

Sephrim's fingers loop through mine. I peek at him between my curls. He still has one arm over his face, but it rests on his forehead now so he can make eye contact. He smiles. "Yeah, he's crazy, or at least acting like it. Feels trap-like."

Darby squats on his other side, one hand tangled in her hair. "I'll see if I can find out more." She scoops up the wires of her digital imager. "Let me do some snooping, buy us some time. I'll be back a little later. Sephrim, try not to move too much. Those ribs need a rest." Darby kisses his cheek, stands, and follows Felix's path out the door.

It clicks shut behind her, and I curl up beside Sephrim, head propped on one arm, the other looped around his waist. So much hangs over us, teeters on an invisible ledge, but at least, for a little bit, I can hang on to something solid and ignore the tug of dread that'll eventually drag me into oblivion. That doesn't mean I can't fulfill my duties as a pseudo-kid sister.

"She likes you." I elongate the "i" until a giggle cuts it off.

He snorts and turns red. Like. Bright red. "Shut up."

"Awww, and you like her too!" My voice squeaks.

"Shu-ut up." Sephrim folds a hand over my mouth and pulls me closer. "But yeah…I kind of do. And don't worry. She'll take care of this. We're safe with her on our side."

Chapter Thirty-Three

Darby

I step out of Cade's and into the rain, soaked almost immediately. It drips off my lashes and into my eyes. Lightning fills pockets in the clouds above. Thunder rattles the gated entrance. The distinct smell of wet concrete saturates the air.

I shiver. Sniff. Wait. Pace.

On my third loop up and down the sidewalk, Felix appears at the entrance. He stops near the edge of the wall of rain with his arms crossed over his chest. Each time lightning rends the sky, it lights his eyes with a sickening glow and casts shadows over his mouth. It gives him the terrifying appearance of a ghoul.

Cracking my knuckles, I glare at him. "What's your play, Felix?"

"Why, Darby, whatever—"

"Save it. I'm not stupid. What are you trying to do, asking that girl to kill those doctors? And don't tell me it's because you care about the Designer Kids, because I know that's not true."

He grins, a mischievous echo of his former self, before Marcus twisted and bent him, before he rebelled against our mother and started his own criminal business. Though once I might have trusted him, I now question his every motive.

"Of course I care about Designer Children," he says. "They're highly trained, expendable labor. If that doctor has her way, very few will be left on the streets for my use."

"And if the other doctor has *her* say, there may not be any on the streets at all," I say. "Or if they are, my guess is they won't be highly trained anymore. I doubt very seriously this is something you haven't considered. What is your play?"

The gate trembles again as thunder punctures the atmosphere and the rain thickens. It mats my hair to the sides of my forehead. I step closer. My boots kick up water.

Felix wiggles his brows. "What do I always say, little sister?"

My jaw clicks as I grind my back teeth together. I let a breath out through my nose. "Always keep a stash of ammo hidden."

Felix came up with that phrase a year or two into his life as a crime lord. He pretends to operate on transparency, verbalizing every plan to his inner circle, but in reality, he always has an angle buttoned up in a pocket. That way no one could ever really foil his plans. Felix always has an out.

"That's my girl. Now don't worry yourself about it." He runs the tip of his thumb over his bottom lip. "Despite what you might think, I don't hate Designer Children, and my plan will make things better for everyone. Just trust me."

"Trust you?" A squeak steals the threat from my voice. "Why the hell should I trust you, Felix?"

"Because I'm going to get our little brother back."

Lightning whitens the world around me, and thunder

erases my initial response. I gape. "What do you mean?"

He jerks his chin up and to the right. Irritation coils through my midsection like a live wire ready to fry an unsuspecting victim, but I turn to look in the direction he indicated. Hellen stands a few feet away. Rain drips from a bright-red umbrella like a curtain of lace across her stony features.

"Hello, dear. We have something very important to discuss."

I lock my arms together and grind my boots into the cement. "No, we don't."

Muffled screams of pain brutalize the silence and carve terror into my chest, spreading ice-cold fear throughout my body. Hellen lifts a small screen from the dark fold of her coat. A video plays on its smooth surface, the violence of which shuts off my windpipe with the same effectiveness of an unforgiving hand.

Hellen takes another step forward. "Yes. We do."

****

Sephrim

A buzz vibrates the floor under my head. It drags me from my half-sleep, and I peel my eyes open. Not long after Darby left, Cal decided to take a shower. Very little time must've passed, because the water's still running in the other room.

I stifle a yawn and pick up my net board. Darby's name blinks across the screen. Weird. Why wouldn't she just come back down? I shrug and hit the answer button. "Hey, what's—"

The look on her face stops me midway through my sentence. Dripping wet and tight-lipped, she looks at something below the screen. Makeup streaks out from the corners of her eyes and smears across both cheeks. Her nostrils flare.

"We need to meet, but not at Cade's," she says. "I found out what's going on with Felix. It'll be better if Cal doesn't hear."

One elbow on the ground, I push myself up and throw a nervous glance at the door to the bathroom. The shower keeps running. "Where do you want to meet? Sam's?"

Silence.

"Darby."

Were it not for the sound of her heavy breathing, the image on the screen might have been nothing more than a picture. Words lie heavy at the edge of my tongue. I hold them there, though every fiber of every muscle, every sinew, burns with an unsettled energy. Three or four questions flit through my brain before Darby finally responds.

Her eyes jerk back and forth, still aimed down, then she nods. "Sam's is fine. Come as soon as you can. Meet me on the roof." She ends the call.

I stare at the black screen. The roof? This coming from the girl terrified of heights? A cold ball of dread forms in my stomach and rolls into my chest. She looked scared, sick. What could she have possibly found out that would shake her so badly? The one and only time I'd ever seen her so frightened was when we confronted Hellen.

With much groaning and gnashing of teeth, I push myself off the floor and ease into my hoodie. "Cal, I'll be back in a bit," I call into the bathroom. "I'll have the net board if you need me."

"You're broken. You shouldn't be going

anywhere."

I chuckle. "I'm not that broken. And I shouldn't be gone long. I'll be careful. Promise."

"Okay, but try not to get more broken if you can possibly avoid it, huh?"

****

I wind through the city soaked in the smell of wet earth. Though I mainly stick to the tunnels, I come up near the garage to check in with Daniel. This time, I'm extra careful to look out for cameras or patrolling Slingers when I push open the sewer lid. My initial scan comes up clear, so I climb the rest of the way out and head to the back door. Faint sunlight peeks through the fast-moving clouds, but it doesn't have much chance to warm the cold humidity. My hand slips on the doorknob.

Locked.

Weird. Daniel never closes up during business hours. I frown and knock. On the street at the other end of the alley, cars rush by, scattering water in every direction. A few birds gather near the steps. They splash in the dirty puddles and ruffle their feathers.

The door opens.

The birds scatter.

I flinch back when one of Daniel's mechanics, a woman named Lex, peers out. Grease smudges one corner of her chin, and a grimace warps her face.

"You." She says the word in a snarl and tightens her grip on the wrench in her hand.

Weird reaction. Lex's never acted real friendly around me, but she's never been antagonistic. I take a backward step. "Is Daniel here?"

Lex's brows smash together. "No. Daniel was arrested. Thanks to you."

The cold ball in my sternum plummets. A loud hum replaces the sounds of the city. I don't need any clarification. Last night at Sam's, Dr. Troy saw Daniel. She must have come after him. Lex is right. This is my fault. If only I'd gone down to the basement like he told me to, this wouldn't have happened.

Back teeth clamped together, I shake my head. Lex is speaking again, and I have to fight to hear her past the roar in my ears.

"…away in handcuffs this morning, while he was packing up to go underground because he blew his cover helping those stupid kids. Damn fool refused to tell them where the runaways were all hiding. But I bet if they got one, they might be willing to let him go."

She lifts her wrench, and I barely block the blow with a forearm. It comes within inches of my head, a terrible defense that sends vibrations down my shoulder and into my battered rib cage. I kick her squarely in the stomach. She stumbles back with a loud grunt.

I shove the door shut and sprint for the sewer without looking back. I run as fast as I dare along the slick ledge, guilt crushing my lungs. My throat collapses in on itself. It chokes out every thin gasp and clouds my head. By the time I reach the manhole closest to Sam's, black spots bubble across my vision.

Both hands pressed into the cold wall, I rest my forehead between them. If I want to help Daniel, I'll have to calm down. He needs me. Darby and Cal need me. Those Designer Kids all need me. And I won't do them any good if I pass out inside the sewer.

When my head stops floating so badly, I climb back out into the damp and the cold. Thick drops of rain hit the ground in mini explosions as I jog toward Sam's.

Small crowds of patrons mill about the front, but no one looks at me. I skirt to the back and find the ladder to the roof.

My ribs burn as I climb. With each rung, I repeat the names of the people counting on me: Darby, Daniel, Cal...Gabe, Lailah, Zad. At the top, I find only a smoking chimney. I frown. Again, weird. Maybe she chickened out and couldn't make it to the top. I glance at the screen in my pocket. No calls.

Arms wrapped around my aching middle, I walk the perimeter. Maybe she's in more trouble than I thought. Maybe she's gotten arrested too.

Maybe anxiety's making me spiral.

I sit on the edge of the roof, legs dangling. I'll wait, at least for a little while. If I leave too soon, I might miss her. Besides, this will give me time to get my breathing under control. I press my palms into the cinder blocks and stare into the blue-black clouds.

They fold together on the horizon. Laced with threads of white lightning, they creep forward like a slow-moving oil spill. Gusts of frigid wind wail from the approaching storm, and drops of rain pelt my face. A flock of birds calls out warnings overhead as they flee in the opposite direction.

I shiver.

A click comes from behind, and I flinch. The distinctive feeling of the barrel of a gun presses into my back between my shoulder blades. All the air evaporates from my lungs as Darby says in a shaky whisper, "Don't move."

I dig my fingers into the cinder block. "What are you doing?"

"I'm sorry." Her voice trembles. "I really am. But

my mom made me a promise…"

"What promise?" The roof rocks, and the names repeat again in my head: Daniel, Cal, Gabe, Lailah, Zad… "Was it about Matt?"

She sniffs. "My mom found out you're the only person who can shut Cal down. She'll let Matty go if you're out of the way… I'm sorry."

The barrel of the gun shakes. My pulse throbs against my temples. If I turn fast enough, I might be able to get the weapon, talk some sense into her. We can save Matt without Hellen's permission. But if I don't move fast enough…

"Darby…"

The bottom of a boot presses into my back. A heavy shove launches me into the open air. For one chest-tightened moment, I hang suspended above the cracked cement.

Daniel, Cal, Gabe, Lailah, Zad, Matt…Darby.

Lightning electrocutes the sky, gravity wraps its strong hands around me, and I drop.

Chapter Thirty-Four

Darby

The thud goes off as loud as a gunshot in my ears. It slams into me so hard I stumble backward. Numb, I grip the roof and stare at the body on the ground. Small rivulets of blood seep out around Sephrim's head, black against the concrete. It creeps along to fill the cracks, both manmade and accidental, and soaks the hoodie he wears, always wears. I imagine the internal bleeding. Broken bones. Pierced organs. Remember that kiss…

An agonized scream builds in my chest as I grip the handle of the gun, but I choke it back down. Why hasn't anyone noticed yet? Called an ambulance? How could the crowd at the front of Sam's not have heard such a loud, soul-rending sound? A sob racks my body, and I sprint to the ladder, scrambling to the street below as fast as my slick boots can carry me. I slide to a stop next to him. My fingers shake when I press them into his throat.

I hold my breath. At first, I don't feel anything. Still. Silent. Dead? Another sob cracks my chest. Like a fatal poison, guilt slithers through every vein, torching its way to my heart. While working for Felix, I've killed so many people, and after the first one, I never let it hurt. Learning to harden myself like a stone, I recited their wrongs as I pumped them with drugs, covered their faces with pillows, or nudged them down the stairs.

Now, touching the cold skin of the boy I'm falling for, they all come back to me, a mass of hard-faced accusers.

Then I feel it, a faint, frail beat against my skin. Tears light the backs of my eyes on fire. There's a chance. With shaking hands, I pull out my mini net board and punch in 911. A healing tube can save him. It *has* to save him. And maybe this will buy me time to get Matty out before Hellen realizes my betrayal. Maybe my plan has, in fact, worked.

The moment I end the call, I sprint into the dark toward Hellen's. By the time I reach the complex, the rain is pounding again. It drums into my skull like a million tiny judges' gavels. A rat. Worse than a rat. The lowest of low scum that exists on the planet. I duck under the overhang and press my palm into the scanner. An electronic voice speaks immediately.

"Welcome, Darby, you are expected."

With a click the door opens. I take a measured breath to calm myself, choke down another wail of pain, and wipe my face. Shield up but slowly crumbling, I march inside. Keeping my hands lifted, I meet the guard at the end of the cold, gray hall. The short-haired woman barely glances at me before she presses a button.

"What is it, Brunwick?" Hellen's voice crackles over the speaker.

"Darby's here."

"Send her in but tell her to wait outside my office."

I swallow a growl. It settles into my back teeth as I brush past Brunwick and into the center of the compound. I don't look up at the bare, windowless walls of the cement rotunda. Hellen sees no point in the decorations and designs Marcus and Felix fawn over. If she can't use it, it has no place with her. She delights only in the beauty and art of weaponry.

Hellen doesn't even keep family pictures.

At my mom's office, a stark room in an obscure hallway, I slump against the wall and watch the people who occupy the compound rush about on various missions. Every step pounds in my ears, all mimicking the sound of Sephrim's body hitting the concrete. I harden my face to stone. A storm of agony rages under it.

Ten bands of Hellen's soldiers pass before I lose count. And when I lose count, thoughts poison my mind. Sephrim. The feeling of his fingers laced through mine, the memory of his smirk, the image of my gun between his shoulder blades, then my boot, then the resistance of his body when I shoved him off the roof. Bits of my last meal kick up into my esophagus. I double over, bent under the guilt.

Five people. In the three years I've worked for my brother, I killed five people. Two women, three men. The first hit brought nightmares with it, the second insomnia, but by the third I'd learned to numb myself.

If Sephrim doesn't survive…

"Oh, suck it up, dear. You know how I feel about signs of weakness."

Teeth clenched, I straighten. "Yes, ma'am."

Hellen stands next to her office door, hands on her hips. "It's done, then? Confirmed?"

"He's out of the way." My head pounds. As long as Hellen believes me, she'll let Matty go. "Now what about our deal?"

Arms crossing, Hellen flutters her lashes as if confused. "And what deal is that?"

Anger blisters my chest. Against my self-control, I grimace. "I thought Felix was the one who played games. You know what deal I mean. Sephrim's out of the way, you're about to have Cal, and I'm taking Matty."

"Are you now?" Her eyes narrow, and she steps forward.

Fear douses the fury in my lungs, and my shoulders crumple inward. I try to find my voice, but it sticks in my throat. A child again, I melt, unable to stand up to my mother, unable to save my brother. And Sephrim died for nothing... I killed him for nothing. Not only scum, but stupid and foolish and easily manipulated. My gaze drops. I blink rapidly to hold back the tears.

"That's what I thought." Hellen sighs. "Maybe I would have honored our bargain, but as you failed to complete your task, I don't see how I can."

My gaze snaps up. "What?"

"Do you honestly think I wouldn't have you watched to be sure the deed was done to my liking? I know what you did."

Legs shaking, I stumble backward. How? How could I have been so stupid? I know my mother, know her paranoia, her precision, her cruelty, and I *should* have known Hellen would never keep the promise she gave.

"Now, you'll either help me, or you'll leave, but either way, your brother isn't going anywhere. I still need him. Together we're going to change the world." Patting me on the chin, Hellen turns and disappears into her office.

Chapter Thirty-Five

Cal

I can't figure out what to do with myself when I get out of the shower. First, I pace, which gets insanely boring after about three treks between the dismantled stove and the bedroom. So instead, I go against my better judgment and fish the other net board from under the couch. Though the news will probably stress me out, curiosity eventually wins. I slide the feed off the screen and up onto the wall.

It snaps, crackles, and pops to life. A reporter with salon-perfect curls and blue-rimmed glasses stands in front of the platform where, soon, the United Nations will meet for the first time in fifteen years. Crowds press into the fence behind the reporter. Some wave at the camera, while others thrust signs into the air and mouth what I can only imagine are profanities.

"Profanity," I say in a mumble as I cross my legs. "Noun. Profane conduct or language, a profane act or utterance. 'Profanity and obscenity entitle people who don't want unpleasant information to close their ears and eyes to you.' Kurt Vonnegut Jr., boys and girls." I blow a raspberry at the screen.

"This will be a historic event that will likely lead to a number of changes in our country," the reporter says. "Now over to Janey Pierce for local news."

The screen switches locations. "Thank you, Laura. I'm here in front of Sam's, a local bar where this evening a young man either jumped or was pushed from the roof."

I drop the board.

"Around five this evening, witnesses saw him fall and land near the back. The strangest part of this case is that his ID chip did not register on the scanners. However, his diagnostics confirmed that he is Sephrim, the runaway Designer Kid who—"

All the power in the room goes out in a loud pop. I gasp in total shock. Sephrim. Someone pushed Sephrim off a roof. Where is he? Did they take him to the hospital? Is he even still alive? Who pushed him?

Before I can process the answers to these questions, the door busts open. I wheel around to face it, ready for a fight. Blue Taser light arches across the room and slams into my chest. My body jerks—head bouncing against the floor—then goes completely limp.

Stun. Verb. To deprive of consciousness or strength by or as if by a blow, fall, etc.

In the pitch black, I can't see who grabs me, but I recognize Felix's cologne. He hauls me over one shoulder and strolls out of the room. All around, the crowd shouts in panic. Blue-white pricks of light flick on as people use flashlights to try to see where they're going.

Then, just as when Matt helped me escape, feeling jolts through me. I bring a knee hard into Felix's stomach. With a loud grunt, he jerks forward, and my feet touch the floor. I wrench an arm against his neck, grip his shoulder, and drive my knee into his midsection again. He slumps to the ground. I aim a kick to his skull, then run toward the tunnel entrance.

I have to find Seph. Figure out what happened to him. Maybe he survived that fall. I've never seen Sam's, but it can't be that tall of a building. Maybe they took him to the hospital and stuffed him in a healing tube. I don't even care about the danger now. I'll break him out if I have to. Use the chip to fight through anyone in my way.

He can't be dead.

Close to the end of the tunnel, the rain erases all other sounds. I see only darkness when I look over my shoulder. Good. My attack must've at least stunned Felix. Even a barefoot blow can do that.

I sprint through the wall of rain. Blinded for a moment, I don't see the arm shoot out in front of me in time to duck. It knocks me backward. I land hard. The world spins, and rain pools thick around my body like blood.

Hellen leans into my dimming vision, protected from the deluge by an umbrella. She smiles. "There you are, Little Shadow. We need to talk."

****

Pain digs in to the back of my neck, and something cold pinches feeling out of my hands and feet. What I hope is water drips from the ends of my hair, weighs down my overalls, and rolls off my nose. All around, unidentified instruments hum. Someone sniffs. I tense at the broken sound. It's definitely not the kind you get with a cold.

Scrunching my eyes shut tighter, I listen. Any information I can gather will help me prepare for the worst. I have to be at Hellen's, no doubt about that. The room smells of antiseptic and—like the first time—I'm restrained, but at least I'm not lying on my face.

It's the little things.

What else do I feel? Tile floor, metal chair, a new sting at the incision site. What else do I hear? Breathing. The sniffer. Matt maybe? Did Hellen find out he helped me? If she hurt him... Anger curls my hands into fists.

"Ah, she is awake."

Well, so much for extensive investigation. I lift my head to see Hellen and Matt at the other end of the lab. At first, I don't recognize Matt. Bruises and blood cover his face, his neck, every square inch of his skin. He sits on the floor, one arm at an odd angle cradled in the other, red-rimmed gaze on his bare feet. Hellen lounges in a chair about an inch away. Legs crossed, hands folded, she doesn't even acknowledge her son but focuses only on me.

She's smiling.

Smile. Verb. To assume a facial expression indicating pleasure, favor, or amusement, but sometimes derision or scorn, characterized by an upturning of the corners of the mouth.

I dig my nails into my palms. When I get free... I focus on Matt. Hellen doesn't deserve one second of my attention. "How's your garden?"

The trembling in his limbs comes to an abrupt halt, and he looks up, his one good eye even bluer in contrast to the black bruise surrounding it. Again, he sniffs. "Growing. Still have the flower I gave you?" His words slur a little, like maybe he's bitten his tongue.

I make a buzzing sound. "Never leave home without it."

Hellen rolls her eyes. "Not that this isn't just so sweet, but if you don't mind, we have more important things to discuss."

I mimic her movement. "Right. Your crazy-lution. Loony-lution. Not sure if there's much to say. All you have to do is take me to that meeting and set me off."

"Again, so smart and to the point."

"I wouldn't want to let you down."

"But you're wrong about one thing," she says. "We do have more to discuss, particularly in regard to the young man who seems to be able to shut off your chip."

My stomach twists in full-on terror. Sephrim. "How'd you know about that?" Last I heard, he'd fallen from a roof. Fallen or…

Hellen grips Matt by the hair. He winces and sniffs again, eye squeezed shut.

"He's quite helpful when he's properly motivated. Why don't you tell her how you let slip a teensy-weensy hint about where my little assassin was hiding? How you broke so damn easily? How you cried when I said I'd use the kill switch if you didn't tell me where she was?"

Fury-induced nausea floods my body, utter shock at Hellen's words. "You ordered a hit on Seph."

Hellen smirks. "I ordered a hit on him. I told Darby to shoot him, but blunt force trauma works just as well. Especially with all the other injuries he's accumulated over the last twenty-four hours. Now you can accomplish your mission, without distraction."

Everything inside me rusts and cracks to bits. Since I saw the news report, I've clung to the hope, the frail, brittle hope, that Sephrim might still be alive, preserved in a healing tube. With Hellen's confirmation, though, that once shiny hope turns to dust.

"I'm sorry, Cal," Matt says, voice thick. "I'm so sorry."

Somewhere, beyond the blare in my ears, I hear him, but I can't react through the numbness no matter how much I want to. Sephrim's gone, and nothing else matters.

Chapter Thirty-Six

Matt

A slip. Hellen called it a slip, but I have a super different word for what I did—betrayal. When my mom didn't find Cal in the false location I'd set up, she got suspicious. Though I'd changed the coordinates to make it look like the chip was moving, Hellen wouldn't accept what she saw. She started with the usual threats. Then came the blows. Finally, she threatened to use the kill switch if I didn't tell her where Cal was.

Out of pure terror, I told her what Cal's friend could do, hoping she'd take Sephrim too, lock him away somewhere. I figured I could help them escape again. I never imagined Hellen would have the guy killed. Or that she would force Darby to do it.

Stupid, *stupid* thought. Hellen never leaves anything to chance. No wonder I couldn't find out anything about her deeper reasons for attacking the New United Nations.

No matter how I plead, reason, beg, Hellen won't let me stay with Cal. After we told her about Sephrim's death, Mom locked me back in my room. Now I slump in the corner with my head propped against the wall again. With the computers all asleep, darkness presses in on me like a living thing. My face and arm throb. The room sways. Every tear stings on the way down.

None of that hurts in comparison to the way Cal

looked at me when she found out what I did. I failed. I promised I'd figure out how to disable the chip. Instead, I told my mom about Sephrim's effect on her. In spite of all my good intentions, Hellen still got her way. Why? Because she loves nothing and no one. She doesn't care about me or Darby or Felix or her own brother. She says she wants the best for the world but steps on people both in her way and out of it to reach her goals.

No more. I grit my teeth. Hellen made Darby kill Sephrim, but I'm not going to let her make Cal kill those dignitaries. And I'm done letting her control me. I'll stop it. I have to.

I force myself onto my knees. No chance of walking to my computers, so I'll crawl. Blood drips from the tip of my nose, splattering the stark white concrete like gory raindrops. Grabbing the edge of the desk with my good arm, I haul myself into the chair.

With trembling fingers, I pull up the code and type *SOS*.

The cursor blinks.

And blinks.

Blink.

Blink.

Blink.

Not good. Dr. Gayle doesn't always answer right away, but she normally answers pretty fast. Even if others are around, they won't understand the message alert as anything suspicious. If she can't answer in full that second, Dr. Gayle sends back some kind of punctuation to let me know she saw it.

I brace myself on an elbow. Blood smears the desk. My injured arm throbs. At least I can make all ten fingers work. Mostly. Paranoia sets in. With Cal captured,

Sephrim dead, and that garage owner, Mr. Todd, arrested, I can only think of worst case scenarios. I have to do something.

Toes curled into the cement floor, I glance at the door, then focus back on my computer. A few keystrokes break into the lab camera system. I scan the rooms and halls until I catch sight of Dr. Gayle next to a healing tube. I squint. My heart nearly busts out of my sternum.

Sephrim.

A pulse throbs in the cavity of his chest. It beats slowly, like the first steps of a race. *Thump, thump, thump…* Then it quickens, not quite to a sprint, but a strong, sort of irregular jog. It pumps the stagnant blood through his veins as the healing tube works, piecing him back together. I bite the end of my tongue, trying to remember how Dr. Gayle described the process, trying to remember how long it would take to fix Sephrim.

Six hours total. I squint at the numbers on the tube. Three have already passed. In just a few more, it will have Sephrim back in one piece. No longer all broken up inside. No longer in critical condition. Good news. News Cal needs to hear. I scowl at the guard standing at the lab door. I'll have to do something about that guy and the evil Dr. Troy who now complains loudly about "damaged product."

As she speaks, Dr. Gayle stares down at Sephrim, gripping the sides of her net board.

Glaring at the glass cover of the healing tube, Dr. Troy taps a nail against its metal base, her face contorted in fury. "This is why we need tighter restraints on those who have expired. If they remained under our supervision and went to the workhouses like they're supposed to rather than running away, things like this wouldn't happen. Now the state will have to spend thousands of dollars putting him back together. Far more than he's worth." She sneers. "I should have brought him in the moment I had him at that wretched bar."

A faint crack comes from Dr. Gayle's screen. "You are quite mistaken, Dr. Troy. This young man, and every child we bring into existence, is valuable, worth far more than money can measure. They should not be treated like lifeless products. They should be treated as what they are, children."

Dr. Troy rolls her eyes up to meet Dr. Gayle's, her lips a pallid, tight line. "You care very deeply for the Designer Children. So deeply, in fact, that you give yourself away."

"Give myself away?" Dr. Gayle lifts her brows.

Fear sparks through my chest. *Uh-oh.*

"I'm not sure I understand your meaning."

"Don't you?" Those nails tap the glass again. "I started monitoring your computer around the time the most recent batch was about to expire, and do you know what I found?"

"No, no, no…" My fingers hover over the keypad. It might be time to open up an escape route.

Dr. Gayle glances at Sephrim. His eyes shift under his lids as his chest rises and falls.

"Similar records to your own, I assume. Or perhaps conversations with my mother in Jamaica?"

"Oh, I certainly found records and conversations, most of them boring and mundane. But then I dug a little further and discovered conversations you were having with someone about blackouts and glitches. When I checked the times, it became quite clear. You have been stealing product and selling it to street criminals." Dr.

Troy smiles, the kind that only affects her lips and leaves her eyes alone.

I curse. She knows. If all my security precautions, all my precious code, failed to keep Dr. Troy in the dark about Dr. Gayle's activities, what else does she know? We don't keep records of the location of the freed Designer Children, but we do have records of businesses friendly to the cause. They arrested Daniel this morning, but what about Meg Sam?

Now they have evidence, and from Dr. Gayle's own computer. How? How did they get past my firewalls? How've I screwed up again? I clench my teeth and start to type, pulse impossibly loud in my ears.

"I assume by your silence you have no defense of your actions." Dr. Troy presses her hands into the glass case.

Dr. Gayle slides her net board into her pocket. "Defense? To the charge of releasing Designer Children before they are taken to be experimented upon at the workhouses, yes. I admit to that. I helped them escape in order to preserve their lives and their sanity. But to the charge of selling them to criminals, I strongly object. I in no way profited from their involvement with any of the crime lords throughout this city or any other."

"Indeed?" Dr. Troy flares her nostrils. "So you wish to add perjury to your crimes? I have records that you received payment from a criminal named Felix Cade. The man this beautiful boy worked for while on the street."

I growl. "Liar."

Arms crossed, Dr. Gayle glares. "Impossible."

"I'm sure that will all come out in the trial," Dr. Troy says, a smile playing at the corners of her mouth. "For now, I would suggest you exercise your right to remain silent. Officer?"

In the half-second the man in uniform reaches for his handcuffs, Dr. Gayle makes her move. She pulls a small, black device from her pocket. I squeeze my eyes shut. The sound of the flash stings my ears even over the computer speakers. Dr. Troy and the police officer both cry out, blinded by the device's light. The buzz dies down, and Dr. Gayle sprints from the room and into the hall. Two officers in uniform race after her.

One tries to tase her.

She weaves out of the way. An incredible move, but she still needs a little digital wizardry. I trap my tongue between my teeth, typing in a code to take control of the automatic doors. Every stroke sends fire up my arm. I ignore it.

Dr. Gayle clears the next set of doors.

I force them into emergency mode. They slam shut behind her, effectively cutting off the two officers.

"Yes!" I fist pound the air, then wince. "Just a little farther, come on, Dr. G." I take control of the side doors, protecting her line of escape until the moment she speeds through the east entrance. Only a few feet to the sewer now. "Come on…come on…"

I lean in closer to the screen. My sweaty, bloody hand latches on to the desk. The doctor lifts the lid. My heart slams into my throat. Then she disappears below ground, and I slump back into my chair.

At least one good guy got away. Now to see if I can help another. Time to go back to the cameras. Wiping my hands on my jeans, I bend forward again and flip back through the video feeds. I wave at the trapped officers, unable to tame a grin.

"Hiya, Matt."

I choke as Uncle Wally steps into the room, holding a new train car. Only half painted, it's completely different from all the others, colorful, unique.

He looks up from it and frowns. "You're hurt. Did Hellie get mad again?" The glasses magnify the tears that immediately fill his eyes.

"It's okay, Uncle Wally. It's okay." I wave a hand and focus again on my computer. "And I want to see your train, but I need a second, okay?"

"Hellie shouldn't do that to you. It's not nice."

"Really, it's okay." I wave at him again, focus still on the screens, clicking back to Sephrim's room. Bashed and bloody, his body truly looks broken, but his chest rises and falls at that steady pace. Still restarting. Nothing to do for him right now, but I can get Cal the truth.

She needs it.

I glance at the door. A door Hellen always locks. A door I could've broken out of countless times. It didn't matter before, my own imprisonment. It wasn't worth the risk, worth losing access to such high-end tech. But now, I have to get out. Uncle Wally could use his card, but then Hellen would know he'd helped and might hurt him too.

Not a chance I'll let that happen. I'll do this on my own. But how do I make absolutely sure Hellen doesn't think Uncle Wally helped me? I swallow. "Uncle Wally, you know what would make me feel better? A peanut butter and jelly sandwich."

He grins broadly. "Okay, Matt, I'll be right back."

I hold my breath while I wait for him to shuffle out of the room. The door snaps shut. I count to ten before I switch to screen number four, Hellen's security system. *Tap, tap, tap, click.* The door slides open again, and I spring from my chair. Blood rushes from my head. I stagger and grip the desk. Cal needs me. I can do this. Even if I have to crawl to get to her.

I glance right down the hallway, no Uncle Wally. Then left, no guards. Air burns hot and tight in my chest as I step out. Supported by the wall, I slog toward the lab Cal's in, the tips of my bare toes catching on the cement floor every few steps. Hellen might still be in there, but if I can tell Cal about Sephrim, I can give her hope, put the fight back in her eyes.

"Matt?"

Hand still on the wall, I freeze, then look over my shoulder. "Uncle Wally, I can explain later, but right now I can't."

His brow furrows. He spins one of the wheels on his train car. "I just wanted to see if you wanted strawberry or grape jelly. Where are you going, Matt?"

My heart pulses in my ears. "Do you remember my friend, the girl who was in my room? She needs my help, but if Mom sees you out here, she's going to think you helped me, and she's going to be mad, and I don't want her to hurt you, so please go."

"But—"

"Hey! What are you doing out of your room?"

Fear coils snake-like through my stomach. I stumble back from the guard running up the hallway.

No, no, no, no.

Then Uncle Wally squats, sets his train on the floor, and shuffles out of the way. The guard steps right on it. Like some kind of wacky cartoon, his foot slips and launches him into the air. His heel wrecks the paint job on the train car and sends it flying.

Uncle Wally lets out an exaggerated gasp, then crouches next to him. "You fell down! Are you okay?" He glances over his shoulder, then waves and whisper-yells the word "go."

I hate to leave him behind, but I have to get to Cal. Gripping the wall again, I peek around the corner, letting out a shocked squeak when I come face-to-face with a most unexpected person. Darby reels back from me, stumbling a few feet before she catches her balance again. The moment she does, she stops to stare at me, eyes wide at first, then narrowing.

She brushes the hair from my face. "Oh, Matty. What did she do to you?"

I flinch from her touch. "No time, I need to tell Cal something."

Her brows shoot up. "You aren't going anywhere near that room. You're coming with me. We're getting out of here. I don't care if I have to knock you out and throw you over my shoulder to do it." She grabs my upper arm before I can back away.

"I have to tell her Sephrim's not dead." I try to pull out of her grip but sway on my feet.

"He's what?" Her voice cracks like an interrupted server.

Another shout—this time from down the hallway—makes me jump. I turn. Black sparks across my vision. A new guard marches in our direction. Darby yanks me around the corner. The ground pitches under my feet, but I manage to keep up. As we run, my sister shoves a small screen into my hand.

"Can you do anything with this?"

A mini net board. "Maybe, but probably not when

I'm about to puke."

"If you don't do something with it now, you'll be right back where you started, and you won't be able to help Cal."

With a hard swallow, I jab the screen with a thumb. Fingers clumsy with pain, thoughts sluggish, I have to try a few times to punch into the system. We slide to a stop at one of the side doors. It doesn't budge. The pound of boots grows louder.

"Come on, come on." I prop myself against the wall. Both thumbs fly across the screen. "Can you buy me some time?"

"With pleasure." She slips past me.

As I keep typing, a slap and a grunt echo off the cement walls. I resist the urge to look back, hold out hope the guard hasn't hurt Uncle Wally. The door pops open. "Darbs, let's go!"

A wet crack splits the air. The sound of a fist against bone. I flinch, and this time I do turn. The quick movement blinds me. I sway again, but a strong hand catches me by the arm and pulls me sideways. I blink in the apathetic sunlight. Fine droplets of rain prick my face. They slap away the dazed feeling in time for me to see the sewer lid.

"Cal…"

"It's okay, buddy," Darby says. "I promise, we'll help her, but we need reinforcements."

Chapter Thirty-Seven

Sephrim

Bright light hovers over me. White, cold, close. Like when Dr. Troy used to examine me. Naked in front of her, I always forced my mind somewhere far away. Since I've never been far away, I made up a special place in my head. Golden, warm, safe. I tried to draw it once, but it didn't come out right. Maybe colors like that don't exist in real life. Only dreams.

A dream carries me now. I soar high above the city, weightless, far removed from the Cades and the lab and the Slingers. Cool air surrounds me. It eases the pain in my ribs and soothes the sting of my cuts and scrapes. I drink sun and starlight, consume the clouds. No one stares. No one touches me. No one debates my value.

But Cal.

This thought drags my gaze to the streets below. I search the ditches, the sidewalks, the sewers, and find her on a rooftop surrounded by a flock of pigeons. Her eyes, no longer blue and brown but black, drift without rest. I try to get her attention, but she walks right through me, crying out in a voice like a brokenhearted dove, "Dead…dead…"

I gulp sterile air. It stabs my throat on the way down. I open my eyes, then squeeze them shut immediately. Rubber tubes wind around my arms, attached to the skin in various places, and cold air puffs out across me. It smells like the lab. With another, more careful breath, I squint into the prying light.

Dr. Troy stands on the other side of a stark white aura, fingers splayed across the glass above me, upper lip hitched in a sneer. She leans so close to the healing tube her nose nearly touches it. "Oh good, you're awake. Right on time. According to the readout, you'll be all healed up in about an hour, ready to be shipped off. Perfect. But don't worry, you won't be transported until tomorrow. After the United Nations agrees to lift their restrictions."

"Shipped—" I cough. "Shipped off? To the workhouse?"

"You know these healing tubes are amazing." Dr. Troy traces her nails across the surface of the machine, over my face. "Broken spine, clavicle, both sets of ribs, shattered pelvis and skull, so much bleeding…internal and external. Thankfully, you landed on your back, protected that pretty face of yours."

"Where am I being shipped to?" Heat fills my chest, burning out the fear I normally experience in Dr. Troy's presence. Cal needs me—I can't get shipped off to some undisclosed location. At least they don't know her hiding place. At least she's safe.

Dr. Troy rolls her eyes. "I suppose legally I am required to tell you where we are delivering you." She smiles. "After the New United Nations meeting, world doctors will put in place a new precedent wherein the scientists who created Designer Babies will have full power over their existence once they expire. In this case, you will be my property to do with as I see fit. Which means you will be transferred to my personal home lab.

The place you were meant to be all along."

I gag. Tension seizes my arms, but when I try to move them, the tubes restrain me. "What?"

"Oh yes." Her smile widens. "You were never going to go to the workhouses. Not you, not my very own special creation. From the beginning I planned to take you home. Now I can do it legally."

"But..." My voice shakes. "What about Dr. Gayle? Technically—"

"Technically, Ms. Gayle is a criminal from justice." Dr. Troy's smile smears again into a sneer. "She escaped our custody. Abandoned you. You, the one she claimed so much to love. Tragic really." She frowns, then caresses the glass. "We're going to have so much fun."

****

Matt

We run through the tunnels, Darby clutching my good arm to keep me steady. I glance at the rank water to our left, positive any minute I'll slip and fall right into it. So many times I sent Designer Kids into these sewers to save their lives. I feel weird running through them myself now.

"Where are we going?" My voice echoes ahead of us, then calls back.

"Sam's. It should be a safe place to figure out what to do," Darby says. "As long as Meg hasn't been taken down by the Slingers." A few ladders later, she slides to a stop. "Wait here. I'll make sure it's clear."

I grip a metal rung and look back down the tunnel. No sign of the guards. I yank the mini net board from my pocket and check the security system. Still on lockdown. Completely sealed up with Cal and Uncle Wally inside.

Fear clenches my stomach.

"All clear, buddy."

Shoving the net board back into my pocket, I dry both hands on my jeans, then climb up after Darby. At the top, I pause. Ash streaks the sides of the buildings, and discarded Taser wires lie scattered across the cement. A woman stands at the back door with a rifle strapped over her shoulder. When she sees Darby and me, her brows shoot up, and she waves us over.

With a hand from my sister, I crawl the rest of the way out of the sewer and half run, half stumble to the woman. She ushers us inside before she speaks a word. The moment the door locks, however, she crosses her arms and blocks Darby.

"Explain yourself, Cade."

"What are—" I stop when I look at my sister.

Green tinges her skin. Her lips move without sound.

Then I figure it out. This woman knows Darby tried to kill Sephrim. My stomach stings. "It's not her fault. It's mine. My mom, Hellen, made me tell her that Sephrim could shut down Cal's chip and—"

The woman holds up a hand. When I flinch, she frowns. "I need to hear this from her."

"I'm sorry, Meg," Darby says, voice trembling.

"I don't need an apology. That belongs to Sephrim. I just need an explanation. We all do evil sometimes. It's the motivation behind them that changes things." She glances at me out of the corner of her eye. "Is it true what he said? Were you trying to help him?"

Darby swallows, and a sob turns into a hiccup. Her cheeks flush. "He's my brother. You see his face? That's nothing compared to what she does to him all the time… Show her, Matty."

E.C. Farrell

Embarrassed heat skitters between my shoulders, itching old scars and recent cuts.

Again, Meg holds up a hand. "It's okay. I don't need to see much more than this." She purses her lips, still glaring.

"She promised..." Darby trails off and gathers her hair into a fist. "She promised to let him go if I got rid of Sephrim. I was supposed to shoot him, but I couldn't. I thought maybe he could survive the fall. I called the ambulance...then our mother went back on her word... I was stupid to believe her in the first place."

A frown tugs at Meg's lips. "Hellen does have a tendency to do that."

"And now we want to help," I say. "My mom has Cal, and the lab has Sephrim and..."

"Matt!"

I turn at the sound of my name and nearly topple over.

Dr. Gayle shoves her way through the small crowd in the middle of the bar. She slides to a halt about a foot away, covering her mouth. "Oh, what has she done to you?"

"You know him?" Meg asks.

"Yes, this is my hacker. He's saved countless Designer Children over the years, and I believe he saved me this morning. It's nice to see you without a screen between us." She smiles and takes one of my shoulders. "Let's get you cleaned up."

Dr. Gayle leads us down to the basement. Meg follows, grabbing a medical kit from a cabinet near the stairs. We sit around a table, and as Dr. Gayle pulls antiseptic wipes from the box, I slide the mini net board from my pocket.

"I can get Sephrim out of the lab, but I need a better computer."

"Why?" Darby asks. "You got us out of Hellen's with that."

I wave a hand, wincing when the doctor dabs my face with a gentle touch. "We're too far away, and this little thing doesn't have enough power. I was able to make contact with Cal before, but Mom made me disable that capability." I grind my teeth. "This is the best chance we have to stop her, to stop the assassination."

Meg walks to the wall and shoves in a panel. It slides aside to reveal a thin, wooden desk and matching chair. More importantly, a large computer spans the wall above it. "Will this do? I hijacked it en route to one of the labs. I keep it around to stay in touch with the network and monitor the bar."

Eye wide, I nod, internally drooling over the beautiful tech. "With that, I could take over the entire government."

Dr. Gayle smiles. "How about we focus on saving Sephrim for now, hmm?"

I crack my knuckles with a thumb. "Let's do this."

Chapter Thirty-Eight

Sephrim

I stare at the ceiling through the glass until Dr. Troy leaves for the meeting of the New United Nations. Shock blares through my body, my no-longer-smashed body. A few hours ago, I was more or less dead. Now if I can't get out of here, I might as well still be a smear on the concrete. A guard hovers near the door. Even if I could find a way out of the wires, then out of the tube, I wouldn't get very far.

The news plays on the wall. Cameras switch focus between crowds milling about the streets, police guarding the government building, and the empty rooftop that will soon fill with dignitaries and scientists. A vulnerable location chosen for the appearance of trust. Or something like that. If Hellen somehow gets Cal to a high point nearby... But she doesn't have Cal.

Does she?

I have no reason to believe Cal isn't still safe at Cade's, except for the fact that Hellen put a bounty on my head and sent Darby to kill me. Anger rolls through my gut. If I ever get out of here, I'll make sure she... I mash my eyes shut. We're going to have to have a really long talk about our relationship, one that will probably involve a lot of cursing on my part, at bare minimum. I tend to be a very forgiving person, but attempting to kill me kind of crosses the line, even if she did believe it would save her brother.

Insane. Completely insane.

Hellen would never let Matty go. Not if he's as good at hacking as Darby claimed. I exhale the angry tension in my stomach. Anger might drive out fear, propel my escape, but it will also cloud my judgment. If Cal's in danger, I need to think clearly.

Now, how to save myself?

I chew the tip of my tongue. Step one, get out of the tubes. Worry about the guard later. I try to lift a hand, but it won't budge from the cool, gel-like bedding. Too many wires. Maybe they only come off with a doctor's code? Panic wraps around my chest.

An image flashes across the glass surface above me. I flinch, then squint up at the face of a kid with a scarred eye and… "Dr. Gayle?"

The doctor smiles and lifts a finger to her lips. "Stay very quiet. Matt is going to get you out of there."

Gaze down, probably aimed at a keypad, the kid frowns. "This is going to sting. Try not to make too much noise."

"Don't worry about me," I say under by breath. "Clearly, I have a high pain tolerance."

Matt hits a button, then looks up at the screen. With a whoosh, the tubes suctioned to my skin detach, leaving fire behind in their wake. I grit my teeth as they unwind and slide back into their compartments. Flexing my fingers and wiggling my toes, I glance down at my body as best I can. Still stark naked, but not hooked to the machine anymore. Progress.

A thrill rushes through my once silent chest. Weird thought. "Nice work." I grin up at the images above me.

"Now I just have to take out the guard."

"He's in no condition to do that," Dr. Gayle says, more to Matt than me. "He has at least half an hour after getting unhooked to regain the full use of his muscles."

Matt squints at something I can't see. "Hang on, I got this."

Overhead, the alarms flash for two bright-red rotations before skull-shattering sirens go off. The guard curses but doesn't move from his spot. I grimace and look back to the screen. Still bent over, Matt keeps typing. His lips move as he works.

A loud clunk snaps my attention back to the guard. As if possessed, the door behind him slides open and slams shut rapidly. Lip curled, the guard glares at it. He leans forward, and electricity sparks across the empty threshold. The man jerks, then collapses half in, half out of the room.

Matt laughs. "That's rough, buddy." He rubs his hands together. "Sephrim, I know you're still a little woozy, but we don't have a lot of time. When I pop the healing tube lid, you've got to get out of there."

A naked getaway, classy.

My head swims, anticipation beats through my veins, but I nod. "I'm ready."

After a few more keystrokes, Matt throws up his hands. The lid pops. With a deep breath, I push it the rest of the way open. Blood bubbles in my head. Gasping, I more or less roll out of the tube and onto the floor. Through wavering vision, I catch sight of a set of scrubs folded on a chair. Relief whooshes through my chest.

Oh good. No streaking today.

With shaking fingers that barely work, I wriggle into the clothes, then turn back to the image on the healing tube.

Matt and Dr. Gayle both gesture and say simultaneously, "East exit."

Muscles quivering, I turn toward the door. Matt's voice stops me.

"Wait!"

I reel back around to face the screen. "What, what?"

"Take the guard's mini board. That way we can stay connected. It's on his belt."

I crouch in the doorway and pull the small screen from the man's hip. Matt's marred face appears on it a second later. He waves again, and I grin.

"East exit, yeah?"

He gives me a thumbs-up. "Coast looks clear right now."

I creep into the hall, look both ways, then shuffle sprint toward the east exit on wobbly legs. Memory collides with reality. Memories of the night Cal and I ran. Most in my birth group sold early on. One by one the others went to families, to dignitaries, to…shady people as Cal called them. Looming expiration, fear, sent us running.

"Guards!" Matt shouts from the mini board. "Duck into the next room. To your left!"

I spring sideways. A door opens seconds before I slam into it. Someone gasps. I jump and round on a small group of Designer Kids. Wide-eyed, they stare, silent even without the finger I put to my lips. In an uneven wave, they all nod and scoot into a corner. Satisfied they'll stay put, I turn to the door and watch a group of guards sprint past. I let out a breath of relief, then choke as one turns back.

Teeth clenched, I shrink into the opposite corner of

the room and again motion for the kids to stay quiet. I can't take multiple guards. Especially not in this state. Not after being more or less dead so recently. Maybe Matt. I reach for my pocket just as the guard steps inside. Her gaze sweeps immediately to me. I curse and spring forward, but my legs tangle, still weak from the healing tube, and I land hard on my knees.

I grab at the guard's boots, but she jumps out of the way and reaches for the radio on her shoulder. Then, just before she jams a finger into the button, the small group of Designer Kids charges. They barrel into her and knock her off her feet.

As they pile on top of the woman, one shouts, "Run!"

I push myself off the floor and sprint into the hallway. Leaving them there sucks, but I have to get out. Cal needs me.

Chapter Thirty-Nine

Cal

Red sunlight stabs through dense clouds. It bleeds to faint oranges and pinks before melting into the blue black beyond. Warmth fans out across my back, but the feeling hardly reaches through the numbness. Hellen and I face away from the sunset and toward the still-deserted government building. Shouts bloom up from the streets below. Some positive, some negative, all loud. Everyone wants to be heard. Everyone believes their opinion deserves a platform.

But too many voices crowd out reason.

"Pathetic, aren't they?" Hellen asks.

"Pathetic, adjective. Causing or evoking pity, sympathetic sadness, sorrow, etc., pitiful, pitiable…miserably or contemptibly inadequate."

Inadequate, the absolute opposite of perfect. I run the tips of my fingers along the inside seams of my overall pockets. The earpiece Hellen fitted me with before we left the compound itches. Obviously, she won't be on the roof once the press conference starts— she has her manifesto to broadcast post assassination, after all.

"Yes. Like my children, most believe everything they're told in spite of facts to the contrary. Fools. They need someone to make decisions for them. I know it might seem…counterintuitive, destroying the government that keeps them under control, but—"

"Are you monologuing?" I ask. "Because you're really bad at it."

She laughs. "I assumed you would want to understand. Considering tonight's events will likely end in your death."

"I don't care." I aim a pointer and middle finger at my temple and make an exploding sound. Somewhere far off, a car engine backfires. "I'm curious, though. Why did Felix decide to help you?"

Hellen takes a step toward the ledge and looks into the street. I lift my hands. One tiny push. A nudge. All I have to do is shove. *Bam. Splat.* No more Hellen. Justice for Seph. Justice he'll never get unless I do something. I let my hands fall again. Without the chip I can't stomach it, and even now I can't bring myself to say the word.

"Felix," she says. "Felix has a softer spot for his little brother than he cares to admit. He claims he needs a hacker, but I'm his mother. I know better. Besides, once I've gained control of the government, he believes I'll put him in charge of something." She waves a hand, then turns back to me. "It's tempting, isn't it, Little Shadow?"

I blink. *Tempting. Adjective. Enticing or inviting.* "What is?"

Head tilted, she takes a step toward me. "To push me off the ledge. End my existence. It would solve all your problems. Wouldn't it? Give you your freedom?"

"Get vengeance for Sephrim." His name cracks in my throat.

Hellen smirks. "Now you understand why those dignitaries must be eliminated. Sometimes eliminating the problem is just easier. Sometimes, people have to die."

****

Sephrim

Though I want to sprint straight to the rooftop to rescue Cal, I need help. Barefoot, I charge through the sewers, then into Sam's. My muscles jitter, fighting me the entire way. Energy drains out of the bottoms of my feet, and my vision blurs. With every footfall I remind myself of Cal.

I pound on Sam's back door, expecting Meg to answer.

Instead, Gabe opens it and drags me in by the arm. "Hurry up, eyes everywhere."

"Gabe? What are you doing here?"

"I'll explain downstairs, come on." The kid pulls me into the basement.

Dozens of teenagers and a handful of adults fill the room. Some have strange eye colors like Lailah, and most look eerily perfect. Designer Kids. Kids I recognize, in fact.

At the bottom of the stairs, I pause, gaping.

"What is this?"

"We're here to help," a twenty-something says. "You and Cal could have kept to yourselves, stayed out of trouble, but instead you kept working with Dr. Gayle to free other Designer Kids. Now we want to return the favor."

I thread my fingers through my hair. "This could be really dangerous."

No matter how old a Designer Kid gets, Slingers never give up their bounty. If any one of us gets caught, tied up by whips or handcuffs, we'll be sent straight to the closest workhouse. Diving into a political crisis almost guarantees this for everyone here. I open my mouth to protest.

"We live in danger on the street every day," another kid says, cutting me off. "We might as well face it for a good cause."

Dr. Gayle shoulders through to the front row and pulls me into a hug. In spite of her own flight from "justice," the scent of coconut and spice still hangs around her. She backs away, offering a smile. "Go save Cal. If you can't stop her, we'll make sure everyone gets off the roof."

I run both hands over my face. The very kids who might be most hurt by this new meeting are willing to risk their lives for those dignitaries. Crazy. I shake my head, overwhelmed. "Okay. But…I can't go there alone. I'm still pretty weak. I need backup."

"I have just the person to go with you," Dr. Gayle says, stepping to one side.

In a corner, tucked into the group, sits Darby, gripping her braid. Rage sets fire to my veins as she stands.

"I know you don't trust me—"

"Damn right, I don't." I clench both hands into fists. "You tried to kill me. Sold Cal out. We were going to help you save Matt, but you decided to trust a lunatic instead."

Tension rolls along Darby's jaw, and her nostrils flare. "You can't do this without me."

"Like hell I can't."

Dr. Gayle touches my shoulder. The smooth skin between her brows puckers. "I understand your hesitation—"

"I'm not hesitant. I'm angry." I cross my arms to keep from pointing an accusing finger at Darby. How? How can Dr. Gayle ask me to do this with the girl who kicked me off a roof?

Her grip tightens. "I understand, I do, but she's right. You can't do this alone, and I'd argue you need her specifically."

I glare as anger boils in my stomach, never looking away from Darby. "Why? Why can't I take literally anybody else in this room?"

Face tight, Dr. Gayle lifts her chin. "Because she knows Hellen better than anyone. If you're going to face her, you need Darby."

I grind my back teeth. No one will blame me for not trusting her. But Dr. Gayle's right. I've barely got use of my limbs, and Darby does know Hellen. I need help. I need *her*.

"Fine." I spit the word. "So long as you swear not to push me off another roof. Or shoot me in the back."

Red flushes Darby's neck, but she nods. "Deal."

"Then let's get to Cal."

"Wait!" Now Matt nudges through the crowd.

In the image in the healing tube, the kid's face looked banged up, but in person, it's way worse. Bruises and cuts smudge nearly every inch of his skin, and one side of his jaw and arm are swollen. No wonder Hellen scared him too much to leave on his own. No wonder Darby was desperate to do anything to rescue him…

"Still have that guard's mini net board?"

I slip it out of my pocket, and Matt grins.

"Perfect. I'm going to try to cut off the mic my mom's using to talk to Cal to buy you some time. She's going to be somewhere inside the building getting ready to broadcast her speech or whatever. I should be able to hack that too, but it'll take time. Also"—he shifts between his feet—"I'm really sorry I told my mom about you. It's not Darby's fault. It's mine. Please—"

"Hey, it's okay. I get it." I give him a weak smile. No matter how mad I am, I can't bawl out a kid with a busted face. I glance at Dr. Gayle, remembering what she taught me about false guilt. "Don't take the blame. All this is all on Hellen."

Dr. Gayle smiles. "Well said." She then lifts a small pile of folded clothes. "So you don't draw too much unnecessary attention. It's not quite like your old hoodie, but it should work well enough to cover your face and will certainly attract less attention than those scrubs. Now, get changed so we can go save the world."

****

Matt

The computers at Sam's work at super speed. I find Hellen's familiar feed—the feed I created for her—with a few keystrokes. A video pops onto my monitor. In spite of my burst of bravery and the safety of many miles, my insides clench in fear. Hellen sits across from a camera. She looks directly into the lens, right at me.

"Not at me," I say out loud, voice shaking. "She can't see me."

Wiping my hands on my jeans—nice unstained jeans Meg Sam gave me—I tap into Hellen's microphone. As she opens her mouth, I cut the connection. Hellen's voice carries over the monitor.

"Can you hear me, Little Shadow?" She waits a moment, then furrows her brow. "Cal? Can you hear me?"

I grin.

"Brunwick, check the security feed."

The camera trembles as the guard obeys orders. I shift my attention to the second video on my monitor. Toes on the very edge of the roof, Cal stands as still as a gargoyle. Everybody thinks gargoyles are scary, dangerous, but really, they protect the cities they overlook.

Stone superheroes.

"She's still there, ma'am," Brunwick says. "Just staring at the crowd. Maybe there's something wrong with the earpiece."

"It was checked before we left the compound," Hellen says through clenched teeth. "How could…"

"Oh darn." I grin at the screen. "Isn't that just a shame? And look at that. Now you're blocked from the national news feeds. Have fun trying to deliver your speech."

I crack my knuckles as Hellen marches to the window. Now I just have to hope Sephrim and Darby can get there before Hellen realizes she's cut off. In the meantime, I've got others to monitor, somebody else to save, and another player to put on the board. Not to mention my own video to broadcast.

I switch my focus to another series of cameras. Two masses of Designer Kids split between Meg and Dr. Gayle take the east and west tunnels, while Sephrim and Darby move north. I bury their digital footprints. Anybody looking for them will have a tough time doing it, especially if they try to use a government programmer. Maybe one day they'll give me a challenge, but so far, I've schooled them all.

Dr. Gayle's lab coat sits on a stool next to me, but she took her medical credentials with her. Though Dr. Troy tried to have her arrested, this still might help her get into the summit, might help them save the dignitaries from assassination if Sephrim fails.

My throat clenches.

A few blocks from the police barricades, on an abandoned street, Dr. Gayle's head pops out of a sewer lid. She holds up a hand and checks their surroundings. When she sees no sign of either citizen or cop, she waves the Designer Kids up onto the sidewalk, and they skim the walls of the closest buildings. Their small group soon meets with the others across the street from the barricades, hidden in the shadows. Some runaways drip with what looks like sewer water, but apart from that they look pretty okay.

I let out a little sigh.

Dr. Gayle turns, steps around a wall, and marches toward the protesting crowds. As she approaches the barricade of soldiers, she lifts both hands. The Designer Kids follow behind at a distance. Nearby reporters all turn at once, the bright lights of their cameras throwing the small group of Designer Kid rebels and their doctor onto the billboard screens.

"That's right," I say in a mutter. "Give me the cameras I need, my minions…"

Dr. Gayle reaches the officer in charge and gestures to the badge on her shirt. The speakers on the computer crackle a little as she speaks. "My name is Dr. Amancia Gayle, and I have a warning for the New UN Council."

The officer glares. "Ma'am, I have a warrant out for your arrest." He taps his finger along the barrel of his gun near the trigger.

I grin. "But do you really?" Another few clicks of the computer keys and the digital copy of the alleged arrest warrant disappears. Like magic.

"I am aware of this, Officer," the doctor says, hands still up, palms out. "And I am risking arrest in order to save the men and women on the roof. In fact, all of these people behind me are risking the same."

"And who are these?"

"Is this a demonstration?" a reporter shouts.

"A protest?" yells another.

"These?" Dr. Gayle smiles. "These are countless Designer Children who have run from the labs, terrified of what Dr. Troy has in store for them in the workhouses. Rather than remain hidden and safe, they are here to protect those who might be swayed to put in place laws that will deny them even more rights than they are already denied. Now please, hear me out."

Chapter Forty

Sephrim

Neither of us speak at first.

We let the rush of water fill the silence. At every turn or curve of the tunnel, my heart skips a beat, my muscles ready to flee packs of Slingers, nerves on high alert for any false move from Darby. My lips tingle at the memory of our kiss, exacerbating the betrayal twisting, knife-like, in my chest. Here in the shadow, with no witnesses, I want to tear into her, let her know just how stupid she was for trusting Hellen. But the mini net board counts down the time until the United Nations meeting.

Ten minutes.

One single delay and we won't make it in time. Hellen will force Cal to kill all those dignitaries and start her revolution.

Then what?

Will the Slingers take Cal into custody? Will the police gun her down without question? An incredible shot and controlled by that chip, Cal could conceivably take out anyone who poses a threat. I don't want to think about the body count.

"Sephrim?" Darby's voice barely rises above the roar of rushing water.

Just the sound of it charges my entire system with fury. I clench and unclench my fists, then finally say,

"What?" My words come out flat, hollow.

"No matter what happens out there, I swear I'll have your back. I'll do whatever I can to make sure you and Cal get out alive."

Great timing. Couldn't have sworn that before you pushed me off a friggin' roof?

I stop at the ladder and look up at the sewer lid. Streetlight beams through the holes like mini spotlights. As a rule, I avoid this area of town. Too many cameras, too many cops. What chance do I have of getting past them now? I swallow and glare back at Darby.

She still won't meet my eyes. My stomach flops. I want her to feel guilty. Because she *is* guilty. But the memory of Matt's battered face flits back through my mind. What if somebody did that to Cal? Had done it for years and I'd already failed to save her once before?

My anger dampens, if only a little.

I give a sharp nod. "Good. I need all the help I can get up there."

She squints at the sewer lid. "Most of the police are probably guarding the actual government building where the meeting's taking place. But I should be able to clear a path if we do run into problems. Is the GPS Matt installed in Cal's chip still working?"

"Yeah, looks like we'll need to go left when we come out up top." I rub the screen against my shirt to absorb the water droplets. A bright dot blinks to indicate Cal's location. So close. I push it back into my jeans pocket. "Ready?"

"I'll go up first, check if the coast is clear."

Darby climbs to the surface and nudges open the sewer lid. After a quick scan of our surroundings, she nods down at me. I followed her up onto the damp asphalt. I keep my head down, hoodie up, as we jog along the empty road in the direction of the blinking dot. Wads of trash roll across the cement like urban tumbleweeds. Off to our right, the crowd around the government building roars.

"How far?" Darby asks.

"About a block, I think—"

"Hey, you two," someone shouts from the other side of the street. "This is a restricted area. Freeze."

"Run." With a hard shove, Darby heaves me forward. "I've got this."

I want to look back. Instead, teeth locked together, I sprint toward the dot. To the west, darkness overtakes the last of the light, leaving a bloody crimson wound on the horizon. Shadows stretch, soaking the alleyways around me. The effects of the healing tube combined with adrenaline shakes my burning muscles.

Five minutes until the UN meeting.

As the building looms, my stomach hitches. I sprint for the nearest fire escape attached to its side. One foot on the garbage bin, I propel myself upward and grab the lowest rung. Great, now just a million-story climb. With a deep gasp I pull myself up. Once or twice along the way, my vision ripples, but a few slow breaths clear it up.

At the top, however, I stop to regain my spent energy. Sweat plasters my T-shirt to my chest, my hair to my forehead. I hook an arm over one of the ladder rungs as my body sways. Considering I was mostly dead a few hours ago, making it to the top is an accomplishment. But exhausted or not, I can't wait much longer. I glance at the mini net board.

One minute.

Lower lip trapped between my teeth, I peek over the short roof wall. Hellen and Cal stand at the other end, facing the government building. As I pull myself up, Hellen steps toward Cal, and leans forward to speak in her ear.

Even this far away I hear it. "Expire."

Chapter Forty-One

Cal

The rifle and tripod in front of me burn into my noggin. Because of a malfunction, Hellen now stands next to me, pinching the worthless earpiece between two fingers, cursing Matt quietly. She lets out a sigh like air escaping a punctured tire. Then her breath sears into my ear along with the dreaded word. The chip drives horror out of me, leaving empty numbness behind. Without my consent, my body lunges forward. I aim at the crowd, pointer finger on the trigger, right eye shut.

Someone shouts my name.

It sweeps across the rooftop like the call of a bird, louder and more powerful even than Hellen's hissed phrase. My heart lifts in a crazy, joyful swoop. I don't have to turn to recognize the voice. Its very sound snakes heat through my muscles. They seize.

Not possible. Sephrim died. Hellen said. Matt confirmed. Pushed from a rooftop and broken to jagged bits inside. It has to be a trick of my mind, the last dying wisps of hope.

"Cal, turn around, turn around and look at me."

"I can't... Seph, I can't." I grit my teeth. My joints burn.

Two forces battle inside me. One tugs at my trigger finger. The other pulls me in Sephrim's direction. I crouch, rusted in place, eyes on the dignitaries. A woman dressed in a bright-blue sari near the back of the small crowd turns her gaze to the stars, a beautiful face carved by age and laughter. Wind lifts strands of black hair threaded with white away from her forehead. I imagine the scent of spice on her robes. A smell similar to Dr. Gayle's. The gun trembles. I growl in the back of my throat.

Whether the voice echoes from the past or exists in the present doesn't matter. I can't kill those men and women. I can't give up and let Hellen—the woman who had Seph murdered—get what she wants.

Another gun clicks.

Hellen's gun.

Horror prickling across my skin, I picture her taking aim at Sephrim. Sephrim, brought back from the dead. With an unhinged scream, I force my hands off the rifle, then spin away from the crowd of dignitaries. Hellen throws up an arm to block the blow. I don't give her a second chance to react. Still fighting the tug of the chip on my muscles, I burst forward and grab her gun. In my peripheral vision I see Sephrim sprinting from the other side of the roof.

Not a memory. Not a trick. Alive, alive, alive again.

Euphoria distracts me. I lose my grip. She levels a kick into my stomach. I let out a dry cough but cling to the gun. Then, with a yell of wild fury, I twist her hand until the fingers bend in the wrong direction. I wrench the weapon free and drive it sideways. It collides with her temple, and she falls, unconscious, her arms and legs at odd angles.

Something sizzles in the back of my head. I yank the rifle off its stand, pin the butt to my shoulder, then aim both guns at Hellen, only vaguely aware of the pound of feet behind me.

"Cal." Sephrim touches my arm.

Out of the corner of my eye, I study his skin. Red dots. Healing tube. I choke on a sob. "You're not broken anymore."

Sephrim reaches for the rifle. "Nah. They fixed me all up."

I hold tight to my weapons. Alive or not, he still can't aim. He might accidentally shoot off one of his own pinky toes or something. "How'd you get away?"

"Your tech-genius friend saved me."

Matt.

The moment the name pops into my head, a scream rends the night. Visceral and heart-wrenching, it cuts through the steady stream of news reports from the billboard screens. Sephrim's grip tightens on my forearm as we both look up at the video about a block away. Images of kids, very clearly Designer Kids, play across the digital surface, victims of the chips, driven to insanity.

Some tear at the backs of their heads, claw at the incision sites, ram themselves into walls to make the pain, the hallucinations stop. Others fight guards and lab techs for scalpels, desperate to free themselves of the technology meant to turn them into mindless soldiers.

Again, my arms shake with anger, but I keep one eye trained on Hellen's still form. Then the feed shifts to something familiar and totally steals my attention. Security cameras scan the lab where me and Sephrim grew up. They flick between the rooms until landing on a memory. Five-year-old Sephrim squirms, one arm gripped by Dr. Troy. Her nails dig into his skin. When he starts to cry, she backhands him.

Beside me, Sephrim makes a choking sound as Dr. Troy drags him into another room on the screen. He looks away, but I keep staring in horrified shock. The second security camera picks up, five-year-old Sephrim whimpers, and… My jaw clicks in fury. I'd known about the abuse. He told me. But seeing it… My gaze darts from the image and lands on the roof with the dignitaries.

No Dr. Troy.

Where'd she go? At a flicker of movement in my peripheral vision, my stomach hitches. My gaze cuts back to Hellen. Still unconscious. "Seph—"

A voice from behind cuts me off. "I thought I might find you up here."

Sephrim gulps, and rage propels me around to face Dr. Troy. She leans against the frame of the roof-access door, hands in her pockets, eyes overshadowed by lowered brows. A red light blinks through the white material of her lab coat. Tracking device. The healing tube.

On the screen, five-year-old Sephrim sobs, and I aim both guns at Dr. Troy. "You Lojacked him."

She purses her lips. "I replaced the identification chip he unlawfully removed, yes, but that's not why I'm here, is it, Hellen?"

At my feet, Hellen groans. I jump and redirect the rifle. Shooting that one-handed won't be very easy, but I can do it if I need to.

Hellen shoves herself upright, a glare aimed at Dr. Troy. "I wondered if you might show up, June. Good. At this distance you'll be easier to kill."

The doctor laughs. "Are you still upset about med school? Is that what this is about?"

"We were in it together," Hellen says. Her voice snaps like a Slinger's whip. "And when we were found out, you hung it all on me. Did you really think I was going to let you succeed after that? Did you really think I'd give up on our grand plans?"

Med school. Matt mentioned that back at the compound. *Well, isn't this a nice little class reunion for Dr. Psycho University. What the what happened there that screwed both of these cuckoo birds up so bad?*

At the moment it doesn't matter. Not with the sound of sirens and helicopters and lab security footage blaring all around us. My thumb inches toward the stun button on Hellen's weapon, but curiosity stops me from hitting it.

"You would have done the same thing had our situations been reversed." Dr. Troy pushes away from the door, hands still in her pockets as if she doesn't have a gun aimed at her. When she moves, Sephrim shrinks backward but doesn't let go of my arm. His breath comes out in short, shallow gasps.

"Maybe now," Hellen says, her voice edging on hysteria, an odd, broken sound. "But not then."

"What's she talking about?" The question pops out of my mouth.

Hellen hisses her response. "You should know. It's only fair. June and I started the tests on the mind-control chips. Everyone else just wanted to treat addiction and bad behavior with brain waves generated by the implants, but we had a bigger vision. Humanity is stupid, lost. They need a stronger voice to make them obey, to protect them from themselves."

My eyes widen in horror.

"So we started creating a different version of the

chips." Hellen leans forward, forcing her next sentence through what sounds like clenched teeth. "I contacted Marcus because of his connections in the underworld. He supplied the chips and promised to help distribute them if we didn't get FDA approval. Then we got caught, and she turned me into a scapegoat, made it look like I did it all on my own."

The doctor merely lifts a brow. "Yes, I know. You were weak, Hellen. Threw yourself at that idiot Marcus Cade and became a *mother*." She says the word with a grimace. "Tell me. Did you have those children because you wanted to or because you wanted subjects to experiment on?"

Sweat slicks my palms as Hellen's nostrils flare, but Dr. Troy continues before she can react.

"And you were going to stop me how? By inciting my former creations against me? By manipulating them into assassinating the New United Nations? What will that accomplish? Other than to aid my appeal to the world for stricter regulations?"

Hellen stands, her mouth cranked in a sneer. "Manipulating? Oh no, June. I solved our previous problem, the one your workhouse labs never could correct. I made the chip work. I figured it out without you. And now I'm going to accomplish our original mission. After you're out of the way."

Dr. Troy's face twitches, but like a tremor under stone, the emotion barely disturbs the surface. "Solved it, did you?" Her gaze flicks to me, then back to Hellen. "Then why isn't your obedient soldier taking me down? Why are the people on that roof still alive?"

Eyes wide and wild, Hellen shouts this time. "Expire."

I flinch, but nothing sparks at the back of my head. No current overtakes my muscles. Resisting the command earlier must've destroyed the device's control. Either that or Matt figured out how to turn it off. I grin. "Offline. Sorry, chief. And since I'm the only one armed here, I think it's time you two start listening to me."

A laugh bursts from Dr. Troy's mouth. Without a word she pulls one hand out of her pocket and aims a small device at Sephrim. With a cry of absolute agony, he buckles beside me, both hands clamped to the back of his head. Something jolts his body from the inside, twisting him at odd angles as blood drips from his ears and nose.

Teeth clenched together so hard my jaw aches, I resist the urge to look away from either Hellen or Dr. Troy. One second of freedom from my aim and they'll pounce. But Sephrim needs me. I have to stop this pain before it kills him. Maybe I can shoot the device out of the doctor's hand.

"You see this, Little Shadow?" Hellen says, her voice grating like a car with worn-out brake pads. "This is what she does. I understand why you didn't want to kill the people on the roof, but this woman, this monster, is the real enemy. Get rid of her, and a great majority of your problems go away. His pain will end."

Get rid of her.

An apparently simple solution. Dr. Troy deserves it. She sees price tags on people's foreheads, uses them for her own purposes, then throws them away when she's done. After the world sees the footage from the labs, everyone will agree justice needs to be served. But will it?

One bullet to the brain. *Squish*. *Splat*. Gone.

"You hurt Sephrim." I cock the handgun with a thumb.

The doctor's eyes widen a fraction. Such a thoroughly satisfying expression.

No one will give Designer Kids justice. Everyone thinks we're products, just like Dr. Troy. Fancy lawyers will argue for her as they always do for the very rich and very powerful. Maybe she'll just get a slap on the wrist. Community service. A verbal apology. Crocodile tears. Forced retirement. No justice. Not for the "not people."

"Do it, Little Shadow," Hellen says.

I twitch my finger toward the trigger. *Bang*. *Crack*. *Squelch*. Justice.

A hand grasps my ankle. Sephrim's hand. Shaking and jerking and twitching. Then comes his voice. "Don't… You're not broken like them…"

Sephrim. *My* Sephrim. Brought back from the dead. Out of the corner of my vision, I see the billboard screen. An image of me now plays in real time. Standing with both guns aimed at Hellen and Dr. Troy, face hard and sharp. I don't look right. I look scary. Mean. Dumb. Just like Dr. Troy wants them to see me. The way Hellen looks when she deals with Matt. If I kill Dr. Troy now, I might get a kind of justice, but after that? A jail cell at best. Workhouses at worst.

Jaw jutted forward, I jam my thumb into the stun button on the gun and fire a stream of electricity. Dr. Troy flies back into the wall. Her hands flail, and as the device bounces on the roof, Sephrim's cries of pain die out.

Rifle still trained on Hellen, I sink next to him, set the handgun down, and touch his blood-streaked face. "Hey. Hey, Sephy."

He grins. "Hey, Cal."

Hellen lets out a deranged scream and lunges for the handgun. She wrenches it from the ground, springs back, and takes aim at Sephrim. Then another gun goes off. *Bang. Crack. Squelch.* Blood and other bits burst from Hellen's forehead. Her arm drops. Her body wavers, then falls. She lands with a dull smack on the cinder-block roof and lies totally still.

Shocked, I gasp, then turn in the direction of the sound. Half propped on the fire escape, half on the roof, Darby crouches with her arm out, a smoking pistol in hand. She stares at her mother, eyes oddly hooded, lips parted and chalk white. Sephrim groans, then sits up.

"Seph—"

"I'm okay…come on."

Hand in hand we run toward the side of the roof. I slide the pistol out of her hand, and Sephrim pulls her up the rest of the way. She shakes as he takes her shoulders.

Darby looks straight through him. "She was going to kill you."

"I know," Sephrim says.

"She was going to kill you."

Sephrim frowns and pulls her close with one arm, then gestures to me with the other. We hold each other in silence for a long time, the boy raised to life, the girl with her mind back, and the one who conquered her greatest fear. Down below, sirens blare, and crowds cheer. Do the dignitaries know how close they came to death? Do they know who saved them?

A loud, electric snap tears me from the safety of Sephrim's arms. I spin to see a Slinger at the other end of the roof under a spotlight created by a news helicopter overhead. I set both weapons on the ground, then sprint forward and drop to my knees.

"I surrender," I say, shouting above the pound of helicopter blades. "I'll explain everything. Just don't use that dumb whip. I'm not an animal."

A second later both Sephrim and Darby sink next to me, their hands up as well. I glance at Sephrim, and as the soldier comes forward, he grins. We've run so long from the Slingers it feels a bit stupid to surrender to them now. But Seph's alive, and I don't care. Together, we can figure it out.

Chapter Forty-Two

Sephrim

The Slinger takes us to the barricade around the government building. Since the rooftop, he hasn't said a word other than to warn us to watch our step when we hitched a ride with the news helicopter. Darby clutches my forearm. I've never flown before and can't decide if I ever want to again. Cal, on the other hand, I have to keep pulling back from the half-open door. I don't mind, though. Every time I grab her, she grins back at me and squeezes my shoulder. Once she even throws her arms around my neck in a strangle-like hug.

Still immobile from the Taser, Dr. Troy sits propped in a seat near the back of the chopper. She eyes Cal and me, but we do our best to ignore her. Every few feet down, Darby glares in the doctor's direction. After glare number four, Dr. Troy shifts her gaze to her feet. I can't blame her. If Darby wants to scare somebody, she does. Even Dr. Evil can't maintain eye contact.

Back on solid ground, Darby and Cal both help me out. My muscles turn to inactive rubber. Before I collapse on the sidewalk, someone comes running through the crowd to embrace me. Her scent gives Dr. Gayle away almost immediately.

"Oh, Sephrim, Cal, you're both all right, thank God." The doctor pulls Cal into her arms, crushing her face against my shoulder.

Tugging in a painful breath, I glance at the Slinger, surprised he hasn't dragged us away. Dr. Gayle releases her death grip on me, and I sink onto the curb.

"Did it work? Did they listen?"

Dr. Gayle smiles. "Come see for yourself."

She guides us through the barricade and into the first floor of the government building. All the dignitaries gather around the ragged band of Designer Kids who rallied earlier at Sam's. Their chatter dies away when we step through the glass double doors. The surprised stillness lasts only a moment before a woman wearing a sari steps forward. I recognize her from the newsreels, Prime Minister Laghari.

She stops a few paces from us and smiles. "Are these the brave children you have spoken so much about, Amancia?"

One hand on our backs, the doctor nods. "Yes. These two are part of the Designer Kid project, and Darby is their friend. They, and Darby's younger brother, are all responsible for stopping the assassination attempt and for bringing attention to the wrongs committed against all Designer Children."

"I am honored to meet you," the prime minister says. "What you've done is no small thing. The truths you have exposed will bring about much change now that our countries have reunited." She lifts her eyes to meet Dr. Gayle's. "Thank you for allowing us to meet them, but I am certain they are all exhausted and in need of rest. We will not keep you any longer tonight."

The other dignitaries and scientists all talk at once, but it sounds like nothing more than meaningless buzz as Dr. Gayle steers us back through the entrance. Outside, we encounter a sight that will forever sear itself into my mind. In front of a police car, handcuffed and red-faced, Dr. Troy sulks. An officer stands in front of her, his lips forming words I can't hear but guess are her rights. Hope leaps in my chest.

"They arrested Dr. Troy?" I ask, only half conscious of the car I climb into, infinitely relieved to be away from all the staring people.

I try not to think about what we all just saw, try to ignore the shame prickling my chest, but it hovers around me like a spotlight I can't find shelter from.

Dr. Gayle slides into the front seat and looks over her shoulder into the back. "Oh yes, that footage Matt leaked has led to world outrage. Like the prime minister said, thanks to you, things are going to change."

"That's great and all, but where are we going, Dr. G?" Cal asks.

"I'm afraid nothing is ever cut and dry. I know you're all tired, but we still have to visit the police station." She frowns into the rearview mirror, and I grimace back.

"Maybe we can get Daniel out while we're there," I say in a mutter.

I let the side of my head rest against the window, exhaustion settling into my burning limbs. The cool of the glass spreads pleasantly across my skin. The Slinger flips his visor and grins into the mirror. Shock returns every ounce of energy.

"Danny-Boy!" Cal throws her arms into the air. "Decided to change your career?"

Daniel grins. "Definitely pays better. But no. While I usually frown on resisting arrest, I knew you kids were in trouble and needed all the help you could get.

Apparently, Matt really is a tech genius. He helped me escape. I'll have some explaining to do right along with you three. Don't worry, you won't have to deal with the police on your own."

Chapter Forty-Three

Sephrim

A million questions and discussions and warnings later, Daniel drives us away from the chaos at the police station and to Dr. Gayle's home. Flashing lights and blaring billboard screens fade as we pass beyond sky-scratching apartments and into more suburban-style houses. Unlike the mansions I steal from, these still reach up instead of out, and no one's dyed the lawns weird colors. Not yet anyway. Half awake, I watch the scenery through smeared vision, aware but only just.

Reality fades in and out for the rest of the night, or maybe morning. Snatches of Meg meeting us at the house with Matt at her side, of Dr. Gayle's living room, her kitchen, the stairs all solidify in my mind but lie under heavy fog. Full consciousness only returns when, while in one of the guest beds in Dr. Gayle's home, Darby appears.

The warmth of her hand on my arm drags me from the thick cocoon of sleep. I gasp, cough, and meet the deep warmth of her eyes. My entire body jumps at once. Every muscle flinches as I take her in. Darby, in a pair of Dr. Gayle's pajamas, long hair hanging around her face like the branches of a weeping willow.

I reel back from her, a grimace twisting my face. Where does she get off sneaking in here in the middle of the night after trying to kill me? "What the hell—"

"Sephrim, I'm sorry." Her voice cracks. "I know, I know you need sleep, and this is a terrible time, but I'm—I just…I know sorry doesn't cut it by a long shot but I just…my mom…Hellen…she…she's…I…"

She gags, and her entire body shakes as more and more color dies away from her skin. The shadows extend across her face, blacking out her eyes so she almost looks like a corpse. A corpse. My stomach cramps as a shiver skitters through me.

"Stop."

She frowns and bows her head in an oddly convulsive jerk.

I inhale slowly but can't get rid of sleep's heaviness. That expression tugs at something in my chest. Again, I remember just how awful Matt looked even after Dr. Gayle took care of him. What would I have done to rescue Cal from something like that? What *had* I done to save her from Hellen? What did Darby do to save all of us?

With another heavy sigh, I place a hand over Darby's. "Climb in."

Her brows shoot up, and for one pure moment, a bit of warmth flushes her skin. Then she slides in beside me, adding her heat to mine the way Cal used to. She clenches both fists at her chin, gaze still down.

I drag my lower lip through my teeth, something I've picked up from Cal, then rub my eyes with a forefinger and thumb. As I focus on the sensation, I take in Darby's expression, consider what she just did to save us. However twisted Hellen was doesn't change who she was to Darby. She was still her mom. Something I've wanted for a very long time.

"I get it." My words come out slow and weighty. "There's nothing you wouldn't do to save Matt, just like there's nothing I wouldn't do to save Cal. What you did…sucked. Maybe you should've known you couldn't trust your mom. I'm still pissed, but…I get it."

With an odd sort of sobbing sound, she wraps both arms around my waist and buries her face in my chest. "It was stupid." Her breath burns across my chest. "I should have known better. But…"

"But she was your mom. I know. It's okay," I say. "Dumb, but okay. Just don't do it again, huh? If you push me off another roof, I'm not sure our friendship will survive."

She sniffs and nods. "Friends."

Chewing my bottom lip, I think the word through. Yeah, she kicked me off a roof, but in the end, she did have my back, killed her own mother to save us. Finally, I sigh. "That okay?"

"I haven't had a friend in a long time."

"Well, you'll keep one if you don't try to kill me again." I grin, then place a kiss on her forehead. "If I wasn't so mad at you for pushing me off a roof, I'd be proud of you for conquering your fear of heights."

She flinches. "I blocked most of that out. Just knew the first time a roof wouldn't have cameras and the second time…" The word trails into a sigh. "I wanted to help. I had to help…even if it meant…"

When she trails off, I don't try to finish for her. Sometimes mourning needs a little silence. Again, Darby's body shakes. She ducks her head so I can't see her tears even if they're impossible not to feel soaking my shirt.

Unable to fight my exhaustion, I yawn.

"Will you do it?" she asks after a few moments, her voice thick.

"Do what?"

She sniffs and wipes her cheeks. "Testify against Dr. Troy?"

My eyes pop open again. "One—" I cough to relieve the suffocating tension wrapping around my throat. "One thing at a time, huh? I helped stop a political assassination and have spent the last…I don't know how long answering questions. I'm exhausted."

Darby squeezes my middle. For the first time in days, my ribs don't ache to the touch. "Fair enough. Plenty of mountains to conquer later." She breathes out, warming my neck. "Twinkle, twinkle…"

"Shut up." I chuckle. "I never should have told you that."

Chapter Forty-Four

Cal

Politics is for the freakin' birds. Although, if Seph decides not to be a mechanic, he'd probably be a pretty good politician. Or at least I think so. I sit on the roof of Daniel's garage, heels beating against the cinder blocks, filing a stubborn piece of metal into the shape of an owl. Down below, cars rush by, the golden-orange sunlight flashing off windshields and side mirrors. The smell of diesel floats up to the roof.

"Where do they think they're going so fast anyway?"

I grin back at Matt. "One's probably going to get into a wreck and have to come right back around to the shop. Good. More work for Daniel. He'll need it to feed all our big mouths."

After the big reveal at the New United Nations—NUN?—Dr. Gayle took over the North American Designer Kids Program. With the changes she made, Daniel was finally able to officially become our legal guardian. It's not officially official—lawyer-y stuff takes time—but no one will arrest Mr. Todd or drag us away.

"Okay if I sit?"

I quirk my lips to one side. Though at first what Matt did felt like betrayal, I figured out pretty fast everything he'd done was to save me. Just like always. While fear kept him from leaving Hellen, ultimately he stayed with her for a bigger reason. To rescue Designer Kids, to sabotage his mother's plans, to be so much braver than anyone gave him credit for. Who wouldn't love that?

Waving a hand over the cinder block, I grin and bob my head. Kind of like a benevolent queen.

All hail Cal, queen of the grease monkeys.

Matt slides onto the ledge next to me. The bruises and cuts trace the soft lines of his face, but time has faded them. He still flinches when people lift a hand around him, but that will fade too. Dr. Gayle says, like the bruises, it will just take time.

"Glad you guys don't have to sleep on the roof anymore?"

"Yeah, but I still kinda like it. It's…" My gaze flicks back and forth across the line of traffic. "It's…quiet. Peaceful."

Plus, I like the dirt, even when rain turns it to sludge.

Lips pursed, Matt joins my heel tapping. "Same at Darby's apartment."

I nudge his shoulder with mine. "How's the new job? Or hobby, I guess."

Dr. Gayle makes sure Matt doesn't spend too much time working. The poor kid just can't stop himself. He loves flowers and his precious computers too much.

A grin overtakes his face, and he lifts a hand.

"Bee orchid!" I throw both arms in the air, and Matt flinches. Annoyed with myself for being so careless, I latch an arm around his shoulders and lower my voice. "Is that from the garden you planted at the Designer Kid home?" I set the gift on my lap, then fish a small, metal plane out of my pocket and press it into Matt's hand. Yep. I'm most sweet on him.

"It's growing like crazy." Matt traces the outline of my little creation with a thumb, still scarred, but no fresh wounds. "There are a lot of computers left to fix, but all the system updates are done. Darby's scaring the crap out of the new security team, and Uncle Wally loves teaching art to the kids."

"Nutshell version." I twirl the flower. "Reality's a bit messier, huh?"

Matt drops his gaze, fear of the people still—what's the phrase? At large?—evident in his eyes. His terror reflects my own. Dr. Troy dug up some world-renowned lawyer to defend her in the upcoming trial, which means Seph and I have to testify. On top of that, countless workhouses still need shutting down, their victims counseling. Nothing settles perfectly, except maybe Hellen's death. Even that didn't lock up quite right. According to Matt's intel, Brunwick now runs things, only with slightly less vehement plans to take over the country.

And Felix? As far as any of us know, he's still plugging along, annoyed at losing some of his workforce and an assassin, but probably finding a way to pivot.

"Yeah. Messy." Matt loops an arm around my waist and lets out a breath. "We'll clean it up."

A new voice comes from behind. "Permission to approach."

I grin and go back to my rhythmic beating. "Do you come bearing gifts, Seph?"

"Burgers and a buddy. Does that count?"

I crane over my shoulder. When I wobble slightly, Matt loops an arm around my shoulders to steady me. A grin bursts across my face, and I give him a loud kiss on the dimple. His cheeks burn bright red, but his smile mirrors mine.

"You may pass." I nod at Seph and Darby, again the kind queen.

A laugh precedes Sephrim as he steps out onto the roof, a bag in hand, Darby at his heels. I pinch my lips against an irritated scowl. Sephrim says I should give Darby a little mercy, the same kind I've given Matt.

Mercy. Noun. Definition... Well, I haven't quite decided on that yet.

Matt must pick up on how I tense, because he distracts me with a shy little kiss that makes Darby snort.

"I could do without the PDA, Matty."

I open my mouth, but Matt beats me to a response. "You're one to talk. And call me Matt. I'm not five anymore."

Though he says it in his own soft, Matt-like way, it's also firm, not leaving room for argument. I squeeze him around the waist, watching Darby's reaction. She lifts her brows. The shadows shift across her face, sharpening it in a way that reminds me a little too much of Hellen. My innards knot up.

Then one corner of her mouth twitches into a half smile, and she gives a slow nod. "No. No, you're right. You're definitely not a little kid anymore, Matt."

Sephrim sits next to me on the cinder blocks, silent as he passes around the burgers and fries, probably a gift from one of the grateful dignitaries. Our shoulders touch, a steadying, solid presence. Even Darby, who sits cross-legged with her back pressed against the half wall, feels like a pillar of our little patchwork family.

Family. Noun. A basic social unit consisting of parents and their children, considered as a group, whether dwelling together or not.

I squeeze Matt's hand. We need another definition for what we are, but whatever noun people decide to call us, I figure the best adjective is one I've hated for so long.

Perfect.

A word about the author...

E.C. Farrell never met a book she didn't like. (Just kidding! Though she's not going to bad-mouth the ones she couldn't finish, she is still mad about the end of Hunger Games.) She likes her characters sassy and her endings surprising.

Farrell graduated from Texas A&M University with a B.A. in Creative Writing and the goal of helping people feel seen through the stories she writes.

Born and bred in the heat of Texas, she spends every spare moment she can writing on her porch or plotting on long walks with the hot sun as her muse. When not writing, you can find her feeding other aspects of her creativity by cooking or enjoying a paint-by-numbers.

~*~

Find E.C. Farrell online at:
https://www.facebook.com/authorecfarrell
https://twitter.com/authorecfarrell

Thank you for purchasing
this publication of The Wild Rose Press, Inc.

For questions or more information
contact us at
info@thewildrosepress.com.

The Wild Rose Press, Inc.
www.thewildrosepress.com